Paul B. Du Chaillu

Ivar the Viking

A Romantic History Based upon Authentic Facts of the Third and Fourth Centuries

Paul B. Du Chaillu

Ivar the Viking

A Romantic History Based upon Authentic Facts of the Third and Fourth Centuries

ISBN/EAN: 9783337064853

Printed in Europe, USA, Canada, Australia, Japan

Cover: Foto ©Raphael Reischuk / pixelio.de

More available books at **www.hansebooks.com**

IVAR THE VIKING

A ROMANTIC HISTORY
BASED UPON AUTHENTIC FACTS OF THE
THIRD AND FOURTH CENTURIES

BY

PAUL DU CHAILLU

AUTHOR OF "THE VIKING AGE," "THE LAND OF THE MIDNIGHT SUN,"
"EXPLORATIONS IN EQUATORIAL AFRICA," "A JOURNEY TO
ASHANGO LAND," ETC.

LONDON
JOHN MURRAY ALBEMARLE STREET
1893

TO GEORGE W. CHILDS

MY DEAR CHILDS: *Years of our unbroken friendship, going back more than a quarter of a century, have passed away, and the recollection of all your kindnesses during that time comes vividly before my mind. Many a time your home in Philadelphia, at the sea-side, or at Wootton has been my home, and many of the happy days of my life have been spent with you and your kind wife. Three years ago I lay on a sick-bed at your house, and all that tender nursing, the skill of the physician, and loving hands could do that winter was done for me, and for all that I am indebted to you and to Mrs. Childs. Now a twenty miles' walk day after day does not fatigue me. "Ivar the Viking" was partly written, after my recovery, under the shade trees of Wootton and in the midst of the perfume of its flowers. To you, my dear old friend, I dedicate the book as a token of the esteem and high regard I have for your noble character, and in grateful remembrance of all you have done for me.*

PAUL DU CHAILLU.

NEW YORK, *September,* 1893.

INTRODUCTION

THE story of " IVAR THE VIKING" depicts the
actual life of Norse chiefs who ruled at the period
therein described, and also gives the customs, religion, life, and mode of thinking which prevailed
among the people. My object in writing this
story is to give a view, in a popular way, of the
life of these early ancestors of the English-speaking peoples, whose seat of power was on the
islands situated in the basin of the Baltic and
the countries known to-day as Scandinavia.

The reader of this volume will gain a correct
idea of the civilization of the Norsemen of that
period, the men who came to the gates of Rome,
and settled in Britain, Gaul, Germania, on the
shores of the Mediterranean, and other countries.

I begin the story of my hero with his birth,
accompanied by the characteristic ceremonies attending it; then I tell of his fostering, his education, his coming of age, of the precepts of wisdom
he is taught, of his foster-brothers, of the sacred
ceremony of foster-brotherhood, of his warlike

expeditions and commercial voyages, of the death and funeral of his father, of his accession to rule, and other similarly typical Viking events.

I speak in the narrative of the dwellings of the people; how they lived; of their "bys," or burgs; of the different grades making up society; of their feasts; of their temples; of their worship, religious ceremonies, and sacrifices; of funerals; of Amazons; of athletic games; of women and maidens; of love; of duels and sports; of dress; of men and women; of marriages. In a word, the book is a life-like picture of the period. The time which I have chosen is the epoch when the Norsemen were most surely and swiftly sapping the power of Rome, and engaged in colonization on the largest scale.

There is not an object, a jewel, either Norse, Roman, or Greek, or a coin mentioned, that has not been found in the present Scandinavia, and is not seen to-day in its museums, and often in great numbers.

The descriptions of customs interwoven in the narrative are derived from authentic records, the sagas, the evidence of graves, and of antiquities in general. These are more fully, scientifically, and technically described in my work published three years ago, "The Viking Age."

The descriptions of dresses of the women have been most carefully drawn from the sagas, and from the handles of three keys seen in "The Viking Age," where three women in full dress are represented. The materials and jewels with which I have adorned them are those found in their graves. The attire of the men is from the garments, weapons, and ornaments of that early period, found in graves and bogs, and from descriptions in the sagas.

"The Viking Age" had hardly been published in England, when a storm of protests and adverse criticisms arose from many quarters of that conservative country; for it is there that the old belief in the Angle and Anglo-Saxon descent of the modern English-speaking peoples is most rooted, having indeed become a religion with many Englishmen.

I fully expected opposition to the new views I propounded. Had not my former accounts of African travels been received with incredulity? Did not the people laugh when I told that I had seen a race of pigmies and been in their villages? Did they not doubt my descriptions of the great equatorial forest, of gorillas, cannibals, etc.? I was before the time. I was too young; and

these circumstances were against me.   But then,
as in the case of "The Viking Age," I found
warm supporters and defenders in England itself.

I knew that it was bold on my part to attack
the Saxon idol which had been worshipped so
long among Englishmen, and to try to destroy
the faith in which they and their fathers had
believed.   Was the glorious Anglo-Saxon name
which the people had been shouting for so long,
even in America, to be overthrown?   What, then,
would become of the sturdy qualities claimed as
inherited from the so-called Anglo-Saxon race?
The qualities are there, only the name of Anglo-
Saxon ought to be changed to that of Norse.

Nothing but absolute conviction made me take
this bold step.   I had never been satisfied with
the assertions of historians, and could see no evidence in their writings for the conclusions at
which they had arrived in regard to the name
Anglo-Saxon and as to who were the conquerors
and settlers of Britain.

When I travelled in the Norselands, to the
northern part of which I gave the name of "The
Land of the Midnight Sun," a name which has
been generally adopted since, I became convinced
that the conquerors of Britain were Norse; for
while visiting their museums, which contained

the Norse antiquities, I saw that these objects were the same as those called in England by antiquarians, Angle, Anglo-Saxon, Anglo-Roman, and in France, Frankish. These facts set me thinking, and ultimately produced "The Viking Age."

As soon as I brought before the public the evidence I had collected, many voices rose and exclaimed: " Woe to him who tries to dispel our belief and destroy our faith!" The world is full of such examples in the treatment of new ideas. How could I escape hostility when I proclaimed that the antiquities called in England by archæologists and others, and classified in the museums as Angle, Anglo-Saxon, Anglo-Roman, are Norse, consequently that the ancestors of the English-speaking people are from the basin of the Baltic and present Scandinavia, and that it is only there that one sees the antiquities of a most warlike and sea-faring race of the period of the so-called *Saxon* maritime expeditions?

Many apply the name of Anglo-Saxon to the people who settled in Britain, without knowing why, except that they had been taught to believe it from their school and college days, or because the majority believe so. I maintain that the earlier England, popularly placed at the southern part of the peninsula of Jutland, is mythical; that such antiquities pointed out as Angle are not found there; that the word "eng" (Swedish äng) is a common appellation all over Scandinavia; that "england," or "äng land," to this day, is the name given to flat, grassy land by the Norse people, as it was in earlier times. The probability is, that the Norsemen, seeing the flat shores of Britain on the North Sea, called it "England," or Land of Meadows; and the people, in the course of time, were called meadow-men, as we say mountaineers, in speaking of people inhabiting mountainous regions.

Some of my critics took up the question of language. The reason they gave for not agreeing with me was, that the English had the definite article "the," and the Icelandic saga-writings did not possess it; this was, according to them, the most positive proof that the earlier English people were not Norse. One might as well have argued that the French language was not derived in great part from the Latin, as it has the definite article, and the Latin had not. Who can ever tell when the definite article was dropped or added in those languages?

I never expected that the appearance of " The

Viking Age" would convert to my views men who had spent their lives in trying to prove, or in maintaining the belief in, the Anglo-Saxon myth, and who believed in the diffuse, contradictory, and often incomprehensible writings of Bede and Nennius, or in the earlier English chronicles, the authorship of which cannot be traced. But I have often wondered why no one has compared thoroughly the Norse archæology of that period with that of Britain, which is claimed as that of the Angle, Anglo-Saxon, as being the early settlers of Britain ; and the only reason I could discover that anyone had for calling these antiquities by those names was because of blind confidence that these settlers were what the historians claimed them to be.

Those who cling to the Anglo-Saxon belief point to here and there a few graves in the ancient Friesland, similar to those found in England, as a proof that the earlier settlers of Britain did not come from the Baltic. As if it were possible that none of these Norsemen, who used to visit Friesland as far back as before the time of Tacitus, could have failed to die there during several centuries! They forget, also, that the Romans never mentioned the people of that country as sea-faring. On the contrary, the mari-

time tribes that harassed them "were living on
the most northern shores of the sea—in the ocean
itself." The antiquities left by these sea-faring
tribes are those that must give us light on the
subject.

One might just as well assert one thousand
years from now that the people of English descent of the present time living at the Cape of
Good Hope were the ones that held sway over
India, because they were nearer than England to
India, or that the solitary graves or little English
cemeteries found between England and India were
those of the people who governed India. A little
more research would prove to them that the
great seat of power was in England. We learn
from archæology where Egypt, Greece, Rome,
and many other fallen empires held their sway.
So we may know, from the traces left, where
the Norsemen held theirs also, and that nowhere
did they hold it more firmly than in Britain.

The controversy, to me, seems very plain. I
have maintained in "The Viking Age," and shall
continue to do so, until I am shown to be mis-
taken, that: It is in the basin of the Baltic, and in
the Norselands, that we see incontestable proofs
as to who were the sea-faring people whom the
Romans called first Sueones and then Saxons, as

shown by the tens of thousands of graves of that
period still existing; that these graves and their
antiquities are the same, and of the same type,
as those of a similar period in England; that
in these Norse graves a great many Roman
coins of gold and silver, and many Roman and
Greek objects are found, showing that these
sea-faring people had intercourse with Rome,
Greece, and the Mediterranean. Nay, do not the
coins antedating the Roman Empire, when patrician families of Rome coined their own money,
tell the tale of how early Norsemen went into
the Mediterranean? Are not Norse graves often
seen on its shores, by the side of the graves of
the Etruscans?

I also maintain that neither at the mouth of
the Elbe, nor anywhere else out of the Norselands, do we see the remains of a dense, warlike,
and maritime population—a population which has
left traces in the number of its graves far greater
than has Rome itself.

How could the host miscalled Saxon by the
later Romans, which overran Europe, till the
downfall of the empire, for four centuries, avoid
leaving such traces? Their population must have
been very dense in order to allow them to send
forth such vast fleets to fight and conquer the

Romans. How is it that the Saxons, whom we know as Saxons, were not a sea-faring people in the time of Charlemagne, as we know they were not? Simply because they never had been. How is it that in Charlemagne's time, on the other hand, the Sueones who must have been the Saxons of the later Romans were dreaded by him as powerful at sea, just as they are described by Tacitus?

Have not the races which have disappeared in America or elsewhere left traces, and must we make an exception of the so-called Saxons of the Romans? This would be against the evidence of everything before us.

It is by comparing the graves and antiquities of the Norselands with those of England that we have the proof that the early settlers of Britain were Norsemen. The scene in this volume, of Ivar going to visit his kinsmen on the banks of the River Cam, in England, has been described, because there is a cemetery there whose antiquities show its Norse origin, and the Roman coins buried with them, of Trajanus, 98–117 A.D.; of Hadrianus, 117–138; Faustina, wife of Antoninus Pius, 138–161; Marcus Aurelius, 161–180; of Maximianus, 286–305, show how early Norse settlements began.

What are the objects found in that cemetery, and described in the beautiful work of the Honorable R. C. Neville, " Saxon Obsequies, Illustrated by Ornaments and Weapons Discovered in a Cemetery near Little Wilbraham, Cambridgeshire," printed in 1852? Swords, axes, umbos, cinerary urns with burned bones, wooden buckets with bronze hoops, bronze tweezers, spear and arrow heads of iron, ear picks, iron knives, iron shears, brooches, beads of glass, and other material fired by cremation.

I will quote the words of Mr. Neville himself : "That so large a number of urns containing human remains should have been discovered in conjunction with skeletons, affords a remarkably satisfactory confirmation of the coexistence of these two modes of burial. My experience enables me to state with confidence that the urns now discovered differ entirely from any [Roman] I had before encountered, and resemble closely those usually met with in Anglo-Saxon buryinggrounds, etc."

If the reader opens "The Viking Age," and looks over its thirteen hundred and sixty illustrations, he will see the same objects as those described and illustrated by Mr. Neville, and the same descriptions of graves.

b

It is time that the views of antiquarians and historians of the old school should be entirely set aside or remodelled; and that the old England, placed popularly as existing in the southern part of the peninsula of Jutland, and comprising a territory of a few square miles, be considered a myth that had no reality, except in the brain of its inventors. When I say that the antiquities found in England are the same and of the same type as those found in the Norselands, I call this a fact and not a theory; and when I say also that these are not found in the Saxon lands, I call this a fact and not a theory. When I say that the antiquities found in England are not found in the so-called earlier England of the historian, I call this a fact and not a theory; and if I am wrong it can be easily disproved.

But let me add, that after the appearance of " The Viking Age," everybody was far from being against me in England. I found there many adherents to my views, and some even went so far as to write to me, that after the publication of the work, and upon seeing its illustrations, they did not believe that Stonehenge was Druidical, but was simply of Norse origin, for there were many graves containing Viking remains in the country round about.

The Roman records are correct. No countries but the islands of the Baltic and Scandinavia correspond to their description. It is there that we find a great number of Roman objects. Coins are there found from the time of the foundation of the empire—those of Augustus 29 B. C. to 14 A. D., of Tiberius 14–37, Claudius 41–54; then in increased number those of Nero 54–68, Vitellius 69, Vespasian 69–79, of Titus 79–81; in still greater number those of Trajan 98–117, Antoninus Pius 138–161, of Faustina the elder, wife of Antoninus Pius, of Marcus Aurelius 161–180, of Faustina his wife, of Commodus 180–192; then in decreasing quantities the coins of the subsequent emperors. By the side of these coins and other Roman objects are Norse objects, and these Norse objects are, as I have said, similar to those found in the England of a corresponding period. The mode of burial is also identical in both countries. These facts tell plainly who were the people who settled in Britain before and after the time of Ivar the Viking and of the Roman occupation.

While the controversy was going on in England, knowing the receptive and impartial mind of Mr. Gladstone, and having been several times the recipient, in years past, of his kind hospitality, and remembering the interest he had taken in my African travels, I took the liberty of addressing to him a request for his opinion in regard to the position I had taken. Mr. Gladstone, who was then in Oxford for the purpose of delivering a lecture on Homer, replied the same day. I append his letter:

DEAR MR. DU CHAILLU:

You have done me great honour by appealing to me, but I fear your appeal is to a person prepossessed and ignorant.

My prepossessions are on your side. But I have not yet been able, although very desirous, to examine the argument on your side as it deserves, nor that of your adversaries.

I am a man of *Scotch* blood only, half Highland, and half Lowland, near the Border. A branch of my family settled in Scandinavia, in the first half, I think, of the seventeenth century.

When I have been in Norway, or Denmark, or among Scandinavians, I have felt something like a cry of nature from within, asserting (credibly or otherwise) my nearness to them. In Norway I have never felt as if in a foreign country; and this, I have learned, is a very common experience with British travellers.

The love of freedom in combination with settled order, which we hope is characteristic of this country, is, I apprehend, markedly characteristic of Norway and of Denmark. I have not spoken of Sweden, simply because I have not been there.

The ethnography of northern and insular Scotland, down even to the Isle of Man, and the history, seem to show a very broad and durable connection.

Still I cannot call these more than feeble generalities. I earnestly hope, when I am a little more free, that I may be able to get some real hold of the subject.

I think a good deal of the argument suggested by our fishing population, and by the *curious* persistency with which, in some districts, Scandinavian terminations have been preserved.

Yours faithfully,
W. E. GLADSTONE.

CONTENTS

CHAPTER XVII

CHAPTER XVIII

CHAPTER XIX

CHAPTER XX

CHAPTER XXI

CHAPTER XXII

CHAPTER XXIII

CHAPTER XXIV

CHAPTER XXV

CHAPTER XXVI

CHAPTER XXVII

CHAPTER XXVIII

CHAPTER XXIX

CHAPTER XXX

CHAPTER XXXI

26. 6. 90

Dear Mr. Duthwailler

You have done me
great honour by appealing
to me but I fear that your
appeal is to a person prepossessed and ignorant.

My prepossessions are on your
side. But I have not yet been
able, although very desirous to
examine the arguments on your
side as it deserves, nor that —

of your adversaries

I am a man of Scotch blood only, half Highland, and half lowland near the Border. A branch of my family settled in Scandinavia, in the first half I think of the seventeenth century.

When I have been in Norway, or Denmark, or among Scandinavians, I have felt something like a cry of Nature within asserting (credibly or otherwise) my nearness to them. In Norway I never felt—as if in a foreign country: and this I have learned is a very common experience with British travellers.

The love of freedom in combination with settled order, which we hope is characteristic of this country, is I suppose hand markedly characteristic of Norway, & of Denmark. I have not spoken of Sweden, simply because I have not been there.

The ethnography and history of northern and insular Scotland, down even to the Isle of Man, and the history, seem to show a very broad and durable connection.

Still I cannot call these more than faint generalities. I earnestly hope when I am a little more free that I may be able to get some real hold of the subject.

I think a good deal of the argument suggested by our fishing population, and by the curious <u>persistency</u> with which in some districts Scandinavian ornamentations have been preserved. Yours faithfully

WEGladstone

IVAR THE VIKING

CHAPTER I

HJORVARD AND GOTLAND

THE mariner sailing in the Baltic, as he skirts the shores of Gotland, sees on a promontory of that island several large cairns and mounds over-looking the sea, and the country that surrounds them. This promontory was the burial-place of a family of great Vikings and rulers who held sway over the whole island a few centuries before and after our era. Among the most conspicuous cairns two are pointed out to the stranger, those of Hjorvard and his son Ivar, the hero of the present narrative.

The events of which I am going to speak to you relate to them, and to what happened during their lives, towards the latter end of the third and the beginning of the fourth century, between the years A.D. 270 and 320, or about sixteen hundred years ago.

Hjorvard, "the wide spreading," so called on account of the widely extended maritime expeditions he had undertaken, was one of the most renowned Vikings of his time. In all his expeditions he had been successful and always victorious in his battles. The Roman fleets had never dared to attack him as he sailed with his numerous ships along the coasts of their wide empire to make war upon the different countries over which they held dominion.

Hjorvard's ancestors, by the side of whom he now lies buried, had been great warriors and seafaring men like himself. They had sailed from the Baltic to the Caspian Sea, by the present Gulf of Finland, and also westward, along the coast of Friesland, Gaul, Britain, and as far south as the Mediterranean. The ships used by them in their river expeditions or along the coast during the summer months were unlike those of the Romans, and were much admired by them. Even in the first century the Romans feared these men of the north on account of the great fleets they possessed, and placed them as living on the most northern shores of the sea, in the very ocean itself. They called them Sueones; and all they knew of their country was what these Sueones told them about it, for the Baltic was an unknown sea to the Romans.

Hjorvard was of high lineage, for he was descended from Odin, and he belonged to that branch of the family of Odin called Ynglingar, which ruled over Svithjod, a realm that embraced a great part of the present Sweden.

Sigrlin, his wife, was a very handsome woman,

and possessed all the accomplishments belonging
to women of her high rank. She was also of
Odin's kin; was a direct descendant of Skjöld (the
Norse word for shield), one of the sons of Odin,
from whom the Skjöldungar are descended. The
Skjöldungar ruled over that part of the land which
to-day is called Denmark, but which was then
called Gotland. Her father was called Halfdan,
and resided at Hleidra, not far from where Copen-
hagen stands to-day, and was one of the great
rulers of the north.

Not far from the cairns and mounds just mentioned was Dampstadir, the head "by," or burg,
the residence of Hjorvard and of the rulers of
Gotland. From this place a long panorama of
coast and land could be seen, and the eye lost
itself in the dim horizon of the sea. There Hjorvard lived in great splendor. The buildings which
made up Dampstadir were among the finest of the
northern lands; they were of different sizes and
varied architecture, and, like all the structures of
those days in the north, were entirely of wood.
They were roofed with shingles, heavily tarred,
their dark color contrasting pleasantly with that
of the log walls of the houses.

All the numerous buildings formed a vast quadrangle, enclosing a large plot of grass called
"tun," or town. From the centre of the square
the sight was extremely beautiful and picturesque, for there were not two buildings of the
same appearance or size. Some were finer than

others, of course, but all were quaint; from their
roofs and sides, gargoyles, representing heads of
horses or dragons and other wild beasts, stuck out
boldly into the air from every side, or looked, with
heads inclined downward, towards the ground.
There were a few houses with towers, called lofts;
in these towers were a number of sleeping-rooms,
and from their tops, in time of war, a sharp look-
out was kept for the enemy's vessels. Many buildings were also used as store-houses.

Before the doors of many houses were porches,
ornamented with carvings, while others had bel-
fries and dark piazzas with ladder-like stairs leading to them, their weather-beaten walls of hard
logs seeming to defy the ravages of time, for
many of them, at that time even, dated centuries
back. Some were specially for the use of the
women members of the family of Hjorvard and
for their household, for it was customary for
women to have their " skemmas," or bowers, all
to themselves. There they received their friends
and spent their time in sewing and embroidering.
There were several festive halls for every-day use.
During the winter long fires ran along the centre of these, the smoke escaping through openings in the roof, which openings could be closed
when necessary. Along the walls ran long benches,
and tables were set in front of them. The light
came in through windows; instead of glass, the
transparent membrane enclosing the new-born calf
was stretched over what were called the light-holes.

The every-day life of Hjorvard was very simple. At the principal, or day meal, Sigrlin sat on the left hand of her husband, the seats next to this, on both sides, being the most dignified for men and women, while the farthest ones, near the door, were the least so. The most high born, oldest, and wisest man—for it was the custom for rulers to have wise men with them who knew the ancient examples and customs of their forefathers—sat on the northern high seat, called the lower high seat, opposite that of Hjorvard, on whose right hand were women, the men being on his left. It was also the custom for chiefs to carry the ale over the fire, and drink to the man opposite the high seat, and it was thought to be a great honor to be toasted by the host.

The most imposing and striking of all the structures along that enormous square was the great banqueting hall; of all the buildings, this was the one in which the chiefs and rulers took the greatest pride, for it was there that they received their most honored guests and gave their most splendid feasts. The banqueting hall at Dampstadir was ranked the sixth for beauty and grandeur in the land of the Vikings, and was very old. Two superb doors at the two ends led into the interior. The door-ways, or jambs, of these were of solid oak, about two and a half feet wide, and several inches thick ; these were adorned with beautiful carvings, representing scenes belonging to the religious history of the race, and varying greatly in depth, so

as to give a fine artistic effect of light and shade.
The doors themselves were of solid oak also, and
were ornamented with intricate designs made with
flat iron bands, of exquisite beauty, and perfect
gems of art. A massive gold knocker adorned
each door. By one door the women entered, by
the other the men.

The inside of this banqueting hall was a sight
not to be soon forgotten. The first artists and
wood-carvers of the North had been employed,
and had shown wonderful skill in the elaboration
and grouping of their designs—the scenes represented including many of the deeds and expeditions of Hjorvard's ancestors. The carvings were
considered so beautiful that even the finest tapestry
was not hung over them, and the wood itself had
become richly dark during the centuries that had
elapsed since the hall had been built. All along
the walls hung shields of variegated designs and
bright colors, ornamented with gold and silver,
overlapping each other, and, of course, adding
much to the gorgeousness of the spectacle.

As was customary, this hall had been built east
and west, the long walls running north and south ;
along the latter were the benches for the guests,
and just in the middle of them were the two high
seats, facing each other. The most important
bench ran along the northern walls, and there the
great high seat, the more honored of the two,
stood facing the sun. It was for the master of the
house ; and to be placed on the high seat opposite

was the greatest honor that could be shown to
any guest, consequently this seat was always assigned to the most prominent men. The nearer
the places on the benches assigned to any one
were to the high seat, the greater the honor; the
places farther away, near the door, being the low-
est. These two high seats were beautifully carved,
with arms on both sides, and two pillars which
were both painted and ornamented with carving
representing historical subjects.

The weapons of Hjorvard hung above his high
seat—his "sax," or single-edged sword, his best
double-edged sword, also his shield, his " brynja,"
or chain-armor, and helmet of gold. His double-
edged sword, called "Hrotti," was a magnificent
weapon. The hilt was all ornamented with gold,
and so was the scabbard; the blade was of most
exquisite damascened workmanship. This sword
was in its sheath, which was wrapped with bands
called " peace bands"—for there was profound
peace over the land at the time we are speaking
of—and no one but Hjorvard could unloose them,
for these were holy, and it was only when war had
been declared that it could be done.

Mementos of the expeditions of Hjorvard and
of his forefathers were scattered here and there,
treasured as heirlooms. Along the walls hung
several Roman swords with Latin inscriptions
upon them, which had been in the family for two
hundred years. There were Roman statuettes,
bronze vessels, and various other bronze objects,

and a collection of Roman coins of every emperor from the time of Augustus, the first Roman
emperor, to the time of Hjorvard. Among the
gems of art were lovely Grecian cups, bowls, and
drinking horns of glass, some of the glass cups
and bowls adorned with charming paintings representing rural scenes, with wild beasts, lions, bulls,
birds of variegated colors, and even men boxing
with boxing gloves, all looking as fresh as the day
they were painted.

At the foot of Dampstadir was a beautiful land-
locked bay where the ships of Hjorvard lay at
anchor, while on its shores were numerous sheds,
under which stood many of the ships which were
thus protected from the weather; there were also
building yards, where busy carpenters were always
at work constructing or repairing vessels.

The finest ships to be seen there were the
"drekis," or dragon ships. These were the largest and most formidable of all war-ships, and derived their names from the fact that their prows
and sterns were ornamented with the head or tail
of one or more dragons. Some were covered with
sheets of solid gold, which gave a superb appearance to the ships, especially when the sun shone
upon their sides. Many of these drekis could
carry a crew of from five hundred to seven hundred men.

Besides the dragon ships there were other war-
vessels called "skeids," "snekkjas," "skutas,"
"buzas," "karfi," "ask," and also many provision

ships which followed the fleets on their expeditions. The skeid was a formidable war-vessel, almost equal in power to the dragon-ships, a very fast
sailer, which carried two hundred and forty men or
more. The snekkja was a smaller ship of the same
general description. The skutta was a smaller
craft still, which could be manœuvred very quickly. It was generally used for boarding other
ships, the upper part of its gunwale being so built
that warriors could more easily leap upon other
vessels. All these vessels, small or large, had only
one mast.

Among these ships could be seen some of the
old-fashioned type which has been described by
Tacitus, with no mast, and entirely propelled by
oars; they were very sharp pointed at both ends,
much like the whale-boats of to-day, about eighty
feet long, and in the widest part ten or eleven
feet broad, with fifteen or sixteen benches about
three feet apart. These boats were propelled
by thirty or thirty-two oars, varying somewhat
in length, and of an average of about twelve feet.
Two men, and sometimes three, pulled each oar,
and a man with a shield protected the oarsmen on
each outer side. The thole-pins were fastened to
the gunwales with " bast " ropes, and were adorned
with graceful carved designs, no two being alike.
On the side, at the stern, was the rudder, resembling a large, broad oar. They were so shaped
that they could be rowed in either direction.
At the time of which we are speaking, this model

of naval architecture was fast going out of fashion, and sailing vessels exclusively were coming into general use. All the vessels were of oak, " clinch-built ; " that is, the planks overlapped each other, and were made fast together by large iron bolts.

The island of Gotland, over which Hjorvard ruled, had a very dense population, and was, on account of its size and geographical position, a great emporium of commerce, and with its war and trading ships occupied at this time about the same position as the England of our days. Its inhabitants were wealthy, and traded extensively, as their fathers had done, with provinces of Rome, with Greece, and the countries round the Caspian, the Black, and the Mediterranean Seas. From such distant lands as these they brought superb bronze vessels, exquisite glass vases, velvets and silks, beautiful objects of leather, embroidered gold and silver textile material for dress, and many other costly objects which the rich prized very highly, as well as wine.

CHAPTER II

THE VIKING LAND, AND THE VIKINGS

AT the period of which I write, the land of the Vikings embraced the islands of the Baltic and those of the small and the great " Belt " leading into that sea, the country known to-day as Scandinavia, which embraces the large peninsula of Sweden and Norway, and the small peninsula of Jutland. The whole land was virtually surrounded by sea. Great fortifications had been built on the southern peninsula of Jutland between the two fjords which enter it from opposite sides, so that no incursion could take place from the land to the south.

The large islands, especially, were seats of great maritime power and wealth. All the tribes were of a common origin and kindred ; they had the same customs and religion, practised the same burial rites, intermarried, and spoke the same language which was called the Norranean tongue.

These Vikings, as we have seen, were quite isolated from Central and Western Europe, and formed a world of their own, having much intercourse with the country forming the present Russia. Between them and Rome stood the inaccessible swamps and forests of Germania, inhabited by wild and barbaric tribes. Great, indeed, was the contrast that existed between the Vikings and the tribes of Germania. All these tribes called themselves Norsemen, or Northmen; they were intensely warlike, and had been sea-faring people from immemorial time. The deeds done on the sea in by-gone ages could only be seen or remembered by graves made venerable by the centuries that had passed over them, or by the large tracings deeply engraved upon the rocks, seen to this day, representing sea-fights, raids, and invasions. Like the hieroglyphics of Egypt, they were the mementos of a great past, forever forgotten.

The Norsemen of our period used only weapons of iron; those of bronze had been given up centuries before, but they were proud of that former civilization, and boasted that at that remote time no one excelled their ancestors in the art of manufacturing arms of bronze—a boast that has not been made vain to this day.

Long even before the time of Hjorvard the country was unable to support its population, and the people had in consequence become more and more aggressive towards the inhabitants of countries to the west of them as years passed away. Through their voyages during the preceding generations and during their own times, they had become thoroughly acquainted with the countries and rivers of Friesland, Gaul, Britain, and other countries, and had been seeking new homes there.

Their fleets swarmed over every sea, and no country was exempt from their attacks. Year after year, an innumerable, irresistible, and apparently inexhaustible host, they poured over Western Europe, and had become complete masters of the sea. Fleet after fleet returned home laden with Roman spoils of all kinds.

These expeditions were undertaken by chiefs living in very different regions of the country, and the people flocked with their ships from every part of the land, to enroll themselves under their standards, when they announced that they were ready to make war on the Roman world. The ever victorious Norsemen called themselves the chosen people of the gods, the loved ones of Odin, and considering themselves the chosen, they never tried to convert other nations; like the Jews of old, they despised every other religion. Wherever they obtained a foothold, they held the land and people under an iron sway. Death had no terror for them; Valhalla, where Odin dwelt, was to be their future abode. They believed also in Frey, Njord, Thor, Freya, and in other gods and goddesses.

There were many conditions of men in the great Viking's land; different grades of society built up the social structure. The whole country was divided into "herads," forming separate realms; some had a much larger tract of territory than others, and were more powerful. Most of the estates composing them were inherited by

laws of primogeniture or entail. Over each herad
ruled a Hersir, which was the highest hereditary
dignity in the land. The title of Drott, "Lord,"
or High Priest, which had come down from
Odin's time, had disappeared and given place
to that of Hersir; the name of king was yet
unknown. Each herad had a head-temple where
the yearly sacrifices for all the people were made.

The Hersir was the head of the community.
He was the leader in war, and the administrator
of justice. He was the high priest in regard to
worship, and as such took care of the temple, and
superintended the sacrifices and other religious
ceremonies. He held the farms and estates belonging to the temple in trust, received a temple
tax from every man for its maintenance and that
of the sacrifices. He presided over the general
assembly of the herad, called Thing, which took
place several times during the year. Through his
position he acquired great wealth, and owned
many landed estates at home and in the countries
he or his forefathers had subjugated. He distributed among his warriors and scalds costly things
and much gold. He stirred up war, reddened the
fields of battle, overthrew his enemies, in order to
rule over more lands and personal property.

The Hersir's wife was generally of Odin's kin,
and their children were wrapped in silk and the
finest of linen; their descendants were the highest
in the land.

Their sons broke horses, bent shields, smoothed

shafts, shook ashen spears, rowed and sailed ships, were believed to be able to write magic runes to save the lives of men; to blunt the edges of weapons and calm the sea by spells; to understand the language of birds; to quench fire, read minds, allay sorrows, and to have the strength and energy of eight men. Their chief occupation was to go to war and fell the enemy. Their hair was fair, their cheeks bright and healthy, and their eyes as keen as those of a young snake.

The Hersir's daughters were slender fingered, their hands and arms were soft, their hearts lighter and their necks whiter than pure snow. They were fair and gentle, endowed with all the accomplishments belonging to high-born women; when they married they were clad in white bridal linen, according to the custom of high-born people, and walked under a bridal veil.

Next in rank to the Hersir were the Haulds, the highest class of dwellers in the land. They lived on the estates that had descended to them for generations. As a body of men, they were the power of the land, and no Hersir could ever rule without their consent.

Their sons, as they grew up, learned how to handle the shield, bend the elm, or make bows, shaft the arrow, throw the spear, ride horses, set on the hounds, brandish the sword, practise swimming, to write runes, play chess, wrestle, and be foremost in all athletic games. They had the same education as the Hersir's children; their daughters were dressed in white, also, when they married.

After the Hauld came another class of land own-ers, the Bondi, whose estates were also entailed. These people throve well on the land, broke oxen, made ploughs, timbered houses, made barns and carts, and drove the plough. Their daughters carried keys hanging at their side, and helped their mothers. When they married, they too were allowed to wear white, like the daughters of Her-sirs and Haulds, to set up a household, and sleep under linen bed-clothes; they divided wealth with their husbands.

There was another class of freemen who rented lands, for they had no estate. The doors of the houses of these were always ajar; there was a fire in the middle of the floor; a lumpy loaf, heavy and thick, hand-mixed, was on the trencher; broth in a bowl, and veal, considered the choicest of dain-ties, were often seen on the table.

A poorer class of freemen existed. Their doors were also always ajar; husband and wife were always busy with their work; his beard was trimmed, his hair lay on his forehead, his shirt was tight. His wife twirled a distaff, stretched out her arms, and made cloth. She wore a head-dress on her head, to show that she was no longer a maiden; a kerchief on her neck, and brooches fastening the folds of the dress on the shoulders.

Then came the slave, distinct from all, dressed always in thick, white woollen stuff, with his hair cropped close, in contrast to the long hair worn by the freeman. Such was his badge of servitude. He was always of foreign birth or origin. He had been captured in war, or bought at a market-place or at a fair in distant lands, and generations of slavery had degraded him; nevertheless he also throve well in the land, but the wrinkled skin and crooked knuckles, the thick fingers, the ugly face, the bent back, the long heels, told the tale of his slavery and of that of his forefathers. His life was passed in trying to learn how much he could endure and bear; his time was employed in binding bark or bast, in making loads, and in carrying these the live-long day. His wife came home in the evening, weary of standing up all day. Scars were on the soles of her feet, her arms were sunburnt, her appearance told of her bondage. After she had come in, she sat down on the middle of the household bench, and her son sat at her side. Husband and wife lived happily with their children; when these grew up, they laid the fences, tended swine, herded goats, cut wood, or dug peat. Such were the classes that made up the population of that great and powerful Viking land.

CHAPTER III

HJORVARD CONSULTS THE ORACLE

THERE was no nobler or bolder heart than that of Hjorvard. He had begun his life of warfare when fifteen years old. Many in the land said that the renown he had gained was the result of folly and hardihood; others thought that he enjoyed his life in doing deeds of honor. He had won fame, and travelled through nine different countries.

Like all the great Hersirs, he had with him twelve champions who formed his body-guard, and had come from every part of the Northern lands; some from the shores of present Norway, others from the islands of the Baltic, and two from Svithjod. The bravest men wanted to serve him, for he was lucky in war, a genial and convivial leader, and most generous with his gold.

All the champions of Hjorvard were berserks, and to be considered the foremost champion was the ambition of every warrior. To attain this proud position was no easy task among so many men in the land who were equally brave and perfectly reckless of their lives, and who were thoroughly skilled in the handling of weapons, and all kinds of athletic games. After such a reputation had been acquired, the champion had either to challenge or be challenged by those who were envious of him, or thought themselves more than his equal ; and these contests, or trials of strength and skill, generally took place before a large assembly of people. The champions of Hjorvard in time of peace often went round the country and challenged men specially famous for their prowess.

Berserks despised chain-armor and all weapons of defence such as shields and helmets. They often even fought without clothing, and could lash themselves into such a state of frenzy that they lost all control over themselves. Often this fury, or berserk rage, came upon them without cause and seized them suddenly, when they would bite their weapons, gnash their teeth, wrestle with trees and rocks, and become reckless of every danger. When in sight of their foes they rushed to the attack with an indescribable fury, and when in conflict with other berserks the fight was deadly. When the berserk fury seized them at home, they would go out, through fear of fighting with their friends, and wrestle with rocks and trees.

Hjorvard had made very stringent rules for his champions and warriors. No man could come under his standard who feared death or uttered words of fright when in danger, or groaned when he received the worst wounds in battle. Nor could these wounds themselves be dressed until the day after they had been received. No man was allowed to have a sword longer than two feet. The swords and saxes of Hjorvard's men were heavier than those of others, so that when they struck a blow it might be most telling.

It was always the custom of Hjorvard to lie with his ships before promontories so that these might be seen by every one. On none of his vessels were tents put up to protect him or his men from the weather. They never reefed a sail during a storm, and he had never more than one hundred and twenty champions on board of his own ship.

He had the honor of chivalry; he bade his warriors not to break men's spirit by putting them in fetters, nor to do any harm to any man's wife, and ordered that every maid should be bought with dowry and with the consent of her father, and that women and their children should not be captured.

Victory always followed him, so that great champions and berserks of the land flocked to his standards when he undertook a warlike expedition. Led by him, they felt sure of victory in advance. No man less than eighteen years old or more than fifty could follow him in warfare. All his warriors had to have strength enough to lift a large stone that stood near his residence. The chiefs who resided in Gotland owed him allegiance, and all were his kinsmen, and all those under him had, by law, to furnish him a certain number of ships and warriors when needed.

During his life he had subdued several chiefs on

the southern shores of the Baltic, and those paid
him tribute willingly, for he was not grasping, and
used his power with moderation ; but all had to
submit once to the humiliating ceremony of let-
ting him put his foot on their necks in acknowl-
edgment of being his vassals.

Though Hjorvard and Sigrlin had been married
a certain number of years, no child had been born
to them, so the Hersir of Gotland made up his
mind to go to Svithjod, the most powerful realm
of the Viking lands, and to Upsalir, the most sacred
of all the places of the north, to consult the gods
and see if he could learn the decrees of fate.

Hjorvard assembled a large fleet, and after bidding farewell to Sigrlin, who accompanied him to
his ship, he sailed directly for the fjord at the head
of which is Lake Malar. The wind was good,
and the second day they came in sight of land.
Here fortified towers and catapults in sight of each
other guarded the narrow arm of the sea on both
sides, whence a storm of missiles could be thrown
on the vessels of an invading host, and in war
times chains were laid across there, preventing the
sudden ascent of ships. As the moon shone
brightly that night, they continued their voyage.
Borne on by a strong and favorable breeze, in due
course of time they came to the narrowest part
of the fjord, called to-day Waxholm. The men
shouted as they sailed past the fortifications, view-
ing which, they said to each other, " No wonder

that Upsalir is impregnable." But the white peace
shields were at the mast-heads, for there had been
peace between Gotland and Svithjod for many a
year.

As the fleet approached Lake Malar the wind
became very light, and the crews had to take to
their oars. Three men were on each; these pulled
the oars so hard that their bodies seemed at times
to be bent in two. Farther on, they came to
the head of the fjord, and sailed amidst the
several islands which are in the river, and upon
which to-day a great part of Stockholm is built.
That place was also fortified; numerous catapults
defended the channels between the islands. Then
they entered the lake, a large sheet of water
about seventy miles long, dotted with fourteen
hundred islands, whose banks were covered with
superb forests of oak of gigantic size, and after
a pleasant journey reached Upsalir. Hjorvard
was received with much honor by Yngvi, his kinsman, the ruler of Svithjod, who descended from
Odin in direct line, and there was great feasting
during his stay.

Many of the dwellings and buildings of Upsalir
dated from the time of Frey, the successor of Odin.
The temple itself was believed to have been built
by Frey. It was of the greatest magnificence and
size, and the most sacred building in the Norselands. From its fantastic and overlapping roof,
gargoyles stretched forth in every direction, or
looked down upon the sacred grounds of the

temple, and the worshippers that came to sacrifice. A gallery ran around the temple, supported by pillars. The temple was built of enormous red fir trees, and its walls had withstood the blasts of centuries. The walls, ceilings, and pillars inside were entirely sheathed with red gold, likewise the altar upon which the holy fire was always burning. The Hersir of Svithjod alone could remain seated during the religious ceremony attending the sacrifice. All the others had to stand until they partook of the flesh of the sacrificed animals.

The door of the temple was round-arched, and a masterpiece of carving, representing Odin offering a sacrifice. On each of its pillars stood a beautiful carved cat. The door itself was ornamented with iron work, with a solid knocker of gold in the centre. Not far from the door outside was the holy spring in which the men sacrificed to Odin were thrown. For a long distance the lands surrounding the temple were sacred. No temple could vie with the temple at Upsalir, none received more yearly taxes and offerings for its sacrifices and maintenance ; large estates belonged to it, and its revenues were very great. People came from every part of the Viking lands to assist in its sacrifices, which were the largest in the North, and on important occasions chiefs met there from all their realms to sacrifice to the gods and learn the decrees of fate.

After his arrival Hjorvard made a great sacrifice. Black oxen and the finest horses had been fat-

tened for this special occasion. The walls of the
temple, inside and outside, were reddened with the
blood of the sacrificed animals, and the Hersirs and
all the people who were present were also sprinkled
with the blood. The gods were invoked, and then
the holy chips that had been dipped in the sacrificed
blood were thrown into the air. The answer came
that Sigrlin would bear a son in about a year;
then with great joy he sailed for Dampstadir to
announce to his wife what the chips had foretold.

After his return he remained at home, waiting
for the event which had been predicted by the
casting of the sacrificing chips. He spent his
time surveying his large estates, and watched over
very carefully the building of a great number
of ships; he often superintended the work in the
fields, for he was a good husbandman; and to
amuse himself, he made several fine damascened
swords. He paid special attention to the fisheries
and seal catching, for these were splendid schools
for future seamen; or he played chess—the squares
of his chess-board were of gold or of silver—or
hunted with his hawks.

CHAPTER IV

ABOUT fourteen months after the return of Hjorvard from Upsalir, towards the year 275, a great event took place at Dampstadir, which filled the hearts of Hjorvard and Sigrlin with joy. The sacrifice which Hjorvard had made to the gods in Upsalir to stop the sterility of his wife had been accepted, and Sigrlin gave birth to a son. While this happened, Hjorvard was in the great banqueting hall, entertaining some of his kinsmen who had come to see him, and was then listening to a poet who was singing the heroic deeds of the ancestors of the race. Messengers were sent to him to apprise him of his good fortune.

Present at the birth of the child were Oddrun, the married sister of Hjorvard, and several other high-born women, and others who lived at or near Dampstadir, and also the female servants; for it was the law of the land that women had to be witnesses of the birth of a child, and none of those who were present could leave the place until they had seen the babe on the breast of his mother. According to custom, the infant was laid on the floor to wait for the arrival of his father.

After Hjorvard had entered the room, the new-born child was put into his lap, and he covered him with the folds of one of the corners of his cloak; doing this he acknowledged the legitimacy of his offspring. Then he looked at his child intently, to judge of his appearance, proportions, luck, and temper. After a thoughtful examination, and satisfying himself that the new-born offspring was well-shaped, he decided that he should live and not be exposed. This custom was similar to that of the Spartans—the father was the only judge to decide if the new-born babe was to live or not.

Then took place the most important and sacred ceremony of " name fastening," equivalent to baptism, or pouring or sprinkling water upon the child, a holy custom which had come down from the remotest time, and was lost in the mist of ages. A vessel filled with water was brought in, and Hjorvard poured water upon the child, and said in a loud voice, so that the people should hear him : " Ivar shall the boy be named after his grandfather; he will of Odin's family the foremost man be called; he will fight many battles, and be much like his mother, and be called his father's son, for he will wage war from early age, and wander far and wide." After this ceremony, the life of Ivar, like that of all other men, was sacred ; his father had not the power to expose him or to take his life, and if he did it would be murder.

Hjorvard gave first, as a " name fastening," a sprig of garlic as a symbol that as the garlic stood

high among the grass, so would little Ivar stand
among men.   Then he placed by his side a double-
edged sword and a sax, a coat of mail, a shield
and a helmet of silver; these had been made
specially beforehand, in case the expected new-
born infant should be a boy, and hence came the
common saying that high-born infants were born
with weapons.   He also gave him two large landed
estates, one called Ringstadir and the other High-
tun.   Every animal born on Hjorvard's numerous
farms on the day of the birth of little Ivar was
to belong to him, with the increase thereof, according to ancient custom.

The champions and warriors of Hjorvard said
that good years were in store for them, as little
Ivar would become in time a mighty warrior who,
like his father and forefathers, would lead them to
victory, as he had the piercing, snake-like eyes of
the Ynglingars.

During the night which followed the ceremony
of name fastening, the utmost silence reigned in
the house where little Ivar and his mother slept.
No one spoke; the utmost darkness prevailed
there, for no lights were burning.   The three
Nornir, Urd "the Past," Verdandi "the Present,"
and Skuld "the Future," were expected to come,
and forecast the life of Ivar that night.

These three genii shaped, or foreordained, the
life of every human being at his birth; their
decrees were final, and the gods had no power
to undo what they predestined.   They carved on

wood tablets the laws for the children of men.
According to the belief of the Norsemen, they
were an inseparable triad, or trinity, who, though
independent of each other, ruled as one the des-
tinies of man.   They were the representatives of
all life—the past, the present, and the future.

Urd was most majestic in appearance; her
long, flowing hair was as white as the purest snow.
The wisdom of the past lighted up her beautiful
countenance.   Her dreamy eyes looked back on
the countless ages of the past.   She remembered
all that had happened since the time of Ginnungagap, or Great Void, before the worlds had been
created, and beheld the successive changes that
were taking place.   From that time change was
constant; no ripple of the sea was as it was an
instant before, for every moment witnessed new
transformations.   Nothing is as it was, and
nothing will be as it has been.   And Urd's contented mind told her that all that happened in
the immensity and evolution of time was for the
best.

Verdandi looked fondly upon Urd, for the present could not exist without the past.   She was
most beautiful; her long, golden chestnut hair,
dyed by countless years in the rays of the sun,
typified the ripening of life, of time, of seasons.
Her face reflected the beauty and the loveliness
of the world in which Ivar's father and mother
lived.   She saw what was constantly happening
in the world—the storms, the wars, the joys, the

pestilences. Once in a while an expression of sadness passed over her countenance, for the woes and sorrows that befell men were brought upon them by themselves, and not by the Nornir.

Skuld was resplendent in beauty and freshness. Butterflies always surrounded her, for she typified immortality. She held in one of her hands the thread of life of every human being. Her garment shone like a silvery cloud ; from her long, flowing hair sprang rays of light, more brilliant than those of the sun, sending their radiance all over the world. With unbounded joy she looked into the future and into immortality. Hope she gave to all the children of men, and hid from their sight the breakers ahead, which wreck so many lives. With one hand she was ready to snap asunder the thread of life, which measured the number of days or hours allotted by the Nornir to every human being that came into the world.

The three Nornir lived in a large hall under the great ash-tree, "Yggdrasil," where the gods give their judgments every day. The ash is the largest and best of trees; it stands ever green ; its branches spread all over the world, and reach up over the heaven; three roots of the tree hold it up, and spread very widely. Under one of the roots is the well in which wisdom and intellect are hidden.

Towards midnight, when every one was profoundly asleep, and deep silence reigned in the house, Urd, Verdandi, and Skuld, according to the belief of the Norse people, came to forecast the fate of little Ivar. They bade him become the most valiant of chiefs, and the best of rulers. They unravelled the golden threads of fate they held, and fastened them in the midst of the heavens; in the east and in the west they hid their ends, and foretold that Ivar should hold land between them; but Skuld flung one thread on northern roads, and bade it to hold forever. This foreshadowed that he would never conquer any country north of Gotland. And it came to pass that the great dream of his life to extend his dominions north was never realized. They bade that he should understand the language of birds; and then they departed from the house to forecast other lives that were coming into the world.

CHAPTER V

THE FOSTERING OF IVAR

IVAR throve well, to the delight of his father and mother, and there was great joy in the family when he cut his first tooth. His father, according to ancient custom, gave him on that occasion a gift called a "tooth-fee." The gift was a knife in a gold sheath attached to a leather belt, sewn and embroidered with gold thread. The buckle was a beautiful work of solid gold. He gave him, also, with this, a large farm not far from Dampstadir, which was to become his residence when he became a man. As time went on, Ivar grew to be a beautiful child; he was fair, and had blue eyes resembling the people of his kin; like all boys of his age he loved to play, and nothing delighted him more than to put in the water a toy boat with a sail, and watch its going to sea.

When he had attained his sixth year, his parents began to think about sending him to be fostered, as it was the custom of the land for boys of prominent and leading men not to be reared at home, for fear they should become effeminate. They were sent to some distinguished friend, known for his bravery, tact, wisdom, and accomplishments, so

that the fostered child could have all the education
his rank in life should require.

Hjorvard and Sigrlin had had many anxious
thoughts in regard to the education of little Ivar,
for they wanted him to become wise, and the most
accomplished of warriors. Their love for him
was unbounded, and it required great strength of
character for both to be willing to part from him
for several years; but they felt that their greatest
duty was the welfare of their son. Their thoughts
had centred upon a noble man as the foster-father
of Ivar, of the name of Gudbrand, a Hersir, who
no longer undertook to lead expeditions into
far-off countries. He ruled over the island of
Engel, which is still called so to this day, and
which is situated in the Cattegat, not far from
the beautiful promontory of Kullen, and close to
the present southern Swedish shore. For him
both husband and wife had the greatest friendship,
esteem, and admiration. No better man could be
found to educate a boy in all the accomplishments
which were necessary for the high-born to possess
in those days.

Gudbrand and Hjorvard were foster-brothers,
and had gone on many warlike expeditions together; many a Roman, Gallic, and British head
had fallen under their saxes and swords; they
had shared and escaped many dangers, and had
received dangerous wounds together, and the love
one bore towards the other was very great.

Gudbrand was not as powerful a Hersir as Hjorvard, and did not possess as many estates and as much gold; but he was closely related to many of the chiefs who ruled over the large peninsula comprising the present Sweden and Norway. He was also of Odin's kin.

Hjorvard and Sigrlin, having made up their minds that Gudbrand should foster Ivar, concluded to send messengers to him to invite him to come and make them a visit, but without telling the reason why. They had told no one of their intentions in regard to the man whom they wanted to foster Ivar. The vessels were made ready to carry the messengers, when an unforeseen event prevented their departure. On the morning of the day appointed for their sailing, a fleet of fifteen sail was signalled from one of the towers as being seen very far off on the horizon. They were so far away that they could not be observed from the shore. Finally they were sighted by those on the beach, and gradually they became more and more distinct as they approached the land, and there was not the slightest doubt that they were steering for Dampstadir; the white peace shields were clearly discerned at the mastheads, also the color of each ship was clearly seen. The sight was beautiful as the vessels came nearer and nearer the land. The shields of the warriors lay side by side, covering each other partly, outside, along the gunwales, and their variegated colors, especially yellow, red, and black, presented a picturesque sight. The striped, colored

3

sails added no little to the beauty of the sight.
Ahead of all was a dragon ship; at its mast-head
a standard embroidered with gold, with an eagle
in the centre, by which the people recognized at
once the dragon ship of Gudbrand.

Hjorvard and Sigrlin, who were watching from
the highest tower, were greatly rejoiced at the
sight. They considered the arrival, at such an
opportune moment, of Gudbrand, whom they
wanted to see so much, as a good omen for the
future of their son. Hjorvard walked towards the
shore to meet his foster-brother, and took a row-
boat to go on board and welcome him as soon as
his ship had cast anchor.

Gudbrand was received with hearty demonstrations of joy and with great honor by Hjorvard,
who had not seen his foster-brother for more than
two years. He was led to the great hall, and seated
on the high seat opposite to that of Hjorvard, and
all the commanders, or " styrmen," as they were
called, of Gudbrand's ships, and his champions
were there also, and seated according to their
rank. There was deep drinking that day; a great
feast took place; the ale and the mead were
passed freely, and served in silver and golden
horns, and there was much merriment until the
early hours of the morning, after which all retired to their separate houses. Gudbrand was
given the finest house, intended for high-born
guests, for his residence while in Dampstadir.

The following day, as Gudbrand was quietly

talking with the champions of Hjorvard in the banqueting hall, and was intensely interested in listening to one of them who was describing a great wrestling contest that had taken place a few days before, Hjorvard entered unnoticed, with Ivar in his arms; and as Gudbrand saluted him, he put little Ivar on his knees, before he was aware of it. It was an ancient custom that the man upon whose knee a child had been thus "knee-seated," as this ceremony was called, was bound to become his fosterer until he became of age. A shout of assent arose from Hjorvard's champions as an approval of the choice of their chief, for whom every one was ready to sacrifice his life. No wonder they approved the choice, for Gudbrand was well known for his wisdom, skill in athletic games, and many other accomplishments.

Hjorvard could have shown no greater proof of friendship, esteem, and regard to Gudbrand than by what he had just done.

Gudbrand promised his companion-in-arms and foster-brother that he would bring up little Ivar to the best of his abilities, and then added, with a thoughtful voice: " Hjorvard, thou knowest well the ancient saying: 'An early sown field shall no man trust, nor his son too soon, for the weather rules the fields, and wits guide the son; each of these is uncertain.' Thou knowest well, also," he continued, "that the Nornir rule unevenly the fates of men. To a few they predestine a happy and contented life; to many, a short or a long one; to some, but little property or praise. Many they have fated to sorrows or to be unlucky; to one man they give great wealth and a miser's heart; to a poor man a most generous disposition. It seems to me that he who has the miser's heart ought to have been poor, and the one that has a giving heart to have been rich. But such are the decrees of the Nornir, and no one can understand or escape them. Fame and poverty are often given to the poet, but his name will endure forever; his mound will always be green in the memory of man, like the deeds of great heroes."

There was great feasting in Dampstadir during the remainder of Gudbrand's stay. Many a warrior drank more than he ought to have done, as was the custom in those times; but hospitality was most unbounded, and chiefs did not want to have the reputation of being miserly.

Many evenings were spent in listening to the songs of poets who recited the great deeds of war of Hjorvard's and Gudbrand's ancestors, and also those that had been accomplished by the two Hersirs. Gudbrand had among the champions who had come with him a man of the name of Ulf, who was a great poet, or scald, and only spoke in verse, and answered also in that manner. His fame was very great, but in despite of offers of great pay by powerful chiefs, he remained with Gudbrand, for he loved him dearly, and to him

the land of Engel was the most beautiful spot he
had ever seen.

One evening, after Gudbrand and all the champions had retired, Hjorvard remained all alone
with Ulf, who composed on the spot a magnificent
song on the deeds of Hjorvard's father, and it
took a great part of the night to recite it. Hjorvard thanked him, and the next day spoke to his
intendant, who had charge of all his treasures, and
after telling him of Ulf's wonderful gift, asked him
how he should reward the scald.

"Shall I give him two trading ships?" said he.

"That is too much, I think," was the treasurer's
reply.

"Other chiefs give costly things—good swords
or good gold bracelets—as rewards for a song
made for them," Hjorvard answered, "but the
ruler of Gotland is above and much richer than
many Hersirs."

So he concluded to present Ulf with a fine trading ship, a new scarlet cloak, a gold ornamented
sword, and a heavy bracelet of gold, and invited
him to come and stay a whole year with him. Ulf
thanked Hjorvard, and said that he would come in
two years, on his return from a visit to his kinsmen in Britain.

After a sojourn of over three weeks, Gudbrand
talked of returning to Engel. Sigrlin tried with
all her power of persuasion to make him stay
longer, and pleaded that Ivar's outfit was not
ready, though she had been busy with her maids,

sewing and making garments for him; and succeeded in inducing him to remain another week.
She was loth to see the day of Gudbrand's departure; the thought of parting with her darling
little son broke her heart.

At last the last day came, when Ivar was to
leave his mother and father, and go and learn
how to become an accomplished man and warrior.
Sigrlin did not sleep that last night. Ivar slept
unconscious in her arms the whole of the night;
she fondled him, and half fancying she was bidding him farewell then, often pressed him so
tightly against her heart that two or three times
during the night she awoke him. No wonder
that her mother's heart grieved, for it was not a
separation of a day from her child. He was not
to be away from her for a month, but for long
years.

When she got up in the morning the rosy hues
of her cheek had disappeared. She dreaded to
look at the sun and to see it rising higher and
higher, for that betokened that noon, the hour
of departure, was getting nearer and nearer; but
Sigrlin was proud, and if it had not been for her
unusual pallor, no one would have guessed the
sorrow and anxiety which she was secretly suffering.

When the morning meal was over, the bustle
which took place told that preparations were
being made for the departure of Gudbrand. Men
were going to their ships, and bidding good-by to

their old or new friends. Many parting bumpers were drunk. Hjorvard had given a great number of costly presents of gold to Gudbrand and to many of his warriors. Finally all the men had gone on board of their respective ships, and only the vessel of Gudbrand remained near the shore. At last the sight of the sun, to the great sorrow of Sigrlin, showed that it was noon. The time had arrived for her to show her courage and hide her emotion, and she must appear cheerful despite her anguish.

The horns for departure were sounded, for everything was ready on board the ships, the sails were unfurled, and the anchors were raised. Father, mother, and all the household, and many people, including the poor slaves, who in despite of their servitude loved their master and mistress, accompanied Gudbrand and Ivar to the shore; the little fellow walked between his parents, chatted merrily as he went along, each one holding one of his hands, and looking down fondly upon him. Finally they reached the gangway, and after wishing each other often good-by, they parted with expressions of great love and friendship. Sigrlin remained on the headland near Dampstadir until the ships had disappeared below the horizon, and then with a deep sigh she retraced her steps homewards, and while alone in her bower the flood-gates of her mother's heart gave way, and she wept long.

The wind was fair, and after an eventless sail of

three days, Gudbrand's fleet reached Hrafnista,
the burg and residence of Gudbrand on Engel.
Sigrid, Gudbrand's wife, was enthusiastically delighted when she saw her husband with little
Ivar to foster, and no wonder; for he was such
a dear little fellow, and so handsome besides.
Sigrid prepared a nice room close to hers for
him, for her first thought was to try to make him
as comfortable as when he was at home. She and
her husband intended to bring him up with the
greatest care and affection, for they felt the great
responsibility that had been thrown upon them.
For a few days Ivar was homesick. He missed his
mother and father very much, and also his play-
mates; everything was new to him in Hrafnista,
but gradually he became reconciled to his new
home, and began to love more and more his foster-
parents.

Gudbrand and Sigrid had a son named Hjalmar,
who was a year older than Ivar. Father and
mother determined that Hjalmar should be edu-
cated at home also, so that the two boys might
become foster-brothers, as was the custom of the
time for children that were brought up together.
A close friendship sprang up between the two
lads, and as they grew up they became inseparable, and in any dispute that one had with other
boys, the other was sure to take the part of his
foster-brother. At times other children of their
age were invited to join them in their play, and
occasionally contests of strength and skill took

place among these young lads for the championship in each of their games, during which they
were applauded and cheered by those of their
elders who were present.

The education of the two boys began in earnest
as they grew older, and both made steady progress. They were taught gymnastic exercises,
games of ball, wrestling, running, jumping, swimming. They also learned how to row, to steer,
and to furl or to reef a sail, and became excellent
riders on horseback, as well as sailors. They were
even taught the practical side of shipbuilding, and
were often to be seen working very hard in the
shipyards. The greatest attention was paid to
their physical training, which was considered of
the highest importance, for skill and agility were
absolutely necessary to a warrior; without them
he could not obtain victory over his foe, or escape
danger, besides which, these exercises made them
strong and healthy.

As time went along, the love between Ivar and
his foster-parents increased greatly. As he became
older he grew in strength and manliness, each following year showing great improvement of mind
and body. Both lads had been taught how to write
runic characters, and also had learned the meaning
of mystic runes—a knowledge that was only acquired by the sons of high-born men—so that when
necessary they might send messages that could
only be deciphered by those for whom they were
intended. They could write beautifully on birch

bark, which was made almost as thin as papyrus for that purpose, or they could engrave runic letters upon wood, stone, and jewels of gold and silver, and inlay mystic letters in the blades of weapons. The art of writing was so ancient in the North that the people believed that it had been taught to them by Odin; but at the period we are speaking of, the Romans, Greeks, and Norsemen were the only people who knew how to read and write in Europe.

Ivar and Hjalmar as they grew older became great athletes, and excelled in skill and dexterity all the lads of their age. They could swim like seals, people said, clad with their armor, and carried then their weapons on their backs. They could throw a spear as well with the left as with the right hand; they could handle a sword, an axe, or a shield in the same manner; and, in a word, could shoot and strike with both hands equally well. They could handle the sword, or sax, with such rapidity of movement that the blade could not be seen in the air, and only its hissing be heard. They could shoot with the bow with an unerring eye, and hit a checker on the head of a man without wounding his scalp; they could throw a stone with a sling with fatal accuracy, and woe to the man for whom the stone was intended. Ivar could leap almost equally well forward or backward, and had even greater dexterity than his foster-brother, and no young man of his age could compete with him in any of the athletic games.

Both foster-brothers were constantly trained in naval exercises, especially when a great number of vessels had come together. They were also taught foreign languages, for it was absolutely necessary for Vikings to understand the language of the countries with which they traded or upon which they made war, for, as we have said, their commercial or warlike expeditions extended far and wide. They could write impromptu poetry, but poetry being a gift of the gods, only its rules and metres were taught to them, for to be a scald one had to be born a scald. They had also learned how to play chess, which was a game much in vogue among the Norsemen.

Gudbrand filled the minds of the lads with the love of fame by recounting to them the great expeditions he had undertaken conjointly with Hjorvard, or sang to them the valorous deeds recorded by the scalds of the old warriors who had gone to Valhalla, so that when the time came they both might emulate their examples.

As Ivar grew older he became deeply inquisitive concerning divers subjects in regard to which he began to take great interest. One early morning he saw Gudbrand seated, as was often his wont, upon the mound of his father, contemplating the sea, and going up to him on a sudden impulse he said : " Foster-father, tell me how things were in the beginning, and about the creation."

Gudbrand answered : " Thou knowest well that our worship is the true one; we belong to Odin,

and are loved by him and by the gods. Before
the creation the universe was a gaping void called
Ginnungagap, and nothing existed. On each side
of this gaping void there were two worlds—
Niflheim, the world of cold ; and Muspelheim, the
world of heat, in the south. The part of the gaping void turning towards the north was filled with
weight of ice and rime, and the opposite side with
drizzle and gusts of wind. The southern part of
Ginnungagap became less heavy, from the sparks
and glowing substances which came flying from
Muspelheim ; and just as the cold and all things
come from Niflheim, the things near Muspelheim
were hot and shining. Ginnungagap was as warm
as windless air, so that when the rime and the
breath of the heat met, the rime melted into drops.
From Elivagar, the stream flowing from the well
Hvergelmir, in Niflheim, spurted drops of poison,
which froze and grew into a Jotun, who was called
Ymir, but the Hrimthursar call him Orgelmir, and
the kin of the Hrimthursar have sprung from him.
When Ymir lived, in early ages, there were neither
sands nor sea, nor cool waves, no earth, no grass,
and no heavens above. There was only Ginnungagap. Numberless years before the earth was
shaped was Bergelmir born. Trudgelmir was his
father, and Orgelmir his grandfather."

"On what did Ymir live, or by what ?" asked
Ivar.

Gudbrand replied: "It happened that when
the hoar frost fell in drops, the cow Audhumla

grew out of it ; four rivers of milk ran from her teats, and she fed Ymir. Audhumla for food licked the rime stones, covered with salt and rime, and the first day she licked them a man's hair came out of them ; the second day a man's head ; the third day a whole man was there. He was called Buri, and was handsome in looks, large and mighty. He had Bor for son, who got Besla, daughter of the Jotun, or Hrimthurs Bolthorn, for a wife, and she had three sons, Odin, Vili, and Ve. From them the Asar, or the kin of Odin, are descended. It is said that the sons of Bor, Odin, Vili, and Ve slew Ymir, and that so much blood flowed from his wounds that he drowned the whole race of the Hrimthursar, except Bergelmir and his wife, who escaped in a flour bin, and from them is descended a new race of Hrimthursar."

" How was the world created ? " asked Ivar.

" From Ymir's flesh the earth was shaped, and from his blood the sea ; the mountains from his bones ; from his hair the trees, and the sky from his skull. From his brow the gods made Midgard for the sons of men, and from his brain the gloomy clouds created. A triad of Asar found on the ground Ask and Embla; they had no breath and no mind, neither blood nor motion nor proper complexion. Odin gave the breath, Hœnir gave the mind, Lodur gave the blood and befitting hues, and from them mankind is descended."

Once in a while Ivar's father would stop at Hrafnista when he passed before Engel with his fleet, bound for some expedition against the Roman provinces, or on his return from them; then there was great joy in the household, and it was with pride that he saw the great progress his son was making in all manly exercises and mental training. His mother came to see him about once in two years, and how proud she was of her son need not be told.

CHAPTER VI

IVAR ATTAINS HIS MAJORITY

ON the last day of the sixth week (the Norse week having but five days) of the month corresponding to our September, Ivar reached his fifteenth year, and by law became of age. The morning of that day Gudbrand presented him with a beautiful ship called the Elidi ; it had on board weapons for a crew of two hundred and forty men. The golden standard which was hoisted at the masthead had been embroidered by his foster-mother, and was called The Victorious, that victory might be sure to follow it wherever it floated. Many spells and incantations had been repeated over it when it was made. The length of the Elidi was one hundred and eighty feet ; it had twenty-five benches for rowers. The poetical name given to the craft was the Stallion of the Surf. Hjalmar also received a beautiful ship as a present, which also had weapons on board for a crew of two hundred and forty men. This vessel was called the Trani, and went under the poetical name of the Deer of the Surf.

The following day Gudbrand with his son and foster-son sailed for the main-land, and after land-

ing they pulled their boat ashore beyond the reach
of the waves, and then entered a great forest of
oaks.   Gudbrand had come for a special purpose
with the two lads.   After building a camp he left
them the following morning, and started out with
his dogs.   He did not return in the evening; the
second day also passed, and still he did not return.
On the third day, towards noon, Ivar and Hjalmar
heard the barking of the dogs, and soon after two
wolves ran quickly by them, and a short time afterwards Gudbrand made his appearance with a large
wolf he had just killed with two arrows.   He had
gone on that hunt for the purpose of killing a wolf,
for he believed firmly that Ivar and Hjalmar after
drinking of its blood and eating of its heart would
become braver than they were before, and would
partake of the fierceness of the wolf while in battle, and that also they would be able to understand the language of birds.

After Gudbrand had rested, he opened the
wolf's carcass, and made the two lads drink a
mouthful of its blood; then he took out its heart,
and going to the fire roasted it on a spit, and
when the blood dripped from it, he thought it
was cooked enough, and dividing it in two, he
gave each a part.   After they had done eating
and drinking of the wolf's heart and blood,
Gudbrand said: "Now I expect you never to
flee from danger or weapons; be brave like your
kinsmen of old."   After this they returned to
Engel.

Gudbrand and Sigrid loved Ivar quite as much as their own son, and resolved to make both equal heirs in their property ; but this act could only be done publicly, and by performing a ceremony which was called " Taking another into one's inheritance," and it had to be done with the approval and consent of the direct heir or heirs, and according to forms of law which were very ancient and precise on the subject.

A day was named by Gudbrand for taking Ivar into his family, so that witnesses might be present, and also those who would otherwise be themselves entitled to his inheritance. Ale from three measures of grain had been brewed, and a bull three winters old had been killed, and the skin was flayed from its right hind leg above the hoof, and from that skin a shoe was made. Then in presence of Hjalmar, his son, who was his direct heir, Gudbrand asked Ivar, his foster-son, to step into the shoe. After Ivar had done this, he asked his own son to do likewise, which Hjalmar did with great willingness. After this ceremony, which was of great antiquity, Ivar was led into the embrace of his foster-father and mother.

Then Gudbrand said, in presence of witnesses : " I lead this man, Ivar Hjorvardson, to my property, and make him conjoint heir with my son Hjalmar ; and this I do with the consent of my kinsmen, who are heirs to my estate." After which he reminded Ivar that he must announce publicly, every twentieth year, that he was con-

4

joint heir with Hjalmar Gudbrandson until he
should get his inheritance. Ivar replied that he
hoped that his foster-father, who had raised him
so tenderly and lovingly, with his foster-mother,
would live long to enjoy his property, and thanked
him for his great kindness and the fatherly care
he had bestowed upon him.

A short time after Ivar had been made co-heir
with Hjalmar, the two foster-brothers resolved to
equip the Elidi and the Trani with a peace crew
of one hundred and twenty men for each vessel.
No one coming to serve on board could be less
than eighteen years old or more than fifty. They
were to have the same laws that Hjorvard had.
It was the first time that both were to command,
or to use the phraseology of the Norsemen, in
which the commanders were called " styrmen," to
steer their own ships. It was quite an event in
their lives, to which they had been looking forward
with great delight.

All the chiefs of the Viking lands had been at
peace with each other for a long time, but inces-
sant expeditions took place, one after another,
against the Roman empire, and the ships returned
home with many spoils and slaves.

It was the intention of the foster-brothers to go
first to Dampstadir, for Ivar wanted very much to
see his mother and father, and to show them how
much he had grown and improved. Both were
yet too young to look like thorough warriors, for
their moustaches had not made their appearance,

and it was the custom of warriors to wear them.
After a visit to Dampstadir, they intended to visit
some of their kinsmen, who ruled over different
realms.

Before leaving Hrafnista, Gudbrand said to
them : " Have you taken costly presents with
you ? " And when the two youths replied " No,"
he continued : " You must take some ; for I never
yet met a man so open-handed or free with his
food that he would not take a gift, nor one so
lavish with his property, that rewards were to him
unwelcome." Then he added : " With weapons
and clothes, such as are most sightly to one's self,
shall friends gladden each other. Givers and re-
ceivers are the longest friends if they give with
good hearts and good wishes." After saying this
he went to one of his store-rooms and brought
to them several gold ornamented swords and saxes
inlaid with gold, several costly foreign cloaks,
beautiful brooches of gold, some superb arm-rings,
or bracelets, and lovely necklaces, all also of gold.
" These objects," said he to them, " you must
give to the high-born men and women you shall
visit. The necklaces will be for their wives and
daughters."

The day before sailing, Gudbrand called Ivar
and Hjalmar, and bade them to sit by him, and saying, " I have called you to give you some advice
which I think may prove useful to you, and
which I hope you will heed," he spoke as follows:
" When you come to a meal among strangers, be

silent or talk little, listen and look on. Speak usefully or not at all; no man will then blame you for ill-breeding. Never mock at a guest or way-farer. Remember that no man is so good that a fault follows him not, nor so bad that he is good for nothing. Never laugh at a hoary wise man, for often it is good and wise what old men say: 'Skilled words come often out of a shrivelled skin.' Remember that loved is the door that is open to all that are in need. Give and be generous; if not, every kind of evil will be wished to you."

That same evening Gudbrand sent for his son Hjalmar, and said to him: "What gladdens me is, that no man will have thy head at his feet, although thou wilt have narrow escapes. Here is a sword, kinsman Hjalmar, which I wish to give thee; its name is Dragvandil, and victory has always followed it. My father took it from the slain Björn Blue-tooth. I have another remark-able weapon, a mighty spear which I took from Harek, but I know it is not manageable by any one who has not reached his full strength."

The day before their ships were ready to sail, the foster-brothers made a great sacrifice to Frey, who ruled over wealth and the seasons. When ready to start, both Sigrid and Gudbrand followed them to their ships, and bade them an affectionate farewell. After a pleasant passage they reached Dampstadir, where they were received with great joy by Hjorvard and Sigrlin. The mother looked with the utmost pride upon her son, who was the

embodiment of manliness, and Hjalmar was treated
in as kindly manner as his foster-brother, for they
loved him dearly also.

Every thing was very quiet in Gotland; the
harvest was taking place, and people were busy
in the fields. The champions of Hjorvard were
absent, and had gone with a large number of
ships to make war in Gaul and Britain, and were
expected to return soon. The two youths spent
a great deal of their time in the practice of athletic games, and every morning they were seen in
the fields where these took place. Ivar visited
his kinsmen and the friends living on the island,
and also occupied himself in learning still more
of the art of shipbuilding, for he wished the
Norsemen to say that his ships were the finest in
the land. He liked good horses and bred them.
Two of his stallions, called Slonjvir, "the flying
one," and Hviting, were known among all the
lovers of horses, and he drove a beautiful, four-
wheeled, wagon-shaped carriage, adorned with
handsome bronze-gilt ornaments, the harness of
the horses being ornamented with gold.

Occupied in these exercises and diversions, Ivar
and his foster-brother remained three years in
Dampstadir,

CHAPTER VII

IVAR'S FIRST EXPEDITION

WHILE in Dampstadir Ivar attained his eighteenth year, and had reached that age when all young men went upon warlike expeditions when the opportunity was offered them, and great warriors and powerful chiefs would have no one younger than this age on board of their ships. Some days after his eighteenth birthday, Hjorvard, who was seated on the mound of his father, sent for Ivar, and after he had arrived he said to him: "From thy grandfather's mound, upon which we are, and whose deeds of valor are known all over the northern lands, and are recited by the poets, and will continue to be until the end of time, thou seest surrounding us the graves of many of thy kinsmen who have also gone to Valhalla. Each of them died valiantly. Among them I want to teach thee the same precepts of wisdom which my father counselled me to follow when I was about thy age. I have found them useful during my life, and they will also be of good service to thee if thou heedest them."

After a pause he continued: "Kinsman, listen to me. It has been the custom from immemo-

e that sons of chiefs should go to war
uire wealth and honor, and that personal
should not be inherited, nor son get it
father, but that it should be placed on
e and in the mound with themselves.
Though their sons get the land and estates, they
cannot hold their rank and dignity, unless they
place themselves and their men in danger and go
to war, earning thus property and honors one after
another, and thus following in the footsteps of
their kinsmen.

"Seek fame and renown in good deeds, for these
never die, and will be remembered by the sons of
men until the end of time. Many a man, since
Odin created the world, has spent his life in getting wealth, and, to obtain it, has become miserly.
Their hearts only delight in the sight of gold.
But not one of these is remembered by mankind ;
their names and their wealth have passed away,
but the names of great scalds, and of the men who
have accomplished great deeds, will live forever,
though the Nornir have shaped their lives so that
they be poor, and die in poverty. So, my son, be
lavish with thy wealth and with the tributes that
will be paid to thee by those thou hast conquered.
Be rich in good deeds. Liberal and valiant men
live best, but the unwise fear everything. A more
faithful friend will a man never get than sound
good sense.

"After a man has been wounded and lies helpless under thy blow on the ground, I need not tell

thee, for thy manhood tells it to thee, not to inflict another wound on him, for then it is murder. If thou diest in the fight, it is because Odin has chosen thee to go to him. If thou art victorious, it is because he has given thee victory; both alternatives are good. Gladsheim is the home of the glad; there the gleaming Valhalla, or the ' Hall of the Slain,' stands, and Odin chooses, every day, men slain by weapons. That hall is easily recognized by those who come there, for it is roofed with shafts, and thatched with shields; the benches are covered with chain-armor; it has five hundred and forty doors; and eight hundred ' einherjar,' for so are called the chosen, pass through it at once. A wolf hangs over the main entrance of Valhalla. Try to be more welcome there than any chief that has reddened the sax and carried far and wide the bloody blade; enter Valhalla bespattered with blood. Odin gives victory to his sons, wealth to some, eloquence and wisdom to a few, songs to poets, luck in love to many, chosen weapons to those he loves, and fair winds to mariners. It is time for thee to go to war, and thus become worthy of thy ancestors and be their equal in fame.

"If thou obtainest renown, be not vain and boastful, for fame is given to thee by the people, and why shouldst thou be proud towards the giver? A quiet demeanor never hurts a man, while people laugh at those who are puffed up in their own pride. Many a man is made a fool by success. The high-born and famous should never be proud."

After saying this, Hjorvard presented Ivar with the sword Angrvadil. It was a superb damascened weapon, with a hilt ornamented with gold. Its scabbard was almost covered with gold. It was celebrated all over the North on account of its quality, and was called by the poets, "Odin's flame," the "gleam of battle," the "injurer of shields," the "leader of victory."

When Ivar had inspected and admired it, his father continued: "Angrvadil has been with our kin for generations, and it is as good to-day as in the days of yore. Thy grandfather and myself have gone into sixty battles with it, and it has gained the victory each time, and it has never been dulled. Never let Angrvadil go out of our family, for misfortune will overtake our kin if it does not remain in the possession of our kinsmen. It will help thee also in duels; courage is in its blade, terror in its point, and luck in its hilt. This sword is infallible," added Hjorvard, pointing to the mystic letters of gold inlaid on the blade near the hilt. "It is death to the one who is wounded by it. Hrotti, my own sword, thou wilt use after my death."

Ivar thanked his father, and said that his gift pleased him better than if it had been gold in abundance, or large estates, and added he did not know what the Nornir had fated him, but that he hoped to die in the midst of victory. He thanked his father, too, for the good counsel he had always given him, and above all for the great love he had

shown towards him; and, with great warmth of
feeling, added that he would try to emulate him
in all his actions, and hoped that none of his kinsmen in Valhalla would ever be ashamed of him.

After leaving his father he went to his mother,
and said to her: "I want thee, mother, to show me
the cloaks which Heid, the sybil, made for my
father a long time ago."

Sigrlin opened a large chest and answered:
"Here they are, and they are almost as good as
new."

Ivar took them up. They were with sleeves,
and a hood at the top, with a covering for the
face; they were wide and long; it was believed that
no iron could cut them, and that weapons could
not damage them, for they had been made with
cunning, witchcraft, and incantations. Ivar took
the two which were the largest. Then he went to
Hringstadir to see the halls and estate which his
father had given him the day that he had "fastened" the name of Ivar upon him.

Ivar remembered all that his father had said
to him, and was anxious to obtain renown and
wealth, and so he and his foster-brother went one
morning to Hjorvard and said: "Now tell us,
father, of the Viking whom thou knowest to be
the bravest and strongest."

Hjorvard replied: "You are young men, yet
you seem to think that no man can withstand
you. But I will tell you of two Vikings of whom
I know. They are called Sigurd and Sigmund;

they are skilled in many things, and very great
warriors."

"How many ships have they?" asked Ivar.

"They have thirty ships," replied Hjorvard,
"and one hundred and twenty men on each
ship."

"Where have they land?" inquired Hjalmar.

"In the southern part of Svithjod," replied
Hjorvard. "They are on land in winter, and lie
on board their warships in summer."

"We will go and try to find where they are, and
fight them," cried both foster-brothers at the same
time. "And we will see who are the foremost
Vikings and champions in the land."

The day after this conversation the champions
of Hjorvard returned with a great deal of booty
they had won in the countries subject to Rome,
and Hjorvard asked some of them to join his
son and Hjalmar. "For," said he, "they are still
inexperienced in the art of war."

The foster-brothers at once set to work to make
their fleet ready, which did not take long, for the
vessels had been subjected to a thorough over-
hauling during the winter. The Elidi had been
fitted up very splendidly, and Ivar placed on board
his body-guard and berserks; the prow defenders
were most carefully selected, for they were to defend his standard. The whole of the crew were
berserks, who surpassed others in strength and
bravery. Picked men were also stationed at the
stern, and the number on board was two hundred

and forty. Ivar's foster-brother Hjalmar had also
a picked crew, among them skilful archers and
sling men, who had not their equal in the land.
The standard of Ivar, which his foster-mother had
made for him, floated on board of the Elidi, and
Hjalmar's on board the Trani.

Two days before the sailing of the fleet of the
foster-brothers, Ivar came to his father, and said
to him: "Tell me, father, some of the omens
that thou thinkest might be useful to men who go
to wage war."

Hjorvard answered: "Many warnings are useful if men know them and heed them. The following of the black raven is good for a warrior, for
it means victory. No man should fight against
the late shining sun, sister of the moon. There is
danger for thee if thou stumblest or fallest from
thy horse when thou rushest into fight, for faithless family spirits stand on either side of thee. If
thou walkest out, and art prepared for a journey,
and meet on the path men ready to praise thee,
and hear wolves under ash trees, good luck wilt
thou get if thou seest the wolves ahead of thee.
Those are a few of the omens that should be a
warning to thee. I want also to give thee some
other advice," he continued. "Wisdom and weapons are not easy to get for the chief that would be
the foremost among men. The sons of men need
often eyes of foresight in the fight. Early should
he rise who wishes to acquire wealth. Seldom does
a sleepy wolf get a thigh bone, or a sleepy man

·victory. Courage is better than the power of swords where the angry must fight. I have seen bold men win victory with a blunt sword. It is better for the bold than for the coward to be in the battle—the game of the Valkyrias. Silent and thoughtful, and bold in battle, should a Hersir's son be. The unwise man thinks he will live forever if he shuns fight, but old age gives him no peace, though spears may spare him." After this they separated.

When the foster-brothers were ready to sail, Hjorvard walked down with them to their ships, and bade them farewell lovingly. They sailed away from Dampstadir with a fair wind, and with their sails set, but after a while it became calm, and the vessels had to be propelled by oars. As they were losing sight of land, a crow flew over the ships with loud caws. Ivar looked at it.

Hjalmar said to his foster-brother, "Does it mean anything to thee?"

"It does," answered Ivar.

Another crow flew over the ship, cawing also. Hjalmar forgot to row, and his oar got loose in his hand.

Ivar said : "Thou art very attentive to the crow ; what does it say?"

"I do not know, for I have some difficulty in understanding them."

Another crow passed over the boat, cawing louder than the two others, and flying nearer the ships. Then Ivar observed : "This signifies much to us. I understand that we will be victorious in our expeditions against the Vikings, for, as my father said to me, the following of the raven is a good omen."

Finally they sighted the coast of Svithjod, and came to a long and somewhat high promontory and they cast anchor there. Afterwards they put tents upon their ships for the night. The lamps were lighted, and the men, to pass away the time before they went to sleep, played chess; the chess-board used on board of vessels had a hole in each square, and each piece a peg to make it fast, so that the rolling of the ship could not upset the game. When tired, they put themselves into their leather bags and went to sleep.

The following morning Ivar went ashore to see if he could discover aught or hear any news, but he saw no houses or people. After walking a while across the promontory, he observed thirty ships lying at anchor and war tents near the beach. The crew was ashore and engaged in practising athletic games; some were wrestling, others were running and jumping, and many were performing warlike exercises with swords and spears, and shooting at targets with arrows.

Sigmund and Sigurd steered these ships, that is, were their commanders; and these two men were the very Vikings whom Hjorvard had mentioned to Ivar and his foster-brother.

Ivar immediately returned to his ships, and told the great news to Hjalmar and his men.

"What shall we do next?" thereupon asked Hjalmar.

"We will divide our men and our ships," Ivar answered, "into two equal squadrons. Thou, Hjalmar, shalt with half the ships pass the cape and raise a battle cry against those who are on shore, and hoist the red shield. I will land from this side with two-thirds of my crew, go along the forest, and with them raise another battle cry. Then perhaps they may be startled by our appearance, and conclude to retire into the forest, and nothing further happen."

Hjalmar rounded the cape with his ships, and Ivar landed with his men, and the plan suggested by Ivar was carried out. Sigmund and Sigurd and their men, however, were not in the least startled when they heard the battle cry of Hjalmar at sea, and another battle cry on land. They stopped their games while the shout lasted, and then continued as before. Hjalmar then went ashore to meet Ivar, and after they met, Ivar said: "I know not for certain whether these men are afraid or not, for they do not seem to mind our war cry."

"What will you have us do?" inquired Hjalmar.

"That is soon told," replied Ivar; "we will not steal upon them; we will stay this night at the cape and remain there until morning."

When morning came, the foster-brothers landed with all their men, and marched towards Sigurd and Sigmund, who had all their men armed and in readiness for a conflict.

When Sigurd and Sigmund saw Hjalmar and Ivar coming towards them, they went to meet them. Sigurd was high-born and a very great Viking; he had travelled far and wide, and seen countries that were unknown to most people; he was short of stature, and had attained the meridian of life; gray hair was beginning to show itself; he was the oldest of the four chiefs.

Sigmund was also high-born, younger than Sigurd, but older than Ivar and Hjalmar. Sigurd asked, when they met, who was their leader. Ivar answered: "There is more than one chief here."

"What is thy name?" asked Sigmund.

"My name is Ivar, son of Hjorvard of Dampstadir; and my foster-brother is Hjalmar, son of Gudbrand of Engel."

"What is your errand here?" said Sigurd.

Ivar answered: "I wish to know which of us is the more powerful."

"How many ships have you?" asked Sigurd.

"We have twenty ships," said Ivar. "And how many have you?"

"We have thirty ships," answered Sigurd.

"That is great odds against us," said Ivar.

"Ten ships' crews shall not take part in the battle," replied Sigurd, "and man shall fight against man."

"This is fair," answered Ivar, "and it is the law of valiant men."

Both sides arrayed their men and made themselves ready for the conflict, which was speedily

begun, and continued all day. Towards night
the peace shield was raised, and Sigurd asked Ivar,
" What thinkest thou of this day's conflict ? "

Ivar answered, " I am well pleased."

" Wilt thou play the game again ? " asked
Sigurd.

" That is my intention," replied Ivar, " for I
never found better and hardier champions. We
will begin the battle again at full daylight."

The men then went to their war booths and
dressed their wounds.

The next morning both sides arrayed their
men for the battle, and fought all day. When it
began to grow dark, the peace shield was again
raised. Sigurd asked Ivar how the fighting
pleased him on that day.

" Very well," was the answer.

" Wilt thou, then," said Sigurd, " try this game
the third day ? "

Ivar then replied, " Then we will finish the
fight."

Hearing this, Sigurd, who was a man of great
common sense, said to Ivar : " May we expect
much booty on your ships if we gain the victory ? "

" Far from it," Ivar replied ; " we have taken
none this summer."

" I think," said Sigurd, " I have nowhere met
more foolish men than here, for we only fight out
of pride and rivalry."

" What wilt thou do, then ? " inquired Ivar.

5

" Let us become foster-brothers," replied Sigurd, " for we are of equal valor."

" Well said," answered Ivar and Hjalmar ; " for we think it right that we should bind our friendship, and swear one another foster-brotherhood. It will be a great boon for us all, as we four will become the greatest warriors and Vikings of the land."

The following morning, preparations were made to carry out the proposal of the preceding afternoon, that Ivar and Hjalmar should become foster-brothers with Sigmund and Sigurd.

It was a common custom, which had come down from the remotest times, formally and solemnly to form ties of friendship between men by swearing one another foster-brotherhood. This relation was of a most sacred and binding character ; those who made the compact pledged themselves to be unselfish and true to each other for life, and to share the same dangers.

These four Vikings first cut three long slices of turf in a semi-circular shape, the ends of which were fastened into the ground, and the loops raised so high that those who were to swear foster-brotherhood could go under them. Under these loops, they placed a spear inlaid with mystic signs, of such a height that a man could reach with his hand the nail fastening the socket of the spear-point to the handle.

The warriors on both sides had assembled to witness the ceremony. It was a beautiful summer day; the sun shone brilliantly, nature was smiling, birds were singing in the groves, butter-flies and bees were flitting from wild flower to wild flower; no one could ever dream of the fierce conflict of the preceding days.

In the midst of profound silence, Sigurd advanced towards Ivar and the three other Vikings, and said to them: "You are aware that from immemorial time, it has been the custom of valiant men, who make this agreement of foster-brotherhood between themselves, that the one that lives the longest should avenge the others, if they are slain with weapons or otherwise."

"Yes," answered Ivar, Hjalmar, and Sigmund.

Then they prepared themselves for the oath of foster-brotherhood, which was sacredly binding, although not taken on the temple ring as oaths generally were. Sigurd, Hjalmar, Sigmund, and Ivar then passed under the loop, and drew blood from the hollow of their hands, and let it run together into the mould which had been cut under the loop of the turf, and mixed together the earth and the blood; thereupon they all fell on their knees, and took oaths to ratify their agreement, and called upon Odin, Frey, Njord, and the other gods as witnesses; and then they all clasped hands, according to ancient custom, as a seal to their oaths.

The four foster-brothers agreed that they would never rob traders and Bondi or other men, except when they must make a raid on land for their men in case of need, in which case they were to pay full value for what they took. Never were they to rob women, though they should find them temptingly rich, nor should women be brought on board their ships against their will; and should a woman show that this had been done against her will, the man of the crew found guilty of such a crime against this law should lose his life for it, whether he were powerful or not.

It was also agreed that they should possess in common the booty they might get on Viking expeditions, and that whichever lived the longest should have a mound raised over the others after the battle or otherwise, and place therein as much property as seemed to him most befitting their rank.

And be it told now, that to their death they loved each other dearly, and never violated in the slightest manner the duties that were imposed upon them by their compact of foster-brotherhood.

The first thing the four foster-brothers concluded to do in concert, after consultation, was to visit Gudmund, Sigurd's father, who was a powerful Hersir, and ruled over the large island, called to-day Oland, near the coast of the present Sweden, and to apprise him of their new relationship. They set sail, and after a short and pleasant voyage, their ships cast anchor in a bay where to-day the quiet little town of Borgholm stands. At that time Gudmund's burg stood there, and near by are still seen many graves and mounds of that period.

The foster-brothers were received with great
kindness, and there was great drinking and feasting. Ivar was seated in the second high seat during their visit. After a stay of a week, they made
their ships ready, intending to sail southward and
visit Gudbrand to apprise him also of their new
relationship. When the time came for them to
depart, Gudmund followed them to the ships, and
as they were ready to embark, presented Sigurd
with three arrows which had a famous name, and
were called Gusi's Followers. The feathers were
gilded, and they were ornamented with gold.

" These arrows," said Gudmund, " Ketil Hœng,
thy great-great-grandfather, took from Gusi, who
ruled over the Fins ; they hit and bite everything
they are aimed at, and were forged in the days of
old by Dvergars."

Sigurd thanked his father, saying : " No gifts
have I which I prize more highly," after which
they sailed away. Soon they came to a beautiful
bay, on the shore of which were seen very many
very ancient cairns, near where to-day the little
sleepy town of Cimbrisham is to be seen. These
graves were filled with beautiful bronze weapons
and many gold objects.

They landed and found the place in great com-
motion, for a trial by ordeal was to take place. A
bond-woman named Hjerka had told Vemund, the
Hersir who ruled there, that she had seen Gunvor,
his wife, and a man of the herad walk together.
Vemund was no longer merry after he heard this,

for he loved his wife dearly, but he wished to be sure that what the bond-woman had said was true, before he took steps to avenge himself. But he had not thus far succeeded, and no one was ever seen with his wife. Nevertheless his jealousy preyed upon him, and one day as he was speaking to her, his sadness was so marked in his countenance that she asked the reason why. Then he told her that he thought she loved another.

Upon hearing this, she was struck speechless with indignation. Her eyes flashed fire, her pure heart revolted against such an accusation or insinuation, her face turned pale and flushed alternately; then a sudden look of despair, of intense pain and sorrow, followed her looks of anger. Was it possible that her husband could believe such a tale ?

Then she said to him: "I will take oaths before thee and many men, upon the white holy stone, that I have not acted with anyone as thou seemest to believe. Send for Halfdan, the ruler of Zeeland, that he may consecrate the boiling caldron."

The foster-brothers were just in time to witness the trial. Halfdan was sent for, and in the presence of hundreds of witnesses who had come to see the ordeal, he consecrated with the sign of the hammer of Thor the caldron before the water was boiling, and the holy white stone used for such an ordeal.

Then Gunvor said with a loud voice, heard

through the hall by those present, " I cannot call on my brothers to avenge such an accusation with the sword, for they are all dead. Look now, men, I am truthful. See how the water boils. Let Herkja go to the cauldron, she who attributes treachery to me."

Herkja put her hand into the cauldron to take the sacred stone, and no one could witness a more pitiful sight than those who beheld how the hands of Herkja were scalded. When the people saw this, they said that Herkja was guilty of false accusation and perjury, and they led the maid into a foul mire, where she met her death.

The following day, Knut, an uncle of Sigurd, who had become very old, felt that his last days were approaching; and as there was universal peace, he could not fall on the battle-field, and so go valiantly to Valhalla, as all warriors did who died fighting the foe. He determined, nevertheless, that he would not die in his bed, for he did not wish to go to Hel. It was the belief of the Norsemen, that those who had not fallen by weapons went to Hel. Hel was one of nine worlds that composed the universe, but in that Hel there was no punishment. So he called his family together, and divided among them his gold and silver and other valuable things, and then told them that he was going to throw himself from a high cliff, for all who did this were believed to go to Valhalla. His family followed him cheerfully, and as he was on the brink of the precipice whence not infrequently men threw themselves down, they bade him a happy journey to Valhalla, and he took forthwith the fatal plunge. A large mound was raised over him, and all the people extolled his courageous deed.

After witnessing the ordeal, and the death of Knut, the four foster-brothers continued their voyage, skirting the shores of the peninsula, passing several beautiful burgs and estates. Several days afterwards, they cast anchor at the mouth of a river almost opposite the island of Engel, for they did not stop at Hrafnista, as Gudbrand and Sigrlin had gone on a visit north, to friends who lived on the shores of the present Christiania fjord.

There ruled a valiant Hersir, named Gautrek the Old, who in his day had been a foremost Viking, but on account of his age had given up warfare. He had nine sons by Alvig the Wise, daughter of Eyvind of Holmgard. They were called Thengil, Ræsir, Gram, Gylfi, Hilmir, Jofur, Tyggi, Skuli, Harri. These nine brothers became so famous in warfare, that in all songs their names are used as names of rank. All fell in battle, having never married.

A great feast was prepared for Ivar, his foster-brothers and his men. Gautrek had a beautiful daughter of the name of Svanhild, and after the guests had been seated, she entered the hall with several maidens, and advanced to the high seat which Ivar occupied, opposite to that of her father; she handed to him a drinking-horn of gold, filled up with mead, and said : " Hail to thee, Ivar, son of Hjorvard! Hail to you all, ye warriors that have come with him!" Then she seated herself by her father.

There was great feasting and drinking during the time they remained with Gautrek, and after a stay of three days, which was the accustomed time for a visit of that kind, Ivar left the place with his fleet, and continued to sail northward. A short summer gale sprang up; during the time it lasted, the Elidi was ahead of all the other ships, for she was very swift, and but few vessels were her equal in speed in the whole northern land. The fleet got shelter behind the numerous islands that line the coast, and made ready to enter the stream which is now known as the Hams river, upon which the town of Hamstad is situated, in the province called to-day by the name of Halland. The peace shields were hoisted at the mastheads, and shields were placed all along the gunwales, and the dragons of red gold shone resplendently in the light of the sun.

Arnfid Hersir ruled over the country. When the ships cast anchor, he was seated on the mound of his father, which overlooked the river and the sea. It was his custom to sit there and hunt with his hawks; these brought him from time to time a hare, black cock, or a partridge. He recognized the Elidi by its pennant, and knew that its commander was Ivar, the son of Hjorvard " the wide spreading," one of his companions in arms and

foster-brother.   The ships often disappeared from
his sight on account of the bends in the river,
which were covered with forests, but finally they
cast anchor below the burg or residence of Arnfid.

Arnfid sent messengers to invite Ivar and his
foster-brothers and their men to come ashore, as
the Gotlanders had never ravaged his realm.   The
invitation was accepted.

Ivar thereupon addressed his friends and followers in this wise: "Let us beware of drinking
too much.   A man carries on the road no better
burden   than   sound   wit   and   common   sense.
Wisdom is needed by him who travels widely.
No provisions on a journey weigh a man to the
ground more than too much ale.   The ale of
the sons of men is not so good as men say it is,
for the more a man drinks the less wit he has.
The spirit that hovers over ale-bouts is called
the 'heron of oblivion;' it steals away men's
senses.   The ale is best when every man gets
his reason back.   Strife and ale have caused
grief of mind to many men; death to some, curses
to others.   Many are the evils of mankind.   Thou
shalt not quarrel with drunken men.   Many an
one's wits wine steals.   Nevertheless, a man may
not send away the cup, but drink moderately."

Ivar and his men dressed themselves in their
best and went ashore, when they were immediately led to the banqueting hall, where a great
feast was prepared in the honor of Ivar and of his
foster-brothers and their following.   Arnfid was

seated in his high seat and welcomed his guests;
he bade Ivar to sit in the high seat opposite
his.

Arnfid had a daughter celebrated for her beauty
and accomplishments; her name was Ingegerd,
and before the feast had begun, she came to
the hall with several handsome maidens who
were visiting her. They were beautifully attired.
Ingegerd herself wore a red dress of thick
woollen material, lavishly embroidered with gold.
The material had been brought to her by her
father on his return from a voyage to the Caspian.
The train, several feet in length, swept gracefully
on the floor. Her hair was braided and fell over
her shoulders gracefully, as was the custom with
young maidens. A beautiful gold band encircled
her forehead. Round her snowy neck hung a
necklace of delicate gold beads. Her tall and
slender form was made to appear still more graceful by a belt of gold of exquisite workmanship
that encircled her waist. Her arms were adorned
by two delicate spiral gold bracelets, and on one
of the fingers of her right hand was a spiral ring
ending in snakes' heads, that had belonged to
her mother.

Before the meal was served, Arnfid announced
that seats were about to be allotted; that men
and women might drink together as many as
could, and that men without companions should
drink by themselves. So they placed lots in a
cloth, each with the name of a guest written upon

it. Arnfid was to pick them out. The lot fell
that Ivar should drink with Ingegerd and sit next
to her that evening.

When ready to sit down, Ingegerd sang haughtily
to Ivar: "What wilt thou do, lad, in my seat? For
seldom, if ever, hast thou given a wolf warm flesh,
nor hast thou seen the raven croak over the battle
field; neither hast thou been where swords meet
and where Valkyrias soar over the fallen."

These words meant that Ivar had never been in
battle, so that neither wolf nor raven nor Valkyrias had followed him; and if this was so, he was
not worthy to sit by her side.

Ivar looked at her beautiful and proud face, and
sang: " I have handled the bloody blade, the ravens
have followed my track; I have made warfare and
been the champion in many games of strength and
skill. Be not so proud, maiden; like thyself, I am
of Odin's kin. The son of Hjorvard follows in
the footsteps of his father."

When Ingegerd heard these words she smiled,
looking at him, and seated herself by his side, and
they drank together and were merry. Many a
maiden was seated by the side of brave and mighty
champions that day—men who had seen many
lands. There was nothing in the world which these
Norse women appreciated more than personal
bravery, and none but the very bravest could
aspire to the hand of those of high lineage. Wine,
ale, beer, and mead were served in drinking cups
of glass from Greece, or in silver cups of great

beauty, with *repoussé* work of gold, representing panther chasing deer, and horses running away. These also had come from the Black Sea, where the Greeks had colonies.

The food was served in silver dishes containing roast pork, veal, birds, and fish. Two sorts of bread were on the table—one kind soft and made of rye; the other flat, almost as thin as wafers, the same kind as is served in Norway to-day.

When the men had begun to be somewhat too merry for the presence of women, Ingegerd and the maidens who had come with her to the feast rose and left the hall, bidding all good-night. But that night Ingegerd herself could not sleep. Her thoughts were always reverting to Ivar, and, without knowing it, she loved him; or, perhaps, her feeling was infatuation rather than love.

Therefore, the next day she prepared the drink of oblivion for Ivar, to cause him to forget the girl he loved—in case he did love another—and sent her maid-servant to invite him to her bower. She had prepared the draught with many incantations and according to a mystic formula. It was of ice-cold sea water, sacrificed blood, a long ling fish, an unripened wheat ear, sacrificed intestine of beast, herbs of every forest, burned acorns, the soot of the hearth, a boiled swine liver, to which were added all kinds of mystic runic letters painted red. After Ivar had come she bade him drink, which he did, but whether it was an efficacious potion or not could not be proven, as he had no sweetheart to forget.

On the third day the foster-brothers made ready to leave. Arnfid wanted them to stay longer, but Ivar said to him : " One should take leave in good time. The guest should not remain too long; the loved one often becomes loathed by staying over many days."

So they parted in great friendship. Arnfid gave Ivar a handsome sword, with hilt and scabbard ornamented with gold ; also an axe inlaid with gold, of very fine workmanship, and costly presents to his foster-brothers and men. Ivar gave also costly presents to Arnfid and his men.

Ingegerd, from her bower, with a heavy heart, watched the ships sailing away, and wondered if she would ever see Ivar again. But, as is often the case among the sons and daughters of men, Ivar and Ingegerd were never to meet again. The Nornir had parted them that day for life, and were to prevent them from continuing the courtship that was written in runic letters of gold upon the heart of Ingegerd. The memory of the hours passed between Ivar and her was all that was to be left. It was but a dream, but how lovely and short was that dream ! Love had germed and grown up in three days, but it was doomed to perish, though that episode of their lives was never to be forgotten. Yet Ingegerd married, and many a time during her life her thoughts wandered back to the days we have just spoken of.

She thought it was wrong to think of them, but we have no command over our thoughts; they will come unawares in spite of our will, and the memory of the past will cling to us until death. How wise it is that no one can read our thoughts! For if it were otherwise, how many happy homes might be made unhappy indeed!

The foster-brothers, after leaving Arnfid, stopped at Engelholm, Gudbrand and Sigrid having returned. There was great joy in Hrafnista on their arrival. Hjalmar was to remain at home that winter.

Ivar sailed to Dampstadir with Sigurd and Sigmund, for he wanted his father to know his two new foster-brothers. They were to spend the winter with him, and all were to meet again the following spring.

Hjorvard and Sigrid were on the shore to meet their son. They had heard of his two new foster-brothers, for Ivar had written them about the fight they had had, and what had followed, and gave them a hearty welcome to Dampstadir.

CHAPTER VIII

THE YULE SACRIFICE

HJORVARD was zealous in the discharge of his ecclesiastical functions, and very observant of all the sacrificial rites. The chief temple of Gotland was at Dampstadir, and every man on the island paid a temple tax to him, for the support of the temple and sacrifice. The sacred building was situated not far from the burg, between it and the mounds where Hjorvard's ancestors lay buried. It was much like many others in the Viking lands, the same general laws being in force in regard to all of them. It was two hundred and fifty feet in length, and one hundred and twenty-five feet wide ; its wooden walls of massive fir-trees had withstood the blasts of centuries. It had numerous and fantastic gargoyles, a long piazza round it, and the interior was divided into two parts, the inmost part being the most holy.

The lands, the groves, and springs within the precincts of the temple were considered most sacred. No one was allowed to enter the temple with weapons, neither those who had committed an offence punishable by law. No quarrels or acts of violence were permitted within its walls. Any one committing any breach of the peace, damaging the temple, or coming armed within its walls, was declared a wolf in the sanctuary, an outlaw who might be slain by anyone.

Inside the main entrance door stood the golden high seats upon which Hjorvard sat as Hersir and High Priest. The timber of the temple, and even the mould under the sacred building, were also considered holy. The walls inside were richly ornamented with gold and silver, and hung with tapestry. The door was adorned with a gold knocker.

In the innermost part of the temple stood the altar, which was constructed with great skill. Upon the altar a fire was constantly kept burning night and day; this fire was called the "holy fire." Upon it also stood a large ring, or bracelet, of gold, on which men took their oaths. The large bowl of copper, in which the blood of the sacrificed animals was put, was there also; and the vessel, as well as the blood from the sacrificed animal, was called holy. Near the entrance outside was the holy or sacrificing spring, in which men that were sacrificed were thrown.

There were three principal sacrifices a year all over the Viking lands, at which the people assembled in the chief temple.

The Winter sacrifice, which took place in the month of Goi, now called October, was to welcome the winter, and on this occasion there were great feasts and much drinking. The second sacrifice, Midwinter, or Yule, sacrifice, was held in

6

the middle of winter, in the month Thor, to insure a good year and peace. This was the great sacrifice to Frey. The third was the Victory sacrifice, in honor of Odin, for luck and victory; it took place in the beginning of spring, in the middle of April, before men began to go on Viking expeditions.

Ivar had returned to Dampstadir after the sacrifice to celebrate the advent of winter had taken place. All the Vikings of the Baltic who had not wintered in foreign lands had come back, for a frozen sea would have prevented their vessels from reaching their destination if they had been late, although the shores of Zeeland and Fyen and the coast of Norway were free from ice during the whole year, with rare exceptions.

Yule was near at hand, and the midwinter sacrifice, the most important of all, was to be on a very great scale at Dampstadir. More animals than usual were to be sacrificed. Black oxen, horses, boars, and falcons had been specially fattened.

Vast numbers of people had flocked daily to Dampstadir, and had brought with them their provisions, also the ale and beer they needed for this festival. The day before Yule, everyone who was to be present at the sacrifice had arrived.

Yule eve, Hjorvard and the large assembly led in procession, as was customary, the atonement boar which had been consecrated to Frey. The animal was very large and handsome, and was so fine that it seemed as if every bristle on it was of gold. According to the sacred rites, the boar was led forward, and those who were to make vows placed one hand upon the head of the sacred animal, and the other upon its bristles. Among the great chiefs who were to make vows were Hersir Hamund the Valiant, the berserk Hromund the Bold, Ingald the Black-eyed, Ivar, and many other chiefs and high-born men.

The first evening the sacrificing ceremonies began, the animals were slaughtered in silence, and their blood was collected in the sacrificing bowl that had been taken from the altar, and after being filled was put back, and then consecrated by Hjorvard making the sign of the hammer of Thor over it ; after which, the altar and the walls of the temple inside and outside, were reddened with the sacrificed blood, and then the people were also sprinkled with the blood, with the sacred twigs used specially for the purpose of sanctification.

After the sprinkling of the people had taken place, the flesh of the slaughtered animal was put in large sacrificial kettles, and these were hung over the holy fires which ran all along the middle of the temple. Then Hjorvard, as High Priest, consecrated the food with the sign of the hammer of Thor. When the food was ready, the horns were filled with ale, then carried round the fires, and were also consecrated. After these ceremonies, the people who had been standing up seated themselves along the walls of the temple, and then ate of the sacrificial meat of oxen and horses.

As customary, the horn, or toast, to Odin was drunk first, for victory and also for the continuation of the power of Hjorvard; then the horn to Thor, for those who trusted in their own strength and power; then the horns to Njord and Frey, for good years and peace. This was followed by the toast to Bragi, the god of poetry. Over this horn, according to custom, vows were made, and these vows had to be made good during the year that followed. This was the most important toast, for men had to keep their word or die in the attempt to accomplish their vows. Many also drank well-filled horns to those of their dead kinsmen who had been great men, and these were called memorial horns.

After this, Hjorvard arose and made a vow that he would drive from the sea every Roman vessel that was to be seen along the coast of Gaul, Britain, Frisia, or die in the undertaking.

Hromund the Bold rose and said: "Slight is thy vow, indeed, Hjorvard, for it requires but little strength and will to drive the Romans from the sea. Make a stronger vow, which will show thy daring and bravery; then I will follow thee and make my own."

Hjorvard answered, "Hromund, thou art right. I vow that I will make war in Gaul and Britain, and come back with great booty; and, furthermore, I will sacrifice the prisoners I make, and redden with their blood the altar of the gods. I take also the oath, that if any vessels of the Romans ever try to come to our land, as they never have tried yet, not one of their men shall return back alive to tell of our country."

"This is a stronger vow than the first, foster-brother," said Hromund the Hersir, "but there is little fear that they will ever come to our land, for they dread our people and our ships; their war-ships flee at the approach of our fleets, but I like the vows thou hast made to attack them in their strongholds of Gaul and Britain."

Then he himself arose and said: "I vow that I will follow thee, Hjorvard, in thy expeditions against the Romans, with all my ships and war-riors; return if thou returnest, or die a warrior's death if thou hast been fated to go to Valhalla in thy undertaking; for as foster-brothers we have sworn to avenge each other."

Then Hamund the Valiant arose and said: "I vow that I will follow you, Hjorvard, and Hro-mund the Bold, with all my ships and warriors, and devastate with you the provinces of the Roman Empire, and go into the Mediterranean. We will show the Romans that they cannot withstand the power of the Norsemen any more on the land than on the sea."

Then Ingald the Black-eyed rose and said: "I take the oath that I will follow you all, and that my standard will float on the shores of Britain, and that I will make upon that island a settlement that the power of the Roman will not dare to attack, or I will perish in the attempt."

Ivar rose and vowed that he would follow his father in that expedition, or die in the undertaking. Many men made vows that night.

After these vows, the memorial toasts to dead kinsmen took place. The scene was solemn and impressive, for many of those that were to be remembered had been living a few years back, and others had died centuries before, in a halo of glory. All had helped to make the land of the Vikings what it was, the most feared of all lands. After the departed kinsmen had been remembered, those present rose and vowed to follow in their footsteps.

Those who could not come to the temple held sacrifices at home. The feast among the people lasted thirteen days, and many spent half of the Yule at each other's farms.

The following April, after the sacrifice to Odin for victory had taken place, all over the Northern lands warriors were getting their ships ready for the general and powerful expeditions that were soon to proceed against the provinces of the Roman Empire; even the shores of the Mediterranean were also to be attacked.

Many of the Vikings intended also to reënforce by their numbers the colonies that had been made by their kinsmen in Britain, Gaul, and Friesland, and other countries, and to settle there.

Hjorvard and all the other powerful chiefs who had taken oaths at the preceding Yule sacrifice at

Dampstadir had not forgotten them; they were making most extensive preparations for war and conquest. Hjorvard was chiefly the cause of the great upheaval. A warlike message had gone to every inhabited place of the land, and every youth wanted to be among those who were going.

Every man who was bound by law to furnish a war-ship or more had been summoned to do so by all the Hersirs. Hjorvard gathered a fleet of several hundred vessels. The greatest enthusiasm prevailed among those who were to follow him. Many doughty champions of the North had come to join his standard, for they knew that victory would follow him. They came from the shores of the present Norway, of the Cattegat, the islands of the Baltic, and the southern shores of that sea. They all knew that they were the chosen of the gods, and were to be victorious.

Weapon Things, or meetings, had taken place everywhere. At these all the freemen were obliged to come and show sword, spear, an axe, a shield, all in perfect order. Each Bondi had to be ready at the place where the war arrow had summoned him, and had to show one bow and two dozen arrows for every bench of the ship or ships he was obliged to furnish.

Hjalmar arrived at Dampstadir from Engel with one hundred ships; the fleets of several of his kinsmen joined him the next day with two hundred ships more. Among these were the berserk Sigvaldi, who came with twenty ships; Tryggvi with fifteen, Trividil with nine. Starkard came with a single skeid manned only with berserks who had constantly the berserk fury upon them. Helsing came with three ships, with a crew composed in great part of skilful archers and sling-men, or stone-throwers. These men came north of the present Christiania fjord. Sigmund and Sigurd also arrived, to the great joy of Ivar and Hjalmar, with fifty fine vessels each. Every one of these had a crew of two hundred and twenty men. The sea before Dampstadir seemed to be like a forest of masts.

There was nothing in the world which the Vikings thought more of than their ships. Upon them they lavished their wealth and skill. They all vied with each other as to who should have the finest craft. Hjorvard's dragon-ship was the most powerful of all the warships assembled before Dampstadir, and his pennant, which floated at its masthead, was embroidered with gold, and in the centre was the representation of Hugin and Munin, the ravens of Odin.

On the eve of their departure, Ivar and Hjalmar went to a sibyl called Helge, who, by rubbing with her hands the bodies of men who were setting out for war, could find out the vulnerable spot that would be wounded unless she protected it by her incantations. The foster-brothers themselves wore charmed chain-armor, which no weapons could penetrate. During the absence of Hjorvard, Sigrlin was to rule over the estates.

The horns for the departure sounded; the ships
soon afterwards were on their way south, and in a
short time were out of sight of the shores of Gotland. New accessions of ships were constantly
made on the way, and after a sail of two days the
fleet reached Hleidra, the head burg of Halfdan,
the powerful ruler of Zeeland. This burg was situated on the arm of the sea which is known to-
day under the name of the Roskilde fjord.

There they met an equally powerful fleet,
which Halfdan had summoned. The vessels were
so numerous that the sound between the present
Helsinor and Helsingborg on the Swedish coast
was but a forest of masts, and the sea could not
be seen.

Halfdan received Hjorvard, his kinsman, and the
high-born men who had come with him, with
great honor. There was great feasting and drinking for several days.

Here the ships were joined by a most imposing
fleet of more than one thousand sail from Svithjod, manned by most valiant men. Then fleet
after fleet arrived; some came from the beautiful
and powerful island of Funen, from the present
island of Bornholm—in a word, from every island
of the Baltic and Cattegat, and also many vessels
from the peninsula of Jutland. At the Lime
fjord, a large arm of the sea on the northern part
of Jutland, the fleets of all the Hersirs of the present Norway, and those living on the Cattegat,
were waiting for the coming of the fleets of the

Baltic.   When all the vessels reached the Lime
fjord, they found there a fleet of over two thousand
craft assembled.   The vessels composing the expedition were of all sizes, from the great dragon-
ships to the small skutas; many of these latter
were intended for shallow water.   There were
also a very great number of provision ships, and
others to carry horses.   Horses were always used
by the Vikings to reconnoitre the land after they
had landed.

At a council of all the commanders, it was
agreed that this great number of vessels would
divide into several fleets, and those into several
squadrons, and that the Roman Empire should be
attacked in many places; also that several squadrons should sail for the Mediterranean, and a time
and special places were fixed for vessels to meet
before the coming of winter.

After the plan of campaign had been settled,
the horns were sounded to order the departure of
the fleets.   They divided themselves as had been
arranged, the red shields were hoisted on the
mastheads, and a mighty shout of war rose from
every ship, far and wide, spreading like the thunder along the sky, or the sound of a mighty tor-
rent breaking everything that existed.   It bade
defiance to the Roman world and empire.

It was no easy matter for each fleet to depart
in the midst of this great forest of masts, but the
good seamanship of the Vikings mastered the
difficulties, and but few casualties took place.

CHAPTER IX

IF one could have been on the most northern extremity of the peninsula of Jutland after the departure of the fleets, he would have seen for several days ship after ship ploughing the sea, rounding Cape Skagen, and then disappearing below the horizon. Some of these were going southward, others westward.

Some were to make warfare in Friesland, others in Gaul and Britain and the Mediterranean. Some were going to Scotland, whence they were to pour their host upon Britain.

Less than two months afterwards, a wail of sorrow and anguish burst in every Roman province bathed by the sea. Couriers went to Rome from every one of these to ask for help, but Rome was powerless to help them, for the Norsemen were masters of the sea, and could land armies wherever they pleased. "The country that owns the sea owns might," they used to say. The whole Roman Empire was in dread and fear of these Vikings, who were continually coming in countless hordes; their number seemed inexhaustible as they poured from the basin of the Baltic and the shores of Norway, year after year, and had done so for two centuries. This last invasion of the provinces of Rome was one of the most, if not the most, formidable that had ever taken place. Fire and sword were carried everywhere by the Norsemen.

Hjorvard had gone to make war in Britain, while his son Ivar, with his three foster-brothers and a large force, had landed on the northern shores of Gaul, where the present Boulogne now stands. There the Romans had built strong fortifications, but many a time their centurions had seen with dismay the Viking fleets pass before them, ascend the Seine, and take possession of many islands.

Before landing, every warrior washed, and combed his hair, and took a good meal, in order to be strong for the day's fight, and was dressed in his best war clothes, so that if he was fated to die he might enter Valhalla as befitted his rank. The red shields had been hoisted as a token of war.

After Ivar had landed his forces and sent men on horseback to reconnoitre, Decius and Curtius, the centurions who commanded the stronghold at Bononia (the modern Boulogne), seeing that the Viking force was much smaller than their own, resolved to attack them, and an overpowering Roman force left their stronghold with the hope of annihilating the Norsemen who had dared to land before their eyes.

When Ivar saw this, he said to his men, " Often the more numerous host does not gain the victory if there are fearless men against it. Many a blunt sword has won the victory in battle. As we are the weakest in number, let us arrange our host in the wedge shape that was taught to our forefathers by Odin himself ; and we will have, besides, another body of men to attack the Romans or protect us, as may be necessary."

When Decius saw this strategy carried out, he marvelled greatly ; for the Romans thought this peculiar war formation, which they called *cuneus*, was only known to them. He had heard from different Roman commanders that the Vikings had this knowledge, but he had not believed them ; and though a moment before, he had boastingly told his soldiers that Rome would soon hear of their victory, he became uneasy as he saw the glittering shields and helmets of the Vikings in their battle array, and the body of archers and horsemen with shining swords, who were ready to go wherever sent.

He then ordered his men to be placed in wedge-shaped formation. When Ivar and his men saw this, they in their turn wondered how it was that the Romans knew this formation, and Hjalmar exclaimed : " They must have learned this from our people ; how could it be otherwise ? "

Before the battle, Ivar issued his orders, saying, "Our horsemen will remain on the lookout, and be ready to support us or to attack the enemy ;

our archers will pour a continuous hail of arrows upon the Romans, and our slingmen will do likewise with stones. The shield-burg should be at the apex of the triangle, and must be guarded by the most skilful warriors; for if it is broken or opened, especially in the beginning of the battle, it will be most fatal to victory. The two other points of the triangle must also be very strongly guarded. It is imperative that great care be taken that our locked formation be not broken or even opened; for disorder in our midst would follow, and might lead to great disaster."

The foster-brothers agreed that as Ivar was the foremost champion among them, he should be at the apex of the triangle with their most valiant men, for this part of the triangle was always the weakest spot of the formation.

Then Ivar said : " Let my standard ' Victory ' be moved forward, and let Alrek, my standard-bearer, be surrounded by berserks. My scalds must stand in the midst of the shield-burg, and so placed as to be able to see the conflict, and praise the deed of the combatants, or of those who fall in the battle."

When Alrek heard this he said: " I have feared for some time past, during the years that this long peace has lasted, that I should die of old age on my bench, and I wished rather to fall in battle, if it had thus been fated me by the Nornir."

Sigmund and Sigurd, with their two standards and their valiant men, were at the two other points

of the array. Hjalmar and a large body of men
were in front of the standards of Ivar to protect the apex of the triangle, or to attack the
Roman host if need be, if these did not come
forward.

The war-horns were sounded on the Norsemen's
side, and the archers and slingmen advanced
towards the Romans, and poured a storm of missiles into them which made many of their host bite
the dust ; then a general attack took place, and
after a fierce conflict of spears and swords, and des-
perate efforts of the Romans to protect themselves
with their shields, their formation was broken after
much slaughter, and they fled in every direction
before the victors. Curtius, one of the centurions,
was killed ; but Decius and a number of his men
escaped under the cover of their fortifications.
From their walls the Roman centurion looked
upon his fallen soldiers and the victorious Norsemen, and exclaimed in a voice full of despair :
" Rome, what has become of thy might, that thou
canst not conquer those men of the sea ? They
defy thy power, and laugh at thy legions sent
against them ! To-day they are here, to-morrow
elsewhere. No province is free from their attacks.
Even if a country is powerful with its legions on
land, it cannot hold sway over the world unless
mighty at sea also."

Sigmund and Hjalmar had been wounded, but
not a word of pain escaped their lips when they

received their wounds, neither did they shrink
when these were dressed, for the foster-brothers
had made a vow that they, like the champions of
Hjorvard, would not wince or utter cries of pain
when wounded or when their wounds were dressed.

After the battle, the slain Norsemen were buried
with their weapons, and their mounds were reddened with the blood of the Roman prisoners who
were sacrificed to Odin for the victory. After the
booty had been carried, according to ancient
custom, round a pole that had been raised, and
divided into four parts, it was distributed among
the men, and many Roman and Gallic captives
were taken to their ships to be sent home.

While the events just recorded were taking
place, the numerous fleets and squadrons of the
Norsemen had not been idle; their colonies had
been reënforced by great accessions, and those
who had been engaged in warfare had collected
a large booty, including a large number of Roman
coins, for they knew their full value for barter;
besides, many of these were to be melted to be
used afterwards in different ways, such as plates,
cups, dishes, etc.

It had been agreed by some Viking chiefs,
while the fleets were at the Lime fjord, that their
ships should meet those of Ivar and his three
foster-brothers at the mouth of the River Somme,
in Valland—for that part of Northern Gaul was
thus called by the Norsemen—and in the autumn
they met at the appointed time.

After a council of war among the commanders, it was decided that they should spend the winter in the Mediterranean. Before undertaking this expedition they made a great sacrifice to Odin, and then sailed away. They had hardly passed the Straits of Gibraltar when they attacked the countries bordering the shores of the Mediterranean. They spread terror as far as the coasts of Greece, took Syracuse by assault, and caused great slaughter there.

On their return, after they had reached the northern part of the coast of Portugal, the fleets divided into several powerful squadrons again, under different leaders, and renewed their attacks upon the seaboard parts of Britain, Gaul, and Friesland. Others sailed for home, loaded with Roman and Greek spoils, and with a large number of Roman coins of gold and silver. They had, besides, many slaves, among whom were many from Britain, Gaul, Friesland, and the Mediterranean. Among them were many handsome young women.

Hjorvard, while his son was in the Mediterranean, had attacked the country lying west of Valland, which is to-day called Brittany, had defeated the Romans in several encounters, and made many prisoners. All had fulfilled the vows of the preceding last Yule. Hromund the Bold had fought by his side ; Ingald the Black-eyed had done likewise ; but he concluded to make a settlement in Britain, on the banks of the Thames, and one of

7

the sons of Hamund the Valiant remained with
Ingald.

After his victories, Hjorvard sent a very fast
sailing vessel to Ivar, who had won great glory in
his expeditions, to tell him that he intended to
return to Dampstadir.

CHAPTER X

IVAR himself had concluded that instead of returning to Gotland, he would go and visit his kinsmen whose forefathers had settled in Britain in the first century. Accordingly, he left the River Loire, and sailed eastward, along the shores of Gaul, visited some of the Gotlanders who had settled peacefully near the sea and on the banks of some of its rivers, and asked them if they wanted help of men and ships. The Romans had left them in peaceful possession of their lands, however, thinking it more prudent to let them alone than to incur their enmity and that of their kinsmen, who they knew were relentless in their hatred.

After passing the mouth of the Thames, upon whose banks were several settlements, the largest ones being where the present Greenwich and Chatham stand, they continued their voyage, sailing along the eastern coast of Britain, which was as flat as it is to-day, and came to the coast of the shire of Norfolk (inhabited by the folk of the north), and cast anchor in an estuary, or bay, to-day called the Wash.

The object of Ivar's visit in this part of Britain was to see his kinsman, Grammar Hersir, a foster-brother of his father, who ruled over a large herad, whose boundary came to the Wash. Nearly two hundred years before, a great-great-uncle of Ivar had married the daughter of one of the Hersirs of Norway. This great-great-uncle was young and adventurous, and had settled somewhat inland of the bay, in the country which is to-day called Cambridgeshire; a great many people from the coast of Norway followed him, and the emigration was chiefly from there.

In those early days, that part of Britain was thinly settled by the aborigines. A great part of the "littoral" along the North Sea was flat and swampy, and the country was covered with oak forests, and on account of this was good for ship-building; for that very reason this settlement had been made. The poor aborigines had received these new-comers kindly, and the extended forest shut them up from the Romans, who had conquered part of the island. On the sea side, the settlers felt secure, as they and the Norsemen were masters on the sea.

Grammar's by, or burg, stood near the shores of the river now called Cam, somewhat near the present hamlet of Wilbraham. The pioneers and the first Norse settlers had chosen this peculiar spot so high up the river, that they might feel safe from the sudden attacks of enemies. Sometimes feuds broke out among the Norse families in Britain and their kinsmen on the Baltic; these would come and claim the inheritance of those that were dead, and war followed. The river-shore here and there was fortified; high towers had been built where high-born men had their estates; from their top a good look-out was kept up, and chains were laid across the river, when they feared hostile incursions, to prevent their ships from ascending the stream.

The following day after their arrival, the ships having the lightest draught, specially built for use in shallow water, were picked out, and then Ivar and his foster-brothers started for Grammar's by. They had to take to the oars, as the wind was very light, and the current was against them. Each craft had fifteen and sixteen benches, and was consequently rowed by thirty or thirty-two oars, three men on each oar, while the other men stood at the prow and stern. The peace shields had been hoisted. When night came, they let down their anchors and raised their tents. Early the following morning they started, and continued the ascent of the stream; they had to row all the way. Here and there, they saw a settlement of the Norsemen, with cultivated land round them, and their ships lying at the wharves near by.

`Finally they came in sight of Grammar's residence, and of the temple overlooking the river, where the worship of Odin, Frey, Njord, Thor. and other gods took place. The structures were similar to those of home, all of wood, and the new-comers might have fancied they were in their own country across the sea.

When Grammar, whose young kinsman's fame had reached him, heard of Ivar's arrival, he sent messengers on board of his ship, and invited him to come and stay with him, with all his men.

Ivar, his foster-brothers, and all the high-born men of his fleet, after landing, went to the banqueting hall, and were received with great honor. Ivar was bid by Grammar to sit on the high seat opposite him, and his men were seated according to their rank. On each side of Ivar were the high-born men of Grammar, and on that of the latter were those of Ivar; Hjalmar being seated on the right of Grammar, and Sigmund on his left; then Sigurd came next, and the others drew lots for seats, for many were of equal birth.

The hall was a fine specimen of Northern architecture, and was somewhat similar to that of Gudbrand at Hrafnista on Engel. The carvings represented the landing of a body of men on shore in war attire, coming to take possession of land in Britain. Tapestry hung along the walls, and a long row of fine shields above the seats encircled the hall.

Grammar was a noble-looking man, and, according to the custom of Hersirs who had come of mature age, he wore a long, flowing beard, which was of a beautiful silver-gray. He was tall and majestic in bearing, and had the deep blue eyes of his kin. His chin and mouth showed great deci-

sion of character, but his benignant smile and soft
eye told of the kindliness of his heart. He ruled
his land according to the ancient customs of the
Norselands. The land had been divided and was
owned as in the Viking's lands generally. He was
a great sacrificer, and loved Frey more than all
the other gods, and sacrificed often to him.

He was a widower, his wife, a daughter of the
Hersir of the island of Fyen, in the Cattegat, having died several years before. He had several
beautiful daughters. The eldest was named Hildigunn, a combination of the names of two Valkyrias, Hild and Gunn, the custom of joining two
names being not uncommon with the Norsemen.
The others were named Brynhild, Sigrun, and
Hervor.

Grammar expressed his great pleasure in seeing
his young kinsman, and told him that he had
fought by the side of his grandfather and father,
and, pointing to a sword hanging over his high
seat, with peace bands fastened around it, he said:
"This sword is called 'Stone-biter' on account of
the sharpness and quality of its blade, and was
given to me, Ivar, by thy grandfather when I
had just begun warfare as a young lad, and was on
board of his own ship. It is a most excellent
weapon, and victory has always followed it. It is
an heirloom in our family."

Then he inquired how Hjorvard and the folks
were in dear Gotland, in Engel, and in old Norway, and added that he hoped to go and see once

more the land of his ancestors before he should go on his burning journey to Valhalla and lie under his mound.

Ivar told him of the great deeds that had taken place since all the fleets had scattered, and what he had himself accomplished in foreign lands.

"Well done," said Grammar; "I can see that thou art a Yngling, and worthy of thy kinsmen who are dead."

Then Ivar presented to him two magnificent velvet cloaks from Greece; a superb coat of mail of exquisite workmanship, made by a smith from Gotland; several brooches to fasten his cloaks with; helmets, saxes, and swords of fine workmanship; a beautiful necklace of gold for Hildigunn, and bracelets for his other daughters. Ivar noticed that the dress of the women and men, the weapons and ornaments, were of the same style as those worn by the people in the Viking lands. Like the emigrants of our days, they had brought their customs, religion, and fashions with them.

A few jewels which had come with the people who had first landed at Wilbraham were still kept as family heirlooms, though most of them had been buried with the dead. These were "fibulæ," or brooches, of cruciform and circular shape, mosaic and glass beads, which were worn by the people in the first and second centuries.

Not far from Grammar's residence and temple, and overlooking the river, was the graveyard of the first Norse settlers who had come to that part

of Britain. There were graves where the bodies
had not been burned; in others the burned bones
were preserved in cinerary urns, or in wooden
buckets with bronze trappings. Weapons, jewels,
ornaments of bronze, tweezers with ear-pickers,
iron spears, iron shears, knives, glass and mosaic
beads, had been put on the pyre and fired or destroyed by its fire. Coins of Trajan, 96–98 A.D.;
Hadrian, 117–138 A.D.; Aurelius, 160–180 A.D.;
Maximus, 286–305 A.D., told the age of the
graveyard, which was a very exact counterpart of
the burial places of the mother country.

One day, while a great feast was taking place,
Hildigunn and her sisters came into the hall. She
was tall and slender; her hair was flaxen, falling
gracefully over her shoulders, far below her waist;
her eyes were of a deep, soft blue, which contrasted
charmingly with her delicate, rosy complexion.
She walked toward Ivar and said to him: "Hail
to thee, my kinsman, we also are of Odin's kin.
Hail you all Ynglingar and Skoldungar and high-
born men who are with us here to-day."

Then, sipping some ale from the horn she held
in her hand, she handed it to Ivar. He took the
horn and her hand at the same time, and said to
her that she must sit by him.

"It is not the custom of Vikings to drink in
pair with women," replied Hildigunn.

Ivar answered that it was, and that he would
rather change the Viking laws if it was the case, so
that he could drink with her. Then she sat down

by his side, and spoke of many things with him during the evening. The poets of Grammar recited the songs which told of the great deeds accomplished by him with Hjorvard, or by their ancestors.

Days passed pleasantly for Ivar and his foster-brothers at Grammar's by, for many maidens had come around from the surrounding estates to welcome the Vikings, and their presence made life so much pleasanter for all.

Every evening these maidens and warriors met in the great banqueting-hall. These fair Viking daughters, in whose veins the blood of the Norsemen flowed, listened to the scalds who had come with Ivar and recited the great deeds of valor the Vikings had accomplished in the expeditions from which they had just returned, and heard with wonder of the hair-breadth escapes of Ivar, and of many of his companions.

No Viking could tell himself of his brave feats, for it was thought unbecoming to do so; but they could tell of the countries they had seen, and of the people they had met in far-off lands, and when they did, the maidens listened to them with wonder and admiration, and their eyes were fixed upon those who told of their strange adventures, and their cheeks flushed with animation.

Finally, the admiration turned into love, without their knowing it; but there could be no mistake, for during the day, while in the skemma, they could not help thinking all the time of the one they admired the most. They wished for the evening entertainment to come, so that they might come into the hall.

The Vikings themselves, especially Ivar and his foster-brothers, wished likewise for the day to pass quickly.

One evening, as the brothers were by themselves, and thought of the beautiful girls they had met, and were talking of love in a general way, Ivar said:

"What men call love springs from the mind, for the mind is the seat and source of all our thoughts; the heart does not think, and cannot love; it palpitates quicker, it is true, with love, but it is only the reflection of the mind. There is a beginning in love, as in everything else that the gods have created—like the flower, it must be born first, grow, bud, and bloom. The bud is the beginning of love, and when love is young it is fickle.

"Trust not love too soon when it is young, for fickle is the mind of man towards woman, and if one searches well, he will find that many a good maiden is fickle to man, for their hearts were shaped like a whirling wheel, and fickleness was laid in their breasts."

The day of parting came at last. The life shaped by the Nornir had to continue; the future was hidden from sight, but what stories of the budding of love could be told, for many a blushing maiden had lost her heart with a brave warrior, and many a Viking had lost his also.

CHAPTER XI

THE DAUGHTERS OF RAN

IT was late in the summer when Ivar and
Hjalmar, who had decided to cross the North
Sea on the Elidi, and their Viking fleet left the
coast of Britain for the Baltic. All on board of the
ships wondered if Ægir and Ran, the god and goddess of the sea and their daughters, would show
themselves in ugly mood on their way home. The
people believed that those who were drowned at
sea went to Ran, those who died by weapons went
to Valhalla, and those who died of natural death in
their beds or chairs went to Hel. The seafaring
people worshipped Ægir, for he governed the sea
and wind. Ran, his wife, received well all ship-
wrecked people in her hall at the bottom of the
sea, and had a net with which she caught men who
came out to sea; drowned men were sure to be
welcomed by her. The Wind and the Fire are the
brothers of Ægir. The Wind is so strong that he
moves large oceans, and stirs up his brother the
Fire.

Ægir and Ran have nine beautiful daughters,
who live in the sea, and the waves are named after
them. These daughters often go three together,

and the winds awake them from their sleep. They are not partial to men, and are always seen in storms. All had names emblematic of the waves. They are called Himinglœfa, the Heaven Glittering; Dufa, the Dove; Blodughadda, the Bloody-haired; Hefring, the Hurling, or Heaving; Ud, the Loving; Hrönn, the Towering; Bylgja, the Billowing, or Swelling; Bara, the Lashing; Kolga, the Cooling.

Ægir and Ran were not to let Ivar's fleet go home quietly. The ships were hardly out of sight of land when the sky became dark and threatening, the clouds hung low and moved with great rapidity, the wind kept increasing in violence, the waves rose higher and higher, and the North Sea was like a sheet of white foam. The sails were reefed on board of several vessels, but Ivar had, like his father, made a vow that he would never reef a sail. The Elidi rose over the waves as if she were a sea-gull, and was so easily steered that the people believed and declared that she understood the human voice. From the south-west, the wind shifted suddenly to the northwest, and alternate gusts of wind and rain followed each other in quick succession.

" It is good," suddenly exclaimed Hjalmar, "that no man knows his fate beforehand; his mind is thus free from anxiety and sorrow."

" The day was fine this morning," answered Ivar, "but after all, a day should be praised at night, a woman after she is buried, a sword after it is tried, ice when it has been crossed over, and a voyage after it is ended."

" Those are wise sayings," replied Hjalmar; and as the Elidi and the other ships were ploughing their way fast through the waves, Ivar said to Hjalmar : "Tell me, foster-brother, tell me of those sea-maidens who wander over the sea and pass their lives in doing harm to many men."

" Those maidens are the daughters of Ægir and Ran," replied Hjalmar; "they are evil-minded and slay men ; they are seldom gentle to us sea-faring people, and the wind arouses them from their sleep, and they look angrily at the ships sailing over the sea.   It is they that are those mountainous waves which we see."

" Who are the maidens," asked Ivar again, " who walk over the reefs, and journey along the fjords and shores?   These white-hooded women have a hard bed, and make little stir in calm weather."

Hjalmar replied : " These are billows and waves, daughters of Ran; they lay themselves on skerries ; their beds are the rocks, and the calm sea stirs them not ; but lo, when the wind blows hard, it rouses their anger, and they send the men that are on the deep to Ran, their mother."

" I fear, foster-brother," said Ivar, " by the look of the sky, that we are going to meet Ægir and Ran and their daughters erelong in their angry mood."

The wind kept increasing.   " The brother of Ægir, who stirs the ocean," said the foster-brother, "wishes to see what kind of men are on board of the Elidi and other ships, and if Ivar and his foster-brothers are fearless men; for, as thou seest, the sea is becoming mountain high."

Then Hjalmar, who was looking at the wake made by the ship, said to Ivar: "Who are those white-helmeted maidens that I seem to see yonder? They are dressed in white, have frowning looks, their breasts heave with passion, and they are coming fast toward the Elidi."

"Those are three of the daughters of Ægir and Ran, and by their size and fierceness must be Hrönn, Bylgja, and Hefring; let us beware of them, for there is anger in their looks; they are coming rapidly toward us, and I think they mean us harm."

Ivar had hardly uttered these words, when there dashed a wave so strongly against the Elidi that it carried away the gunwales. It was Hrönn, they fancied, that had come against the ship. Then another wave followed Hrönn; it carried away part of the bows of the Elidi. It was Bylgja. Right after Bylgja, in the wink of an eye, came another wave that swamped the deck of the ship, and flung four men overboard, who were all lost.

Then Hjalmar said: "It is Hefring, who has carried those four men to Ran, and Hrœsvelg (the wind) is flapping his wings with great force at heaven's end so that the tempest may blow still harder." "It is likely," said Ivar, "that some more of our men will visit Ran, for the storm is increasing; we shall not be thought fit to come to her hall and in her presence unless we prepare ourselves well for her welcome." Then he cut asunder several large arm-rings of gold, and divided them among his men; "for," said he, "I think it right that every man should carry some gold with him, and appear before Ran as befits the rank of every high-born man. We have cut the red rings which the rich father of Hjorvard owned, before Ægir slays us—gold shall be seen on the guests in the middle of the hall of Ran if we need night quarters there." Then in a musing voice he added: "Ran is handling us roughly, and has taken many of my kin to herself. Verily the land of Ægir's daughter is not always safe."

It had become very cold, and Ivar said: "Fire and the sight of the sun are the best things among the sons of men, also their good health and a blameless life, if they can keep them. It is better to be merry than to be down-hearted, whatever may come to hand. Glad and cheerful should every man be until he meets his death."

The fleet was behaving splendidly in the tempest; the ships rode over the waves as if they had been birds of storms.

The dragon ships of Sigmund and Sigurd came within hailing distance of the Elidi, and Ivar shouted to them: "Foster-brothers, have the daughters of Ran treated you roughly?"

"Yes," shouted each in turn. "Several of our men have gone to the hall of Ran, and we have

prepared ourselves for this journey, for we are
fearless men."

The wind shifted, and the ships were driven
toward the dangerous coast of Norway, and came
in sight of the shores of a large island with great
weird cliffs hanging over the sea. The storm
seemed then to be at its height, the vessels had
to run before the wind, every sail had been un-
reefed to allow them to make their utmost speed,
so that they might not be swamped by the huge
seas that advanced toward them from behind.
"Witch-craft moves the storm," cried Hjalmar,
"and we had better sail under the lee of the
island for protection, for we cannot contend with
Ægir, nor Ran, and their daughters."

The Elidi and the other vessels came to the lee-
ward of the island, where it was comparatively
calm, and there the Vikings waited for better
weather. During the night the storm abated and
the wind became fair. On the morrow they sailed
away and had good weather for a time, but the
wind became stronger and stronger after they
were far out to sea, and they were once more in
the midst of a great storm; the daughters of Ran
once again were roused, and the waves became
very high and threatening. Then a snow-storm
arose, and the snow fell so thickly that the men in
the stern and the prow of the ships could not see
each other, and the waves broke over the ships
and filled them with water, so the men had to
bale for their lives.

8

"He who travels widely, steadily," said Ivar, "must meet good and evil."

"That is certain, foster-brother," answered Hjalmar. "Now is the time for brave men to be tried, and show that they do not fear death."

The great waves continued to dash against the Elidi, and Ivar burst forth into a chant, singing: "We, the renowned warriors of chiefs, have come on the deep, and land is out of sight, and I see all the men that defend the Elidi baling the ship."

The snow fell so fast and thick that they could not discern anything; the night came, and those who were not on the watch put themselves in their leather bags to sleep, and thus protect themselves against wet and cold. Ivar and Hjalmar steered the Elidi alternately. Toward morning they thought they saw nine Valkyrias, helmet-clad and with shining spears, riding in the air, over their ships, and then the storm ceased.

"They have come to protect us and hush the storm; the decree of the Nornir in regard to our death is not yet to be fulfilled," said Ivar.

Soon after, they saw land, but as it was all covered with snow they could not make out the place, as it is very difficult for mariners to do when snow covers the ground.

Then the fleet hove to for a while, and afterward sailed cautiously along the coast, keeping out of the way of the breakers and islands which rose only to the level of the sea; they came to the mouth of a fjord, and then recognized the land, and saw that they had been driven out of their course. Continuing their voyage southward until they came to Engel, they were received by Gudbrand and Sigrid with great demonstrations of joy; after a short stay they separated, each going his own way, Hjalmar remaining at home during the winter.

CHAPTER XII

SIGURD, with his own dragon-ship, sailed northward, and landed on a large island where there
were many inhabitants. He wished to visit a fos-
ter-sister of his, called Ingebjorg, whom he loved
dearly, and who received him with many demonstrations of joy. He was very proud of her, for
she was extremely beautiful, had dark brown hair
and hazel eyes, and was gifted with all the accomplishments that belonged to high-born women, as
well as possessed of a gentle and lovable character.

In the evening he betook himself to a large hall,
where there was an elaborate entertainment, and
there were many guests present. He was enthusiastically received, for many had heard of him.
A very skilful performer was playing on the harp,
and Sigurd enjoyed it greatly, so long was it since
he had heard aught but the clangor of battle, and
the roar of the winds and waves. Near him sat
three charming maidens, fair to look upon, with
whom he talked much. Their names were Thordis, Ragnild, and Thorana.

Thordis was beautiful, and had charming little
ways of her own. She was noticeably dignified in

manner, had a graceful figure, was dressed coquettishly, and possessed an exquisite pair of almond-
shaped bluish eyes which seemed the incarnation
of love.   She was every inch a Hersir's daughter,
and was a great favorite among the Vikings, to
whom her liberal ways and kind heart, as well
as her beauty and accomplishments, made her
extremely attractive.

Ragnild was twenty years old, tall and slender;
her hair was fair and silky, her complexion as delicate as that of the apple blossom.   The blue dress
she wore that evening was in delightful contrast
to her fair skin and hair.   Her big blue eyes were
like nests filled with little Cupids ready to send
their arrows right and left into the hearts of those
who came within their range.

Thorana, the shortest of the three, was twenty-
two years of age, and possessed a very graceful
figure, with a pair of small eyes full of mischief.
Her head was adorned with thick chestnut hair of
rich color, with streaks as of burnished gold here
and there.   She was full of life, had great in-
dividuality, and, in general, had very much her
own way, as she was an only daughter.   All three
maidens loved the society of scalds and warriors.

The mothers of these three girls were handsome women, and all had brought up their
daughters with tender love and care, and taught
them all the accomplishments which were required
of maidens of high birth.

Thordis had lost her father, and she and her

mother mourned his death greatly. She had a brother, a most charming and handsome fellow, whom Sigurd liked at once.

A very few days after this entertainment, Thordis, Thorana, Ragnild, and Sigurd had become fast friends, and called themselves cousins. They saw each other every day, and met often in the banqueting hall in the evening. One day Sigurd received a message from a friend, written in mystic runes, in which Thordis, whose home was elsewhere, was casually mentioned as visiting on the island, and the message also said that she held large estates in her own right. This latter part of the message did not please Sigurd, for he liked Thordis for her own sake and her charming ways.

One day, when Thordis was seated by the side of her mother, Sigurd appeared, and, after saluting them in his usual way, he said, with a laughing expression: "Cousin Thordis, I have received a message, written in mystic runes, in which your name is mentioned. It is sad news to me, indeed. I wish I had never received it."

At these words, Thordis's big, beautiful eyes became twice as large as they were before, and, with an inquiring and startled look, she said: "Cousin Sigurd, I insist on knowing what your friend has written, and who he is."

"No," said Sigurd, "you will never know who he is."

"Then what did he say?" asked Thordis. "I insist upon knowing."

"If you wish to know," replied Sigurd, "I will
tell you that. He wrote that you were a lovely
maiden, but that you possessed great wealth in
your own right; and this last part was sad news,
indeed, to me. I wish I had never received the
message. I never cared or knew if you were
rich, and I like you for your own charming ways
and for yourself, and——"

"Well," replied Thordis, with apparently a feeling of great relief, "your friend has deceived you;"
to which assertion her mother nodded assent.

"Certainly not in the first part of the message,
where he says you are a charming girl," said
Sigurd.

"There, also, he made a mistake," she replied,
laughing. "But never mind, Cousin Sigurd."

The following day, Ragnild, Thordis, and her
brother, with Sigurd, drove up to Eagle Mountain
from which a beautiful view of the sea, of the burg,
and of the island could be seen.

Every day that passed away bound the friendship of these three maidens with Sigurd stronger
than before.

Alas! a day came when Ragnild's mother, who
was also a visitor on the island, received a runic
message from home, that they must return. Poor
Ragnild did not like it. She wanted to stay, for
it was so pleasant on the island. Sigurd was at
least no better pleased, nor were Thordis and
Thorana, and it was with great regret that they
parted; they followed her to the ship, but not

before they promised to meet again in the winter.
Ragnild was very much missed by them in all the
entertainments that followed, and Sigurd thought
often afterwards of lovely Ragnild.

One day Sigurd proposed to Thordis and
Thorana a moonlight drive, as the weather was
beautiful, and at that time, the beginning of September, the moon was very brilliant. It was
agreed that two other friends were to go. They
were pleasant men, full of life and jollity.

It was a beautiful night; not a cloud was seen
in the sky. The full moon, queen of the night,
shone in all her glory; the stars glittered and
twinkled brilliantly in the deep azure of the firma-
ment.

Waiting in front of the "skemma," or bower,
of Thordis and Thorana stood a splendid four-
wheeled carriage, wagon-like in shape, drawn by
two of the fleetest horses known in the country.
The horses were very restive. They champed
the bit, pawed the ground, and snorted incessantly.
Two men held the fiery steeds firmly by the bridle,
and it took all their might, and in despite of this
they could hardly prevent them from getting
away from them.

Sigurd and his two companions were anxiously
waiting for the coming of the two Vikings' daughters. Thorana and Thordis at last made their
appearance, clad in their warm, graceful evening
cloaks. Their faces were radiant with expectation,
for both had been looking forward to that drive

by moonlight and the sail on Eagle Lake, and were anticipating great delight. Accompanying them was a middle-aged friend, a woman who was to act, as we say in our modern way, as a chaperon. She was very skilled in embroidery, and had great talent in representing on canvas all kinds of scenery, views of the sea or landscape, either weird or charming.

They had hardly entered the carriage, and had had no time to be seated, when the horses, becoming apparently unmanageable, dashed forward, and, as they rounded the corner of the way leading to the high road, the vehicle seemed fairly to bend like a bow, and was on the point of being overturned. Fortunately the great skill of the driver was equal to the emergency. Then the carriage fairly flew over the ground, an irresistible power seeming to impel the fiery steeds forward in their furious speed.

The excitement was very great among all. Sigurd exclaimed that even Sleipnir, the eight-footed horse of Odin, could not go faster, neither could clouds, pushed before the tempest, fly forward more quickly. The moonlight imparted a weird appearance to the landscape, the strange shadows of the trees seemed to play all round them, and the shadows of the rocks and of the hills appeared and disappeared, one after another, in quick succession, like phantoms or ghosts.

Here and there they entered a part of the road densely wooded and where the rays of the moon could not penetrate ; then came a less dense part of the forest, where tall, conical-shaped pines extended their phantom-like shadows out upon the road and over themselves ; then groves of aspens came in sight, with their leaves quivering and frolicking as so many merry maids. The heaven was their banqueting hall, the stars their lights, and the murmur of the wind the music.

All were speechless and spell-bound at the speed of the coursers and the unearthly beauty of all that passed swiftly before them, but once in a while an exclamation of delight or of wonderment escaped from the lips of Thordis and Thorana.

Sigurd, who had been silent for some time, suddenly seemed to see far off in the sky nine Valkyrias riding in the air on fiery white steeds. Skuld, the Norn personifying the future, was preceding them, and Sigurd wondered why Skuld was with them, and what her appearance forbode. She accompanied them evidently to see that the decrees of the Nornir, who had shaped the lives of each of them at their birth, should be fulfilled at the particular time. What were those decrees no human being knew. Then Sigurd said to himself, "It was well ordered that no one should know his fate beforehand." He did not know that they had fated him to be in love with Thorana or Thordis. Suddenly the Valkyrias and Skuld appeared to vanish from his gaze.

As the carriage sped along, the horses ran faster than before ; it seemed hardly possible that the axles could stand the strain put upon them. Such was the rattling, that every part of the vehicle seemed on the point of coming to pieces. All shouted that they did not mind, that the wild fun would be still greater than ever. In a word, the excitement had rendered every one perfectly reckless of danger. "Why should the daughters of Viking heroes be afraid?" exclaimed Thordis; and Thorana shouted at the top of her voice: "It is good that our mothers are not with us; my mother would have died of fright or faint, and then we should have missed all our sport."

Glimpses of Eagle Lake were finally seen through the foliage of the trees, and soon afterwards they stopped before a solitary cabin near its shores, their horses fairly covered with foam.

Every one declared that never had he driven so fast, or seen such superb driving, or been so excited in his life. In a few moments two boats were seen gliding out upon the waters of Eagle Lake, which was nestled in the midst of wooded hills, while yonder was Eagle Mountain towering above all. In one boat were Sigurd and Thorana; in the other, were Thordis and her two friends. Sigurd wished that Thordis had been also in his boat.

The scene was most enchanting; not a ripple was seen on the crystal-like water, which the moon had transformed into a mirror, in which the stars coquettishly looked at themselves, while images of the hills and trees were reflected along the shores.

"O mother Earth," said Sigurd to himself as he contemplated that never-to-be-forgotten night. "How beautiful thou art, when the moon rules over thee instead of the sun! The moon gives us the night, the sun the day. Some say that the nights were created for the sons of men to sleep, but if it is so, why should the nights be so beautiful to behold, when the moon shines, and the stars tremble and glitter in the blue of the sky? Do not the nightingales sing their songs of love at night when the moon is their sun? Love was born of the night; the nights of the moon are the lover's days, for the moon shines upon them, and kisses them with her radiant and soft light."

Thorana insisted on rowing herself. Her graceful figure bent forward and backward at each stroke of the oars, her cousin Sigurd silently admiring her all the time. Their companion enlivened the time by his bright conversation and the recital of his numerous adventures, for he had been in many distant countries, and his anecdotes were full of wit. The weird echo repeated their words in the deep silence of that night, which was only disturbed at intervals by the falling of the oars upon the water.

The two boats for a while drew wide apart, and their occupants amused themselves by listening to the echo. Once Sigurd thought he saw Hugin and Munin, the ravens of Odin, flying above his head on their way to Valhalla, to tell the Ruler of Hosts all that was happening in the world.

Then again, appeared to him the nine Valkyrias with Skuld, who had followed them all the way; their spears glittered in the moonlight. Skuld's hair sent rays of light out over the night. For a while she hovered over their boat, and then threw down upon the earth a superb ball of fire, a shooting star; then with the Valkyrias she disappeared in the direction of the Well of Urd. Every day the Nornir take the holy water from the well, and, mixing it with the clay that lies round it, pour it over the ash tree, Yggdrasil, that the branches may not dry up or decay.

When the two boats came close together again, Sigurd saw two shadows reflected in the water, more beautiful to him than those of stars and of all that had been reflected in the water since Odin had made the world. They were the shadows of Thorana and of Thordis. Their beautiful faces, their graceful forms, their long hair, were like an apparition from the deep. It was as if the two beautiful daughters of Ægir and Ran, Dufa "the dove," and Ud the "loving," had come to see the men who were in the boats.

Sigurd remained spell-bound before the sight, when, by a motion of the boat, the shadow disappeared, never to reappear on the beautiful waters of Eagle Lake, and in a short time they found themselves once more on the shore.

Sigurd mentioned to no one that he had beheld Valkyrias with Skuld, and the beautiful shadows of Thorana and Thordis, but all these visions had made a deep impression on his mind, and he remained thoughtful all the way home. The following day he made a sacrifice to the goddess Var, who, as we have said, listens to the vows of love men make ; but no one ever heard of that vow. But we may safely say that the drive that beautiful night and the row on Eagle Lake was never forgotten by any of those who were there, as long as they lived.

A few days after the events we have just mentioned, Thorana and Thordis made ready to go to their respective homes. The last evening of their stay saw the same party together in the hall where they met first. Nothing save death could have prevented Sigurd from being present. The following morning all met on board of the ship that was to take his two lovely cousins away from the island. A host of friends came to bid them good-by, all apparently happy, for none had yet realized how they would miss each other, and the good time they had all had, and that regrets were soon to follow, and all wondered· if all of them would meet again.

They parted with many expressions of love and friendship, and the following day a messenger came and handed to Sigurd a message written in mystic runes. It was from his cousins, who had written it on their way home. These magic words were : " With best love, from your broken-hearted cousins ! " and a flush of joy overspread his face when he read this loving message. He immediately sent a messenger to them with another message, telling of his lonely feelings.

Sigurd felt utterly wretched after the departure of his two cousins, though they were to meet again. A feeling of intense loneliness came over him; all that was bright and cheerful in the island had gone; the wind moaned; the waves, as they struck the shores, seemed to sing mournfully in his ears, "Thy three cousins are gone, the rocky cliffs will see them no more." He even dreaded to pass the skemma where they had stayed. No maiden could cheer him, for in his eyes none were so lovely and accomplished as Thorana, Ragnild, and Thordis.

He whiled away the time by writing on birchbark a saga, in which he recounted all that had happened on the island. Finally he concluded to depart, and after sailing a few days he came to a burg where a foster-brother by the name of Thorkel and he had been brought up together. But Thorkel had been dead for several years. Sigurd wanted to see his grave, and, after landing and telling his errand to the people, he went towards the mound where Thorkel and his wife lay silently side by side. They had been married but a short time ere Skuld snapped asunder the thread that measured the days of their lives. He ascended the mound and murmured to himself, "Here Thorkel and his wife lie. The thinking minds that guided and moved their actions during their lives have left them. Helpless, motionless, and without life they sleep."

Looking up, he saw a butterfly of brilliant colors, with wings of gold and rainbow tints, full of life, going merrily from one flower to another, drinking of their nectar.

Whilst watching his joyous course, Sigurd exclaimed musingly: "All life is ephemeral! Man and woman, like this butterfly and the flower, are but the creatures of a day in the immensity of time and in the world which the gods have made. What a beautiful life is that of the butterfly! He lives in the air; his life is that of love and immortality. He spends his days in caressing and kissing flowers, and becomes intoxicated with their sweetness. Like love, he feeds on love. As soon as he has fulfilled his destiny, and filled brimful the cup of love and drunk it, he dies as a brilliant meteor that burst into life for an instant, like the twinkling of a star that never returns. Thus the flower is born to show her tempting beauty, her sweetness, and intoxicating nectar to the butterfly. The flower was created for the butterfly, and the butterfly for the flower; so were man and woman created for one another, and to love each other, and, like love, their minds are immortal. Short is the life of the butterfly and of the flower, but their existence in the immensity of time is apparently not shorter than that of man. If the lives of the butterfly and the flower are ephemeral, so also is the life of man. In the immensity of time since the 'Great Void,' the lives of all created things appear to the gods of the same duration. Man is born, ushered into the present, and then into the future, and thenceforth belongs to the past. We are tossed," said Sigurd, "on the sea of life, like a rudderless ship, and we sail from day to day towards the unknown called by us the future, not knowing where we are going, nor how the Nornir have shaped our lives; always hoping and hoping for something we have not been able to grasp."

In this reflective mood of mind, Sigurd left the mound, under which lay two hearts which had been bound together by love during their lives, and returned to his ship, wondering what were the number of days the Nornir had decreed at his birth he should live, and also if he would ever find a woman that he would love so much as to be impelled to ask her to become his wife.

Then he sailed for Dampstadir, and there met Ivar and his two foster-brothers waiting for him.

CHAPTER XIII

A VOYAGE TO THE CASPIAN

THE following spring, Ivar and his foster-brothers made preparations to go to the Caspian Sea, by the Volga. They had sent word to several of their young kinsmen, asking them if they would join them in their voyage. The proposal had been accepted with eagerness by them all, for most of those to whom the invitation had been sent had never gone so far south, and they longed to see the lands of which they had heard so much, or from which so many costly things came; but two or three among those invited had been there before to trade, and had made on their return great profits on their goods, and they wished to try their luck again.

It was not a small undertaking to make a voyage to the Caspian, for it was tedious, and took a long time. Ivar chose three vessels of very light draught, that could sail easily on the rivers of the present Russia, leading to that sea. Special vessels were built for such voyages, and the models of these craft were beautiful, and could not even to-day be improved upon for that sort of navigation. One vessel, very much like those of Ivar, was found at Tune, in Norway, and can be seen at Christiania to-day.

Provisions were collected, among which was a great deal of hard bread, very much like that used to-day in Scandinavia. Various articles necessary for barter were also collected, such as scales and weights; a great quantity of gold spiral rods of certain size and weight, which were to be cut into smaller or larger pieces if necessary, and then weighed, for the Norsemen had no coins, and these rings or pieces were the medium of exchange. Their scale of value was according to weight. Their intercourse with Rome, however, had made them acquainted with Roman coins of gold and silver, and they knew exactly their worth, and often brought them home and kept them until they visited again the Roman province. They also had a measure called an ell, two feet in length, to measure the beautiful fabrics they intended to buy, and also a measure for wine, for they were to bring back wines with them.

A man named Ulf was to go with them. He was familiar with the navigation of the Dnieper, the Don, and the Volga, and had sailed several times from the Baltic to the Black Sea. He had lived chiefly upon the River Don, where he had a large trading establishment. He was a great trader and sea-farer, whose business was to go on trading voyages to various countries. Sometimes he went by sea, at other times by land. He was an old friend of Hjorvard, who often ordered

him to buy goods for him, and had been very often
to Gotland. Ulf was just the man for such an expedition, and the foster-brothers and their friends
congratulated themselves on his going with them.

In the beginning of June, as soon as the ice
allowed them to sail, they left Dampstadir, and
sailed through the Gulf of Finland ; thence, after a
difficult navigation through lakes and rivers, and
some hard rowing, they reached the great River
Volga, and, descending the stream, they came to
a place called Novgrad, a great mart, where a
fair was held once a year in summer. Novgrad
was in the great realm of Holmgard, and they
found there many friends, for the people were of
the same kindred. Many Vikings had married
the daughters of the Holmgard people, and much
intercourse took place between them and the
Norsemen. Both peoples had in common the
same religious belief.

During the fair, many kinds of people were to
be seen there with their wares. They came from
the Caucasus, from the Ural Mountains, from the
shores of the Caspian, from Turkestan, even from
China, and many other lands. Slaves were also sold
at Novgrad in the market-places. Peace reigned
at the Novgrad fair, as it did at all the fairs of the
Norsemen, or at the temple or assemblies of the
people. No strife or shedding of blood was allowed to take place, and no one was molested.
Ivar and his friends bought nothing at Novgrad,
intending to come back and do so on their return.

From Novgrad they sailed down the Volga, using their oars when there was no wind. They stopped here and there at several places, and were well received everywhere.

While on board, every one of the crew had to be cook, for it was then the custom of traders not to have cooks, all the messmates drawing lots to see which of them should do the cooking each day. All shipmates also had to drink together, and a tub with a lid over it stood near the mast for this purpose.

When finally they reached the Caspian without any serious mishaps, there was great rejoicing on board. Ulf was the recipient of many praises for his skilful pilotage. But the most difficult part of the journey was not yet accomplished—that of crossing the Caspian to the Persian shores, and the ascent of the Oxus River remained to be done. Before undertaking the second part of the voyage, the ships were drawn ashore, scraped, repaired, and painted, for their bottoms had become foul. During those days the Vikings spent much of their time practising athletic games when they were ashore, for on no account were these exercises to be neglected.

When the ships were ready, they crossed the Caspian without encountering one of those storms that make the water of that shallow sea, so full of shoals, dangerous to mariners; and after landing they wondered much at the people they saw, for they differed greatly from the Vikings. They

worshipped the sun and fire; some wore large tur-
bans like the Turks of to-day, were very indus-
trious, and many led a nomadic life with their
herds. Their women were beautiful, and the men
were courteous and hospitable. The Vikings
bought a good deal of beautiful velvet, which
they called pell, and much rich cloth embroidered
with gold and silver, brocades, and also superb
linen tablecloths and napkins.

They ascended afterward the River Oxus, the
ascent of which was very tedious. The current
was strong and against them, but no one tried to
molest them, and every one was anxious to barter
with them. There they bought silk goods and
velvets, and spent the beginning of the winter on
the river, and the later winter months on the Caspian, whence they sailed and rowed up the Volga
before the melting of the snow and ice in the
north; and by the time these had melted, and
swelled the stream and made the current very
rapid, they were far up. Here they waited until
the river should have fallen to its usual size, remaining all the time on board of their ships,
spending their days in playing chess or gambling
with dice, for almost all the Vikings were great
gamblers. Their voyage northward was far more
tedious than that southward. It was necessary to
place three men at each oar on account of the
current, and the end of September found them
once more in the Baltic, with their ships loaded
with precious merchandise.

Hjorvard and the Gotlanders were delighted to see Ivar and all his companions back. Not a single death had occurred during the voyage. Ulf had had an eye to business, and a good part of the cargo belonged to him. Ivar presented his father with several casks of wine and many precious objects, and to his mother he gave costly woollen, velvets, and silk stuff.

The fame of Ivar had spread far and wide all over the land. Scalds in the halls of Hersirs recounted his brilliant warlike exploits. He was very mature for his age, and gifted with great tact. People said he would be exactly like his father. He had reached the age when parents think about looking for a wife for their sons.

One morning, accordingly, Hjorvard called Ivar and said to him: "Listen to what I am going to tell thee. We have been told Frey had seated himself on Hlidskjalf, the high seat from which Odin could see over all worlds. When he looked to the north he saw on an estate, or farm, a large and fine house towards which a woman was walking. When she lifted her arms to open the door, a light shone from them on the sea, and the air and all the worlds were brightened by her. This woman, as thou knowest, was Gerd, the daughter of Gymir by his wife Orboda, and was the most beautiful of all women. Frey's great boldness in sitting down on the holy seat was thus punished, for he went away full of sorrow, having fallen deeply in love with her. When he returned home

he did not speak, nor could he sleep or drink, and
no one dared to question him. Then Njord called
Skirnir, the page of Frey, and told him to go to
him and ask Frey with whom he was so angry
that he would not speak to anyone. Skirnir
obeyed, though unwillingly, and when he came to
Frey he asked him why he was so sad and did not
speak to anyone. Frey answered that he had
seen a beautiful woman, and for her sake he was
full of grief. ' Now thou shalt go,' he said, ' and
ask her in marriage for me, and bring her home
hither, whether her father be willing or not. I
will reward thee well for the deed.'

"Skirnir replied that he would go and deliver
this message if Frey gave him his sword. This
sword was so powerful that it fought of itself.
Frey gave it to him, and then Skirnir departed
and asked the woman of Gymir in marriage for
·Frey, and Gerd promised him that she would come
after three nights, and keep her wedding with
Frey.

"When Skirnir had told Frey of the result of
his journey, Frey sang: ' Long is one night, long
is another. How can I endure three? Often a
month to me seemed shorter than one-half this
forthcoming wedding night.'"

Hjorvard having thus told the story of Frey,
said: "Ivar, my son, when I look from Dampstadir over the sea, I see yonder, towards the
west, where we often behold so many grand sun·
sets, a beautiful maiden, nay, three beautiful ones,

walking in the green paths leading to Upsalir. These three maidens are the daughters of Yngvi, the Hersir of Svithjod, and, as thou knowest, their beauty and accomplishments are known all over our northern lands. Thou hast come to that age when it is time for thee to find a wife, and I have thought of a match for thee, kinsman, if thou wilt follow my advice, and nothing would please me more than to have thee marry one of Yngvi's daughters. Thou mightest visit many countries and find no maidens more accomplished than they are, and it would be of good advantage to our family and to Gotland if thou didst marry one of them, and bring our kinship still closer than it was before with the Hersir of Svithjod."

Ivar replied that he knew how much his father had his welfare at heart, but said: "Thou must not forget, father, that the daughters of Yngvi have the highest pedigree in all the Northern lands, and the realm of Gotland may not be large enough for their ambition. It may be possible that these daughters may wish to wed men having greater possessions than myself. I think it would be prudent, before thou and our kinsmen propose the match, that I obtain greater renown than I have."

"There is no difficulty, my son, about thy pedigree, for we are all of Odin's kin, and you would be equally matched."

The conversation ended there for the present, Ivar leaving the matter of his marriage in his father's hands, though he thought much of what Hjorvard had said, and of his earnest wish to have him happily and honorably married. He knew, too, that Yngvi and Hjorvard were great friends, and visited one another, and gave feasts to each other, and that a connection by marriage between the two families would be very advantageous and agreeable to his parents.

CHAPTER XIV

HAKI'S BURNING JOURNEY TO VALHALLA

ON their return from the Caspian, the four foster-brothers had found the country very much disturbed; several Vikings from abroad, with a great number of ships, had been plundering here and there among the people. Peace had deserted the land, and great distress from these incursions prevailed everywhere. Among the greatest plunderers were two famous brothers of the name of Haki and Hagbard; they were great Vikings, and had a large host and a great number of powerful and swift ships. These had gray sails, and were painted of such a color that their vessels could not be seen far away. Haki and Hagbard had no lands; they lived on their ships, and never slept under a roof, nor did they ever drink at the fireside; their men had no homes, and had left their country, preferring a life of adventure and warfare with two such famous chiefs. They attacked people ashore everywhere, and plundered them, and afterwards returned with their booty to their ships; they wintered in the rivers, and defied the power of Rome, and of all the Hersirs in the land. When their ships were old, they bought new ones or captured others. They had at last become tired of Western countries, had returned to the Norseland, and had been outlawed by all the Things, or assemblies, of the people of every realm.

Haki had with him twelve champions, among whom were Starkad the old, and Ulf the valiant. All his men were berserks, who were often seized by the berserk fury. Starkad and Ulf were old men, who had been through many a bloody fight, and had served under Haki's father, who had never himself slept under a roof. They all had taken an oath at a great sacrifice that they would never die in a bed; neither would they ever throw themselves from a rock in order to go to Odin and Valhalla, but that they would all die by weapons in battle. Haki himself was one of the greatest of champions, and so agile as well as powerful, that he was a most dangerous enemy to deal with.

One day Haki went with his host against Thorkel, a great Hersir, without warning, for he ruthlessly disregarded the laws of war, so that Thorkel had hardly time to collect his warriors. The latter had also twelve champions, among whom were the brothers Svidpad and Geigad, both far-famed in the North. A fierce battle took place, and Valhalla was destined to receive many men that day. When the battle was at its height, Svidpad and Geigad made a furious assault on Haki's men, and many of them never saw the light again. All of Haki's champions were badly wounded, and could fight no more, being too weak on account of loss of blood. Then he went forward and broke the shield-burg of Thorkel and slew him, as well as his standard-bearer, and also Svidpad and Geigad. He conquered the land and took possession of it, and became the ruler of the herad of Thorkel. He stayed at home during the winter, and ruled the land he had conquered, after which his champions sailed away to southern lands, on Viking expeditions, and earned much wealth for themselves.

Among other great Vikings who never slept under a roof or drank by the fire-side, and who disturbed the land and had been outlawed, were the brothers Eirick and Jorund. After a great battle in which they had slain the Hersir of Gautaland, they thought themselves far greater men than before, and wished to try their strength against Haki and Hagbard, and avenge the disgrace put upon Thorkel, their kinsman ; so, when they heard that Haki had allowed his champions to go away, they collected a large host. When it was known that they had come to reconquer the land for their kinsmen, the people from all the country round flocked to their standards in large numbers, and a great host marched against Haki. A mighty battle soon took place. For a long time victory was undecided, champion fighting against champion. Finally, Haki rushed forward, and fought with such irresistible force, that he slew

all near him, among them Eirick, and cut down
the standard-bearers of the brothers, whereupon
Jorund fled to his ships with his men.

But Haki had received such severe wounds that
he foresaw that his remaining days would be few.
He had made ready a vessel which he prized very
highly on account of its swiftness, beauty, and
war power. He had it loaded with the bodies of
high-born warriors that had fallen in battle, together with their weapons, and had a large pyre
of tarred wood made on the ship. Then he bade his
followers farewell, and told them that he was going
to Odin, and ordered men to carry him, in full
war-dress, with chain armor, helmet, sword, and
shield, on board of his ship. Then he bade them
to build a large pyre near the prow, and to lay
him upon it.

After they had done so, he had the rudder ad-
justed and the sail hoisted and set, and much gold
and many weapons placed on board. Then the
tarred wood was kindled. The wind blew from the
shore seaward; the burning ship sailed away, and
the warriors bade Haki and his men a happy journey to Valhalla. Farther and farther the funeral
pyre of Haki and his men went on its way. The
flames rose higher and higher towards the sky;
the sail burned, and at last the mast, looking like
a tower of fire, fell upon the deck. The people
believed that the higher the flames rose, the
greater would be the welcome in Valhalla. Then
the lurid glare of the flames became less and less

brilliant, and, on a sudden, the ship went down into the deep. But Haki and his warriors had sailed to Valhalla, and the people said that this great deed of Haki would live forever in the memory of man, and would be sung by the scalds to the end of time.

During this time, Ivar and his foster-brothers had gathered a large host and made his vessels ready, for he intended to make war on the Viking raiders who infested the sea and brought trouble and insecurity upon the land. As they were being launched, Hjalmar's ship struck one man as it came down the rollers, and killed him. This accident happened once in a great while at the launching of ships—an operation that was always attended with danger, the more so if it were not carefully done. Such an accident was called "roller-reddening," and was considered a very bad omen, therefore the intended expedition was abandoned. Ivar and his foster-brothers thought that some faithless family spirits wished them evil, and had abandoned their watch over them.

The next day, when Ivar and Hjalmar were walking together, Ivar thought he saw a pet goat of his, which had been always in the habit of coming into the courtyard. No one was allowed to drive him away. Suddenly he said: "This is strange!"

"What dost thou see that seems strange to thee?" asked Hjalmar.

"It seems to me," Ivar answered, "that the goat which lies in this hollow place is covered with blood."

Hjalmar, astonished, answered him that there was no goat there, nor anything else.

"What is it, then?" inquired Ivar.

"I am afraid," Hjalmar returned, "that thou must be a death-fated man, and that thou hast seen the spirit that follows and protects thee, warning thee of danger; and if not thyself, some of thy kinsmen may, perhaps, be fated to die. Guard thyself well, foster-brother. I will also watch carefully over thee, so will Sigurd and Sigmund."

"That will not serve," cried Ivar, "if death is fated to me, for no man can change his fate; but I will fall bravely."

These two successive omens made a deep impression upon Ivar; the ships were dragged ashore, and put under the sheds, and it was announced that no expeditions were to take place that year.

Then Ivar made a special sacrifice to Frey, for he loved Frey more than all the other gods, and often sacrificed to him, and that day he offered up four black oxen, and two of his most valuable horses. The following day, Hjalmar said to Ivar: "Let us find out the decrees that fate has in store for us, for I do not like the 'roller-reddening' that has taken place at the launching of our ships, or the vision of the bloody goat. Let us consult the oracles, as well as sacrifice to Frey. I still fear some impending misfortune is going to happen to some of us, and that some great sorrow will over-take us. Let us make ready and beware of treach-ery. Perhaps we may meet a witch full of evil on the way; then it is better to walk on than to lodge in her house, though the night may be stormy. Often wicked women sit near the road, who blunt both swords and sense. Let us never go out of doors without our weapons, for it is hard to know, when out on the roads, if a man may need his spear. The sons of men need eyes of foresight."

They made, therefore, another sacrifice, and dipped the sacrificial chips into the blood of the sacrificed animal, that was kept in the sacred cop-per bowl which stood on the altar of the temple. The sacrificing chips were thrown into the air, and the answer was that Ivar would not die, but must remain at home that year, and that a kins-man very dear to him would be killed in battle. So Ivar stayed quietly at home.

The following summer Ivar made the Elidi ready and sailed for Norway; but on the voyage, while in the Cattegat, he was obliged to stay on an island on account of head winds. There they threw the sacrificial chips again to get fair winds, and, as they fell, they indicated that Odin was to receive one man out of their host before a fair wind would come. They then sailed toward the coast and cast anchor, and there they landed. Not far from their place of landing was a great sacrificing

10

ring, in the midst of which lay a huge stone, or altar. The people were in the habit of coming there from the surrounding country to make human sacrifice and to break the backs of men given to Odin on that altar. Agnar was the name of the man whom the oracles, speaking through the sacrificial chips, had designated, and upon the altar his back was broken, and he was given to Odin, and they reddened the altar with his blood. After this the men returned to their ships and sailed away with a fair wind. This sacrificing ring where Agnar was given to Odin is seen to this day near Blomholm in the province of Bohuslan, where a large ring composed of eleven stones is still standing, with a sacrificial boulder in the centre.

CHAPTER XV

DEATH AND BURNING OF HJORVARD

THE warning of so many bad omens proved to be true. During a terrific sea-battle, in which many ships were engaged, between Hjorvard and Starkad, a powerful Hersir with whom he had long had a feud on account of a disputed inheritance, Hjorvard received his death wound. During this fierce conflict, weapons buried themselves in bloody wounds, and sank deep into men's bodies; rivers of blood gushed out on the armor; the whirlwinds of the Valkyrias, as the poetical Norsemen called battles, were abroad among men; arrows and spears played round the shields in the midst of the "tempest of Odin." Many swords were broken, many shields were rent asunder, many suits of chain-armor were cut to pieces, and many of the host took their journey to Valhalla.

Suddenly Hjorvard thought he saw during the battle a Valkyria, the mighty Skogul, leaning on her spear-shaft, and heard her say: " Now the elect of Odin are coming; a great host will enter Valhalla to-day before night." Then looking up he thought he saw Valkyrias on horseback, in front of Skogul and Gondul, bearing themselves

nobly, helmeted, with shields, with their hair
floating in the air behind their backs, and with
spears from which rays of light sprung.

Then Hjorvard exclaimed, "Gondul and Skogul,
Odin has sent to choose among chiefs who of the
Ynglingar kin should to him go, and in Valhalla
dwell." It seemed to him that the Valkyrias
hovered over him. He was then clad with helmet
and chain-armor, and standing under his war standard; the oars had dropped, the battle was then
raging most fiercely, the spears hissed, the arrows
quivered, flames of fire came from the swords.
Hjorvard urged the Gotlanders and his champions
to the fight; the "play of the Valkyrias" was wax-
ing hotter and hotter. Hjorvard's sword cut into
the "cloth of Odin," for such was the name which
Norsemen gave to chain armor, as if it were water,
and reddened the ships with the blood of men.

Suddenly Hjorvard beheld, as in a vision, Skuld
the Norn at the head of the Valkyrias, and about
to sever the thread of his own life. He was right.
Odin guided a spear towards him, and Hjorvard received his death-wound. The following morning
he lay on the deck of his ship amidst many dead
champions. In his delirium he murmured, "Why
hast thou decided the battle as thou didst, mighty
Skogul? We surely deserved victory from the
gods." And Skogul seemed to answer: "We have
caused thee to keep the field, and thy foes to flee.
We shall now ride to Valhalla to tell Odin that
Hjorvard the Wide-spreading, and his fallen host,

are coming;" and in his dying ears seemed to sound the voice of Odin saying: "Hermod and Bragi, go forth to meet Hjorvard, the valiant Hersir of Gotland, for he is coming this way to the hall; he is bespattered with blood, and has a mighty host following him." And as he dreamed of entering the portals of Valhalla he heard again the voice of Odin saying: "Welcome, Hjorvard! Thou shalt have peace with 'the chosen,' and cheer from the Asars; thou fighter of men, and wise ruler, who didst take care of the sacrifices and temples, thou hast more than many a chief, in many a land, reddened the sword, and carried forward the bloody blade. Twice welcome, Hjorvard! My maids, the Valkyrias, will carry wine to thee, and wait upon thee, and carry ale to those who have come with thee."

Hjorvard awoke partially, however, from his dying swoon, and lived long enough to be brought home in his ship; and before expiring he said to Sigrlin: "Wife, let my burning journey be worthy of our kinsmen; let a wide and high mound be raised over me; let the mortuary chamber be roomy; surround the mound with tents, shields, weapons of all kinds, for it is good to have them for every-day fight in Valhalla; let foreign linen, silk, and costly garments, and riding gear go with me. Place me on the pyre in full war dress, clad with my gold helmet, my costliest chain-armor, and gird me with one of my best swords. Let many horses be killed and follow me, also my hawks, so that I may enter Valhalla as it befits a great chief and a Ynglingar; and throw gold and silver on the pyre, and throw also many weapons, so that the shining golden doors of Valhalla be not shut against me and my warriors that have fallen. Thus our journey will not be poor, for the wealth that we have earned during our life and not given away will go with us. Place by me also the sharp sword that lay between thee and me before we were wedded, while I courted thee, for thy person was holy, and that sword defended thee and guarded thy honor."

He had hardly uttered these words when he expired, and, according to holy custom, his eyes and mouth were closed and his nostrils pinched, his body and head carefully washed, and his hair combed.

The people said that Odin himself had steered the ship of Hjorvard during the battle.

Ivar was not in the fleet when the fight which caused his father's death took place, nor was he at home, but two days after his father's demise he returned to Dampstadir. He had left his ships on the other side of the island on account of contrary winds, and crossed the country on horseback. On his arrival he went immediately to the great hall, as it was his custom when he returned from an expedition, to drink with his men. He little dreamed then of the sad news that awaited him, for no one on the way had been willing to tell him of his father's death. He had hardly seated himself on the high seat opposite to that of his father, when his eye caught sight of what he had not noticed at first on his entrance. He saw the walls covered with black and gray hangings. This had been done by his mother, for it was the custom upon occasions of this kind and importance to drape the great hall in mourning, and the hangings told of the great sorrow and loss which Gotland had sustained. By this Ivar then knew that the death of a great kinsman had taken place, and his face at once betrayed an expression of profound anxiety.

Shortly afterwards his mother came in, and seated herself by his side. Ivar looked intently at her, and after noticing the pallor of her face, said to her: "Thou must have ordered, mother, the hall to be thus draped; tell me for what purpose and for whom are those tokens of mourning?"

Sigrlin answered: "My husband, the Hersir of Gotland, is no more. Hjorvard, thy father, is dead, but fell gloriously in the midst of victory."

"The tokens that forbode the death of a kinsman have then proved true," said Ivar, with a deep sigh; "the sacrificial chips foretold this." Then he added sorrowfully, and with a voice full of emotion: "A death-fated man cannot be saved. All is dangerous to the death-fated. A man who is not death-fated cannot receive his death wound, he will escape in some way or other; but every one must die the day he is death-fated. The decrees which the Nornir made the day of my father's birth had to be fulfilled."

Sigrlin was inconsolable at the death of her husband, but she did not weep, nor wring her hands, nor wail, as women often do. Very wise men came forward, who tried to console her heavy heart, but they did not succeed, for though unable to weep, her sorrow was great, and her heart broken.

The high-born brides of powerful chiefs and warriors sat gold-adorned by her side, trying to soothe her sorrow ; each of them related her woes, the bitterest sorrow she had suffered. The sister of Gjuki said : " No woman on earth lacks love more than I. I have suffered the loss of two husbands, of three daughters, of eight brothers, and of four sisters, and yet I live." Still Sigrlin could not weep.

Then said Herborg : " I have a harder sorrow to tell. My seven sons and my husband fell among the slain in the southern lands. The brother of Ægir, the Wind, and the nine daughters of Ran, played with my father and mother, and with my four brothers on the deep; they were dashed against the gunwale of their ship, and they were killed. I myself had to wash, to dress, to handle, and to bury their bodies. All that I suffered in a single year, and no man gave me help. The same year I became a bond-woman. I had to dress and to tie the shoes of a Hersir's wife every morning. She threatened me because of jealousy, and struck

me with hard blows; nowhere found I a better housemaster, nor anywhere a worse house-
wife."

Still Sigrlin could not weep.

Then Gullrond spoke thus to them: "Little
comfort can you give by speaking as you have
done to Sigrlin, wise though you are." Thereupon
she bade them uncover the body of Hjorvard,
when she drew the sheet from it, and threw it on
the ground at the feet of Sigrlin, saying to her:
" Look on thy beloved husband ; put thy mouth to
his now silent lips, as thou wert wont when thou
didst embrace him."

Sigrlin looked at her dead husband, and she saw
the wound on his breast, the lips that could not
speak, the ears that could not hear, the eyes that
could not see, and the hands that could not caress;
the checks were pale, and the mind and life had
gone.   At the sight, she sank down upon the
pillow where the dead Hjorvard's head rested.
Flushed were her checks, and a tear fell upon her
tresses, then upon her knees; and from those
springs called the eyes, rivers of sorrow flowed
copiously, and she was comforted.

Five days after the death of Hjorvard, his funeral, or his burning journey to Valhalla, took place,
for it was the law of the land that men should be
laid under mound not later than the fifth day after
their demise.   The people believed that Odin had
enacted the same laws in the northern lands as
formerly prevailed among the Asar.   Thus he

ordered that all dead men should be burned, and
that on the pyre should be placed their property,
promising that with the same amount of wealth
should they come to Valhalla as was burned with
them; also that they should enjoy what they
themselves buried in the ground, and that their
ashes should be thrown into the sea or buried in
the earth; that over great men, mounds should
be raised as memorials, and over men that had
especially distinguished themselves for manliness,
memorial stones should be erected.

It had been agreed by Ivar and his kinsmen
that Hjorvard's burning journey should be on
board a ship, and that the ship should not be sent
to sea, but burned ashore. A fine Skuta of fifteen
benches, beautifully ornamented, was chosen for
the pyre, their powerful war ships never being used
on such occasions. The Skuta was propped to
stand up as if it were in the water; the prow
looked towards the sea, as if ready to be launched
for an expedition. A large quantity of tarred wood
surrounded it, and in the prow of the ship the resting place of Hjorvard had been erected. When all
the preparations were ready, Hjorvard's body was
carried upon the bed on which he lay; he was
dressed in full war costume, clad with helmet and
chain-armor, with sword by his right side and
shield on his breast; spears were laid by his left
hand, and at his feet lay his golden spurs.

Ivar then brought forward his own saddle-horse,

magnificently harnessed and equipped.   Then followed a superb and profusely decorated four-wheeled carriage, with a single seat standing high in the middle, and twelve horses; the horses and falcons were slaughtered, and the carriage broken and thrown upon the pyre.   Then Ivar, just as the torch was applied, bade Hjorvard his kinsman to sail, ride, or drive to Valhalla, as he liked best; and all his champions, warriors, and multitudes of people bade him a happy journey, and expressed the hope that he would welcome them there, at the proper time, when the decrees of the Nornir should be fulfilled in regard to them.   So that his journey to Valhalla might be worthy of him, they threw into the pyre many costly things, weapons and quantities of gold and silver.   The loose property which Hjorvard had won or got during his life, and that had remained in his possession, was also thrown into the funeral pile.   All the weapons that were to follow him to Valhalla were, according to ancient customs, rendered useless. Swords and spear-heads were bent, and their edges indented; shafts were broken, shields were rent asunder, and shield-bosses cut.   Roman and Greek objects were partly destroyed, and with Roman coins were also thrown into the ship.   Solemn and grand was the spectacle, and lurid the glare. Gradually the flames became less and less high, the noise of the cracking wood became fainter and fainter, and finally nothing was seen but the burning embers.

Then the charred bones of Hjorvard were gathered in the midst of solemn silence. The ashes were scattered to the wind and fell into the sea. The burned bones were put in a beautiful Roman bronze vessel, and with them Roman coins of Diocletian's time, the spear-point that had caused his death-wound, also a few draughtsmen belonging to his chess-board, and two dice. Twelve shield-bosses, with their convex side downward, were made a lid for the vase, and lay over the bones; a bent sword was placed over the cinerary urn, which was put in the mortuary chamber that had been prepared; and a large cairn, which took several days to build, was raised over Hjorvard's remains; and a large memorial stone, with runic inscription, put on the top. Thus went to Valhalla Hjorvard, the Hersir of Gotland.

"It is wise," said Ivar to his foster-brother Hjalmar as they were mournfully conversing upon the sad ceremonies of the past few days, "that Odin has ordered that the wealth of a man, his gold and silver and his movable property, should go on his burning journey with him. This thought makes him generous during his life, and he gives away lavishly the wealth that he acquires, thus preventing his heart from being hardened towards those who are in need. So Hersirs and prominent men should not be miserly. The wealth that is thus given during one's life is given back to them in Valhalla."

Then after a pause he added musingly: "Foster-brother, I have often thought of Helgi, my first cousin, the son of Halfdan, and that if he had lived he would have been the Hersir of Gotland, instead of my father.   Then I should not now be ruler over the sacrifices.   How strange are the decrees of the Nornir!"

CHAPTER XVI

HELGI AND THE VALKYRIAS

IVAR had spoken of Helgi because he had often heard his father mention his brother, but he has not been referred to in this narrative before, for he had been dead many years. Halfdan had married Thurid, a beautiful daughter of the Hersir of Zeeland, and loved her passionately. She died about a year after their marriage, in giving birth to a son. Halfdan was so grieved at the death of his wife, that he ordered the child who was the cause of such great misfortune to him to be exposed. The infant was laid in a cradle, and a piece of pork was put in his mouth ; the cradle was taken to a wood at some distance from Dampstadir, and put near the root of a tree, in such a manner that the infant should be protected against the wind and the bad weather, and thus die easily. No name had been fastened upon him, as water had not been poured upon him.

A short time after the child had been exposed, an uncle of Hjorvard was passing through the forest. He heard the cries of the little one, and following the direction of the noise, he was profoundly touched at the sight, and took compassion upon the babe, and brought him up secretly on his estate, his sister taking great care of him, and both loving him tenderly.

Halfdan never married again, for his love for Thurid was far too great, and in his eyes no woman could equal her. His memory and love for her never faded from his mind to his death, and the last word he uttered was her name.

As the child grew older he became a very handsome boy, but he had not the power of talking, and his uncle mourned that the Nornir had fated him to be dumb, and began to think that perhaps it would have been better to have left him exposed. But one day, as the boy was seated on a mound, he saw afar off gleams of light flashing in the sky, coming toward him, and imagined that he beheld nine Valkyrias riding in the air, over the sea, clad with helmet and chain-armor, and with glittering spears in their hands. One of them was the foremost, and as she rode above him, she fastened a name upon him and sang: "Helgi shall thy name be; thou wilt rule over great wealth on the plains of Rodalsvellir, in far-off lands." Immediately Helgi began to speak.

After Helgi had grown up, he went on warlike expeditions in foreign lands, and never returned to his birthplace and to his kinsmen; but no one wondered at this, for in those days warriors often conquered far-off realms and settled there, and never came back, or else perished, and no tidings of them reached home.

After the death of Helgi's father, men were sent into every land in search of Helgi, to tell him to come and get his inheritance; but no tidings were heard from him, and Hjorvard took the rule over Gotland, after the inheritance feast of Half-dan his brother had taken place.

As time went on and years passed away, great tidings were told of Helgi in the Norseland, and his life began to be sung by the scalds. The people said and believed that the Valkyria that had given him his name was called Bodvild, and that Skuld had given him the power of speech, as the Nornir had only fated him to be speechless during part of his boyhood; that Bodvild was the daughter of a Hersir called Hogni, who ruled over a large realm in southern lands, not far from the Black Sea; and that Bodvild at times was a Valkyria, and when tired of that life came among men and became as other women; then again she would disappear and be a Valkyria.

They believed that Bodvild was Svafa re-born. Svafa had been the daughter of one of the great rulers of the North in ancient times, and led the life Bodvild was supposed to lead. It was the belief among the people that sometimes the thinking mind of a person came again to dwell among men and women; that it was only the body that was unlike.

The story told of Helgi that had come to Gotland was as follows: Orvar was a powerful ruler who lived at Svaringshaug. He had many sons; among them were Gunnar, Gudmund, Starkad, and Hogni. Hodbrod had gone to an appointed meeting of Hersirs, and there he betrothed himself to Bodvild, with the consent of Hogni, her father, but without her knowledge, for she was not at home. It often happened that fathers betrothed their daughters without their consent and knowledge, when these owned no entailed lands in their own rights.

When Bodvild heard that she had been betrothed by her father without her consent, she grieved deeply, for she loved Helgi, and had made her mind to marry him. Then she went with Valkyrias, for she had taken their shape, and rode over land and sea in search of Helgi, to tell him the sad tidings of her fate. One day Bodvild saw Helgi; he was then at the Loga Mountains, and there had fought against the sons of Hunding, a powerful Hersir who ruled over a large realm. In that battle he slew Alf, Eyjolf, and Hervard; he was very weary of the fight, and sat down at a place called Eaglestone. When Bodvild came to him, she threw her arms round his neck and kissed him, and told him of her errand.

Helgi was "under helmet," and was then naturally thinking of war, for he had many foes, but his thoughts turned towards the fair maiden who was by his side. She said that she loved him with all her mind, for she had heard of his great deeds, and told him how she had been betrothed to Hodbrod by her father. "But another chief I wanted to have, and that chief is thyself. I fear the anger of my kinsmen, for I have broken the marriage which my father had made his mind for me to have; but Hogni's daughter wants the love of Helgi, and of no one else."

Helgi answered: "Do not care for the wrath of thy father, nor the ill will of thy kinsmen. Thou wilt, young maiden, live with me; thy kinsmen I do not fear. I will marry thee." Then she betrothed herself to Helgi, and on that account war was declared by Hogni, her father, and by all her kinsmen, against Helgi. Hodbrod, who was a widower, joined them with his sons.

Helgi gathered a large fleet and sailed towards Frekastein, the place appointed for the battle. They had hardly lost sight of land when a great tempest arose; it thundered, lightning darted and fell among the ships; it seemed as if the fleet were to founder in the midst of the sea, for the ships had become unmanageable, and the men made preparations to meet Ran. Ægir and his brother the Wind were in an ugly mood. The daughters of Ran were all round the ships and showered upon them blow after blow.

When lo! Helgi thought he saw three times nine Valkyrias riding in the air, and hovering over the ships, and said to his men: "Behold the maidens of Odin! How beautiful they are as they look down upon us from their magnificent coursers!" Among them and foremost was Skuld, the youngest of the Nornir; then came Bodvild, helmet clad, with her long hair flowing in the air, as her steed speeded along. Suddenly the storm abated, and Helgi believed that Bodvild had come to shelter him. The fleet continued its course, and sailed along the shore and came to Freka-stein. In the background rose the Loga Mountains.

Gudmund, one of the sons of Orvar, and a land-defender whose name was Egil had been watching silently the ships of Helgi. Suddenly Gudmund shouted: "Who is the chief that steers the ship that has a gold embroidered battle standard hoisted on the prow? Those in the van seem not to be peace-like people. The redness of war is thrown upon them; the red shield stands high at the top of the mast."

Egil the land-defender answered: "Here can Gudmund know Helgi, the hater of flight, standing in the midst of the fleet; he holds the birth-land of thy kin, the Fjörsungs' heritage which he has taken from them."

Gudmund rode home with the news of war. Then all the sons of Orvar gathered together a host. Many great chiefs repaired to their standards; there was Hogni, the father of Bodvild, and his sons Bragi and Dag, and also Hodbrod.

The hostile hosts met at the appointed field of battle that had been "hazelled," or marked out with stakes. A great battle took place; there was immense din of weapons, clashing of swords and of spears, many helmets were rent asunder, many shields were broken, and a great host de-

parted for Valhalla. Gleams flashed from the
Loga Mountains, and Valkyrias riding helmet covered and mail clad hovered over the battle-field.
Their chain-armor was blood-bespattered, and
from their spears rays of light sprang. It was
getting towards the end of the day when from her
horse, Bodvild, the daughter of Hogni, hushed the
clatter of shields, and immediately a truce took
place.

Helgi invited the Valkyrias to come to a feast
that night with him; his chiefs were to be there,
but Bodvild said: " I think we have other work to
do than to drink with thee to-night; we have to
carry the elect to Valhalla," and they disappeared.

The next day the battle continued, and Helgi
was victorious. In that battle all the sons of
Orvar fell, and all the chiefs except Dag, son of
Hogni, whose life was spared, for loth was Helgi
to destroy the life of the brother of Bodvild.

Bodvild went about among the slain, and found
Hodbrod near death's door, and when she saw
him she sang: " Bodvild, the daughter of Hogni,
will not fall into thy arms, Hodbrod, and will never
be betrothed to thee or marry thee. Gone is the
life of Hodbrod, Adil's son; the wolves will tear
to pieces many corpses to-day, and the ravens will
have food."

Afterwards she met Helgi, mortally wounded,
who, as he saw her, said: " All is not given to
thee, fair maiden, everything is not in thy power;
the Nornir have great might over the fates of

men. This morning fell at Frekastein, Hodbrod, Hogni and all the sons of Orvar, and I was their slayer, for I fought one after the other. But, in my turn, I fear I have not long to live."

And in truth, Dag met Helgi at Fjorturland the next day, and thrust his spear through him, and Helgi fell there dead. Then Dag rode to the Seva Mountains and told Bodvild the tidings thus : " Loth I am, sister, to tell thee, for very unwilling I am to make thee weep. This morning fell at Fjorturland, the land he had conquered, the man who stood with his foot on the neck of many chiefs who had to pay him tribute."

Bodvild was wild with grief when she heard the sorrowful news. Then beside herself with passion, and with eyes flashing fire, she cursed Dag, her brother, and cried : " By the clear water of the River Leiptir, which runs by Fjorturland, and in the sea, the ship shall not move that carries thee, though a fair wind blow. The horse shall not run which is to run with thee, though thou hast to escape from thy foes. The sword shall not bite which thou drawest, except when it sings about thy own head. If thou wert an outlaw, hiding in the forest, and hadst not food unless thou tearedst corpses, then, and not before all these curses be fulfilled, will the death of Helgi be avenged."

To which Dag answered : " Mad art thou, sister, and out of thy mind, as thou invokest curses on thy brother. Odin alone causes all strife between kinsmen."

Then Dag offered indemnity, or " weregild," to his sister—a temple and large estates, half of his lands, and a large amount of gold; but she refused to be indemnified for Helgi's death. She was short lived, and died early from grief for her lover; and as Helgi was dead, the rule over Gotland had come into the hands of Hjorvard.

CHAPTER XVII

THE INHERITANCE FEAST OF HJORVARD

AFTER the death of his father, Ivar did not become the Hersir of Gotland before the Thing, or assembly, of the people had ratified his hersirship; for though it was hereditary, no one could rule without the consent of the Thingmen, who could, when occasion became necessary, deprive a man of his dignity and of his hersirship, for the Hersir had to obey the laws as well as the humblest man of the land, and the greatest power of the land was the Thing.

Before assuming the dignity of Hersir, and consequently that of High Priest of Gotland, Ivar made a sacrifice before the people, and according to ancient custom, he killed a ram, reddening his hands in its blood, and then declared the godship of Hjorvard to be his; after this ceremony he was to rule over the sacrifices at Dampstadir.

He remained at home waiting till the "arvel," or inheritance feast, of his father had taken place, for he could not get his inheritance before that time. According to ancient custom, the inheritance feast had to be made during the year in which the person died for whom the inheritance feast was made, and the man who gave it could not occupy the high seat of him from whom he inherited until the "arvel" was drunk. Hjorvard, being of Odin's family and a powerful Hersir, the feast was to be of great splendor. Ivar and his kinsmen decided that it should take place ten months after Hjorvard's burning journey. Ivar sent ships and messengers all over the Viking lands to bid high-born men and kinsmen to come and make the feast with him, and arrange that all possible honor should be paid to Hjorvard, his father.

According to ancient laws, the high seat of Hjorvard was to remain vacant until the "arvel" should take place. When warriors gathered into the hall, the empty high seat of the departed Hersir and great Viking chief reminded them of their absent friend, who had so many times drunk with them, and with whom they had gone to war and won victory and wealth. In the evenings the scalds, who had been with him in all his fights, recited before the assembled guests the great deeds he had accomplished, and which they had seen as they looked upon the contending foemen from the shield-burg, or wall of shields, that surrounded them and the standards. They told of many fatal combats between champion and champion, or between ship and ship that had grappled each other, and how Hjorvard had twice, during his life, cleared of warriors the decks of two ships.

Things followed the even tenor of their way in

Dampstadir. Sigrlin continued to superintend the
estate, as she had done in her husband's time when
he was on Viking expeditions. Ivar helped her,
and saw that the ships were kept in perfect order
and well tarred and painted, and that new ones
were built. The slaves, dressed in their white
woollen coarse stuff, with short cropped hair,
were busy with the different tasks assigned to
them, and the free servants attended to their
work.

Ivar himself superintended the cultivation of the
lands, for he was a good husbandman, and sometimes was seen forging a sword, or superintending
the construction of a ship. As a pastime, he
often played chess with the old land defenders of
his father, or went hawking, but above all, he
loved to sit on Hjorvard's mound ; from there he
contemplated the sea. The paths which every ship
had made, ploughing its way, were unseen, and
for this reason one of the figurative names given
to the sea by the Norsemen was the Unseen
Path.

One day, as Ivar was seated with Hjalmar on the
mound of Hjovard, and was in one of his meditative moods, he said : "After all, Hjalmar, a man
is not utterly unhappy, even though he be in ill
health ; some are happy in sons or in daughters,
some in kinsmen, some in much wealth, some in
good deeds, and some in friends. To his friend
a man should be a friend, to him and to his friend,
but no man should be the friend of his enemy's

friend. If thou hast a friend whom thou trustest well, and if thou wilt get good from him, thou must blend thoughts with him, and go often and meet him. Be never the first to forsake the company of thy friends; sorrow eats the heart of him who cannot tell all his mind to one. I was young once, I travelled, and missed my way. When I met another man I thought myself wealthy. Man is the delight of man. The fir tree withers that stands on a fenced field; neither bark nor foliage shelters it. Thus is a man whom no one loves. Why should he live long? Brand is kindled from brand, till it is burned out. Fire is kindled from fire. A man gets knowledge by talking with man. It is long out of one's way to go to one you do not like, though he lives near by; but to a good friend there are short paths, though he be far off. I came much too early to many places, and too late to some; the ale was drunk, or it was unbrewed. An unwelcome man seldom finds the ale ready."

Then he added: "A homestead is best, though it be small; for a man is at home there, though he have but two goats and a straw-thatched house. We contemplate many a humble dwelling from here; in many of these happiness and joy are to be found—more so, almost always, than in the halls of the wealthy. The fire and the sight of the sun are the best things among the sons of men; then his good health and a blameless life, if he can keep them."

Ivar had taken great pains that nothing should be wanting to make the " arvel " of his father more famous than any one that had taken place in the Norseland within the memory of man. He had had two large festive halls built for a great number of guests who were coming. Nothing had been spared to give wide-spread fame to the arvel, which was to last two weeks.

Several great Hersirs had sent word to him that they were coming to make the arvel with him, and so arrange that as much honor as possible should be paid to Hjorvard, his father. The Hersirs of Svithjod, Gardariki, Holmgard, Fyen, and Zeeland were to be among the guests.

A fortnight before the time that had been decided for the arvel, the people who lived the farthest began to arrive, for they wanted to make sure that no contrary winds or other obstacle should cause their absence. The day appointed for the beginning of the feast, every guest was present.

It was according to ancient custom that when an " arvel " was held after the death of Hersirs and high-born men, he who gave it and was to receive the inheritance should sit on the step in front of the high seat of the deceased until the horn, called Bragi's horn, was brought in, when he had to rise, take the horn, make a vow, and drain it to the bottom. After this he was to be led to the high seat of his deceased kinsman, and was then the owner of the inheritance.

Before taking his inheritance, in presence of all the assembled guests, Ivar seated himself on the steps leading to the high seat of Hjorvard, his father. On the first evening many horns were filled and drunk to the memory of the departed kinsman. The second night the horns to Odin, Njord, and Frey were drunk, after which the horn to Bragi was filled, and over it vows were made. The scene was very impressive. Vow after vow was sworn by prominent men to accomplish some great deeds that would be known all over the northern lands.

Then Ivar rose and made the vow that, within two years, he would avenge the death of his father, or die in the attempt, closing with " So help me, Odin, Njord, and Frey." After this oath, his kinsmen led him into the high seat of Hjorvard, his father, and thenceforth he was entitled to his father's inheritance.

After the feast was over, Ivar gave costly gifts to all the prominent men who had come to help him by their presence, and minor ones to those less prominent who had come with them, and all departed with many protestations of friendship, declaring that it was the greatest inheritance feast they had ever seen.

A short time after Ivar had given his inheritance feast, another death in the family took place. As he was drinking with his men, a messenger came to him with the news that Ingimund, one of his uncles, living in the eastern part of the

island, on the shore of a bay to-day called Tang-
vide, had died suddenly in his high seat. The
death of Ingimund caused great sorrow among all
the people, for he was much beloved, and many
went to him for advice, for he had an excellent
knowledge of the laws. The sorrow about his
death was the greater, because he had not thrown
himself down from some high cliff, from whence
he would have gone to Valhalla, as he had never
been fated by the Nornir to die on the battle-
field and by weapons. He had intended to do so,
and had often said that he did not want to die in
bed, for it was the custom for warriors overtaken
by old age to die by throwing themselves from
cliffs, and going to Odin, thus showing that they
were not afraid of death.

Ivar and many of the people of Dampstadir
made ready to go to the funeral of Ingimund.
When they reached his home, a large mortuary
chamber of solid timber was made, and a cairn
thrown over it, leaving the entrance to the chamber free.

Great preparations were made for the journey
of Ingimund to Hel, the world of the dead who
had not died in arms, or sought Valhalla of themselves. After Ivar's arrival, the sons of Ingimund
came to him and said: " Thou art the head of our
kinsmen, and thou knowest that it is the custom
from immemorial time when a man does not die
by weapons to make him ready for his journey to
Hel. We ask of thee to put the Hel-shoes on the

feet of our dead father, for, as thou knowest, the
ancient faith that has come down to us tells us
that such shoes should go to Hel with the man
that takes that journey.   Therefore we will dress
Ingimund splendidly, for when a man dresses well
when he goes out of our world, and is a long
time in dressing, he is said to prepare himself for
Hel."

Ivar answered: "I will put and tie the Hel-shoes
on Ingimund's feet, as you ask me."

The shoes were put on. After he had tied them,
Ivar said: "I know not how to tie Hel-shoes if
these are unfastened on the journey to Hel."

Then he asked the people to see if they were
well tied. After looking at them, those that were
present said: "Well done, Ivar; these shoes cannot possibly be untied, and the journey of Ingimund to Hel will be without mishap."

The body of Ingimund was dressed superbly.
He was clad in his war apparel: he had on his gold
chain-armor, and wore his helmet; his ornamented
shield was laid on his breast, and his sword by his
side; his rings and bracelets of gold were on his
hands and arms, and thus he was laid on a bed in
the mortuary chamber.   At his feet and at his
head were put several beautiful Roman and Greek
bronze vases; some exquisitely beautiful Grecian
cups of glass, ornamented with fine paintings; a
Samian vase; a Roman sieve of bronze; a pair of
tweezers of gold; a fine bone-comb, and other objects, among which were several coins of Diocle-

tian, who was Roman emperor at the time. Then, as the chamber was closed, all present wished Ingimund a happy journey to Hel; and to this day the stranger sees, as he sails along the eastern shores of Gotland, among the large cairns that overlook the sea, that of Ingimund.

CHAPTER XVIII

IVAR SPURNS STARKAD'S INDEMNITY

STARKAD, who had given the mortal wound to Hjorvard, feared Ivar's enmity, and that of his kinsmen and foster-brothers, and wished to pay "were-gild," or indemnity, for his death. He had heard of the vow of Ivar, and knew that sooner or later he would avenge the death of his father, for there was a saying, that there was a wolf's mind in a son. Accordingly, he sent a man called Nidud, a great warrior, to Dampstadir, to offer Ivar indemnity.

When Nidud came to the banqueting-hall, the men were seated on the benches round the fires, drinking their beloved beer, mead, and ale. On his arrival all became silent, for the warriors knew that great news was to be told. Ivar bade Nidud to sit on the second high seat, and it was not long before the silence was interrupted by the rising of Nidud, who, in a chilling voice, said: "Starkad has sent me here to thee, Ivar, with costly presents, and I have ridden through the length of Gotland to bid thee, and also thy foster-brothers, to his hall, and to the benches facing the tables. Come all, with your eagle-beaked helmets, to get honor and large gifts, helmets and shields, swords and saxes, chain-armor, horses, and costly garments, gold and silver, and large estates.   Thou, Ivar, will get indemnity for thy father's death, and be reconciled to Starkad."

Ivar wondered if Starkad had a wolf's mind, and meant, cunningly and treacherously, to attack him with an overwhelming host if he came with but few men.   He answered: " I and my foster-brothers own seven halls full of swords; their hilts are of gold, and their scabbards are orna-mented also with gold.   Our swords and saxes are the sharpest, our 'brynjas' are the whitest and brightest, our arrows are the fleetest, our spears the surest, our horses the best; we have no lack of gold and silver, for our treasures are among the greatest in the northern lands."

Nidud replied: " Here is the message and invi-tation in writing which Starkad sends thee, Ivar. It is written in mystic runes;" and he handed a stick on which the invitation had been written.

Then Ivar read the message, and turning his head to his foster-brothers said to them in a low voice : " I shall not accept his invitation and the indemnity he offers to me."

" I wonder at his offer," replied Hjalmar.   " He has seldom done this before, for he is of a miserly mind.   Let us confer together alone."   So Ivar told Nidud they would give him an answer the next day; and, bidding his champions to entertain Nidud and his men until he came back, left the hall with his foster-brother.

12

"I am surprised at the costly things Starkad has sent thee," said Sigurd. "But among them I noticed a ring with a wolf's hair attached to it. I think some one warns thee and us that he has a wolf's mind towards us, and means treachery."

"It must be some woman who loves us," replied Ivar. "Whom do we know among women in Starkad's realm? Let us try and recall."

After a silence which lasted some time, during which the two foster-brothers remained plunged in thought, Hjalmar said: "Herborg the Lovely must have tied this wolf's hair there," pointing to the ring. "She is his sister, and thinks well of us all."

"I am sure she loves thee, Hjalmar," said Ivar.

"I think not," replied his foster-brother; "but I believe she likes us very much, and has for us the greatest friendship. It is just like a woman—kind-hearted, noble in friendship, and true to the end of life."

Then they looked carefully at the "kelfi," or stick, upon which runic messages were carved or written, when suddenly they discovered that some of the letters had been changed with a great deal of skill. Then they inspected most minutely every letter, and found that with the invitation there was also a warning for Ivar not to come, or if he came, to bring many warriors and champions with him.

In the meantime, Nidud, and the men who had come with him, and the champions of Ivar drank merrily, Nidud praising highly the gifts the champions were to receive when they came to visit Starkad.

Sigrlin was not long in hearing of the invitation of Starkad, and the following morning she came to Ivar just as he was making ready to go to the banqueting hall, and said to him: "Ivar, I had a dream last night which I am going to tell thee. It is a warning of the gods, and thou must not go."

"What was the dream, mother?" Ivar inquired.

"It seemed to me thy sheets burned in fire, and that a mighty flame burst through thy house."

"Here lie linen clothes, for which thou carest little; they will soon burn," answered Ivar. "This is where thou didst see sheets burning."

"But," Sigrlin continued, "I thought a white bear had come in here. He broke through the walls; he shook his paws so that we were frightened; he caught many of us in his grasp, so that we were helpless, and there was a great struggle amongst us to be free from him."

"That," said Ivar, "is a storm that will arise, and soon become violent, and thy white bear will prove a rain-storm from the east."

"I thought an eagle flew in here," persisted Sigrlin, "through the length of the house; it bespattered us with blood. That forebode, I thought, a heavy fight. It was the shape of Starkad."

"We kill cattle speedily when we see blood; it

often means oxen when we dream of eagles," replied Ivar, reassuringly.

" I fancied I saw a gallows made for thee, and
that thou wert going to hang thereon. I thought
I buried thee alive. I saw also a bloody sword
drawn out of thy body; a spear, I thought, had
pierced thy side ; wolves howled at both its ends.
It is sad to tell of such a dream to such a son as
thou art ; but thou art all I have in the world, and
I think our own Disirs, or family spirits, warn us
of danger, Ivar."

" They were dogs that ran, instead of wolves ;
they were barking loudly."

" It seemed to me that a river ran through the
length of the house, roaring in anger, rushing over
the benches, bruising the feet of thy foster-brothers; the water spared nothing. This forbode
something, I am sure. It seemed to me, also, that
dead women came hither this night ; they bade
thee to come quickly to them and their benches.
This must forebode something. I say again, that
I fear that the guardian spirits of our family have
abandoned thee, and that they are to be faithless
to us."

" Mother, be not afraid," returned Ivar, earnestly. " Dreams are not always warnings from
the gods, though I must say that what thou tell-
est me is strange ; but thou knowest well that no
one can escape his fate, and what the Nornir have
decreed must take place."

Then they separated, and Ivar went to the hall,

his mother following him soon afterwards, and found there the messengers waiting for his answer to the invitation of Starkad.

The hall was filled with guests, and the ale was passed round. A hush fell upon the throng as Ivar entered, and in the midst of expectant attention, anxious looks, and profound silence, he said, with a voice loud, but full of emotion: "Nidud, and you men who have come with him, go and tell Starkad, your lord, that I have vowed at the arvel of my father, in presence of my kinsmen and kinswomen, and of the high-born of the land, and of the men of great renown who came from Gaul, Britain, and the remotest countries where Norsemen have settled, that I would within two years avenge the death of Hjorvard, my father, or perish in the attempt. Tell him, also, that my foster-brothers and my kinsmen will avenge his death and mine if I fall. Tell Starkad that there is no weregild large enough to indemnify me for the death of my father, and that when he slew him, he slew one of the bravest and most high-minded of men. Tell him that the time of revenge is soon coming."

"Well answered, my son," shouted Sigrlin at the top of her voice; "the kinsmen of Hjorvard are not all dead yet, and Starkad will find it out."

These utterances were received with loud assent on the part of Ivar's followers present, and with mortification and chagrin by the messengers of Starkad, who immediately took their departure.

CHAPTER XIX

THE SLAYING OF STARKAD

AFTER the departure of the messengers of Starkad, Ivar summoned a Thing, at which it was resolved that war should be declared against Starkad the following spring. Then Ivar sent word of his intention far and wide, to all his kinsmen, and called on all his tributary chiefs to be ready to join him in the expedition. The war arrows were forwarded by messengers, who carried them on fully-manned ships, by night and by day, or on the high roads. The law was, that if a man neglected to carry the arrow he became an outlaw; if the messenger came to where a woman lived alone, she was bound to procure ships, food, and men, if she could, if not the arrow was to be carried onward; if a man remained seated quietly after he had received the arrow, and paid no attention to it, he was outlawed.

Messengers, who were the highest-born men of the land, were sent to Starkad to tell him that Ivar and a large host would advance against him the following spring, and to choose, as he was the challenged man, according to ancient custom, the battle-field where the conflict should take place, and to "enhazel," or stake out with hazel poles, the field.

Starkad sent word back that he had chosen a battle-field near his burg, which was in the southern part of the peninsula of Jutland. Then Starkad himself sent out the war arrow, and summoned men from all his realm, and all the chiefs who paid him tribute. Every male from fifteen years of age was under obligation to come, and every horse three years old was to be drafted.

On both sides the time was thenceforward employed in making preparations, and in the spring Ivar set sail with a very large fleet for the place appointed as the field of battle. On the day of his departure from Dampstadir he said: "The dark ravens have awakened early this morning; thus of yore screamed the hawks of Gun the Valkyria before chiefs were death fated; then the birds of Odin, Hugin and Munin, came to tell him of the fray, so that he should make Valhalla ready."

Many champions came to join the standards of Starkad. Among the foremost was Atli the Valiant, who had come with a great host—Svein, Gnepi the Old, Gard, Brand, Teit, Hjalti, Storkud. In his body-guard were the champions Borgar, Barri and Toki. Ubi the Frisian was one of the foremost and most renowned of warriors, and many others who were destined to perform great deeds of valor on the battle-field came also.

The Hersirs who had also come with a great host were Tryggvy and Alrek, both very skilled with their swords, and Stein, and Styr the Strong.

Among the Amazons who had come to Starkad were Heid and Visma, each of whom had come with a numerous host. Visma carried the standard of Starkad. With her were the champions Kari and Milva. Many Vends, a people living on the southeastern shores of the Baltic, were in her following. They were easily recognized, for they had long swords and elongated, narrow shields. She herself was a superb woman of twenty-five summers, with long, fair hair floating from under her golden helmet, reaching far below her waist, and resting on the back of her horse. Her sword was of the best and sharpest. She had accustomed herself from her childhood so well to the use of shield and sword and chain-armor, that she was one of the foremost in horsemanship and in the handling of weapons, and the champions who could successfully compete with her were very few. She always rode a magnificent white charger.

Heid had also come with many renowned champions. She was twenty-eight years old, above medium height, full chested, her limbs of splendid proportions. Her hair was of the color of ripened wheat, and glossy, and, like Visma's, fell far below her waist. She rode a superb black steed, and when under helmet and chain-armor, and with shield and sword, was the perfect ideal of a shield-maiden.

Many great chiefs had joined Ivar's standard. He had gathered men from many realms—from all over Svithjod, Gotland, from the shores of the

Cattegat, from Gautaland, from many herads of the present Norway, and even men of Norse ancestry from Britain and Gaul.

Of the foremost champions of Ivar were Hersir Ali the Brave, and Storkud the Old, who had travelled far and wide, and had fought under many Hersirs during their lives; Rognvald the Tall; Ragnar, who was the greatest of all his champions, and who was always foremost at the point of the wedge; Thrond and Thorir; Helgi the White; Half; Erling the Snake-eyed; Holmstein, and Einar.

The great champions of Svithjod were Aki, Eyvind and Egil.

The Hersirs who had come with hosts of their own were Hrani, Svein the Reaper, Soknarsoti, Hrolf the Woman-loving, Dag the Stout, Gerdar the Glad, Glum the Fearless, Saxi the Plunderer, and many other champions who were eager to show their prowess.

Among the shield-maidens, or Amazons, was Vejborg. A great host and many chiefs and champions followed her. Vejborg was the personification of a fury; she was extremely beautiful, had an exquisite figure, light blue eyes, flaxen hair. Her eyes when under the excitement of battle seemed to throw fire, and she looked superb under helmet and chain-armor. Her horse was of a dark chestnut color.

Great, indeed, was the assemblage of warriors on both sides. On the side of Ivar were thirty-three

"Fylkings," or legions, and five thousand men were in each Fylking.

On the side of Starkad were twenty-six Fylkings, with a less number of men than Ivar had in each Fylking.

When they had reached the neighborhood of the chosen battle-field, they pitched their war tents and slept during the night.

The host of Starkad lay likewise in their tents, not far off, while Starkad went alone to consult his mother, who was a woman of great experience and wisdom. He told her that there would be not less than two to one against him.

She replied: "I would have reared thee in my wool chest if I had been certain that thou wouldst live forever. Better is it to die with honor than to live in shame. Take this standard, which I have made with my best skill, and which I believe will be victorious for those before whom it is carried."

The standard, covered with exquisite handiwork, was in the shape of a raven, and when the wind blew on it, it seemed as if the raven spread his wings. Starkad became very angry at his mother's words, and left her and did not take her standard.

The belligerents arranged their hosts in battle array, and much thought and skill were required. Part of the host on each side was arranged in wedge shape.

Bruni was considered very wise, and arranged the host of Starkad. On the apex of the wedge, or array, he put the shield-maiden Heid with her standard. With her were one hundred champions who were all berserks. They formed the shield-burg; among these were the scalds Eivind and Amund. On one of the other points of the wedge he put Visma with her standard and powerful following; on the other wing was Toki. The standards were carried in front of him. There were many great champions with him; among them were Alfar and Alfarin, sons of Gandalf the Hersir, who had been in the body-guard of Starkad's father.

Herlief was considered the wisest in the host of Ivar, and Ivar bade him arrange his host in battle order, and to assign to each man the standard under which he was to fight.

At the apex of the wedge he placed the shield-maiden Vejborg with one hundred berserks, who guarded her standard and formed the shield-burg, and among these were the most valiant men of the land.

In front of the standards of the host of Ivar stood Adils the Gay, from Upsalir; he was not in the Fylkings. With him were the champions Sigvaldi, who had come with eleven ships; Tryggvy and Tvividil, each of whom had come with twelve dragon-ships; Lœsir, who had only one skeid, a most beautiful and formidable craft, entirely manned by berserks; Eirik, from Helsing, who had come with a large dragon-ship, manned also by berserks. Besides these great champions, there were others of equal valor. Among them were

Thorkel the Stubborn, Thorlief the Overbearing, Hadd the Hard.

When all the preparations for the conflict were ready, Ivar sent Herlief to see how Starkad had drawn up his host, and how many men he had, and to stake the battle-field with him. Herlief reported that Starkad also had drawn up most of his men in wedge shape.

Starkad, in his turn, sent Bruni to see how Ivar had arranged his men.

When the hosts were ready for battle, Visma said to her champions: "Make your weapons ready, and thou, Eivind, ride to the host of Ivar the Gotlander, and challenge him to battle."

Eivind did so, and, according to the custom, sent an arrow over the host, and shouted to them: "Odin owns you all."

Then Ivar sent Alrek towards the host of Starkad, and he threw a spear into the host, and shouted also: "Odin owns you all."

Both sides had the war-horn sounded and the red shields raised, and gave their war-cries. Then Ivar said: "If Odin does not want to grant me victory, as he has always done before, may he let me fall in the battle with all my host, and all the men who fall on this battle-field I give to Odin."

The arrays met, and the battle from the first raged fiercely. Soon the champion Ubi the Frisian advanced in front of the host of Ivar, and attacked the apex of the array of Vejborg, and first of all the champion Rognvald. The single

combat ended by Rognvald's fall, and then Ubi
rushed at Tryggvy and gave him his death-wound.
When the sons of Alrek saw Ubi's furious rush
into the host, they sought him out, but he slew
them both, and then every one retreated before
him.

Meantime Hjalti, a champion of Starkad, attacked Ivar, and the contest lasted long, but
finally Ivar with a blow of his sword gave him
his death-wound. Then the champion Gnepi
the Old met Ivar, and they fiercely attacked
each other ; but at last Gnepi too fell, pierced
with many wounds, but displaying great courage
to the end.

Then Ivar seeing the havoc made by Ubi,
and fearful that his host would become demor-
alized by such an onslaught, said to Sigmund, his
foster-brother, " Thou hadst better ride to Vejborg
and tell her how matters stand." Vejborg, when
apprised of the great danger that menaced Ivar,
made a terrible onset on Starkad's host. First
she attacked the champion Barri, dealing him
blow after blow, and so quickly that he could only
protect himself with his shield, and this only for
a time, for one of her lightning strokes soon cleft
his shield, and giving him a wound that disabled
him, she left him. Then Styr the Strong met
her. They attacked each other with great fierceness, but the throng of warriors was so great that
they were separated against their will. Finally,
after slaying Toki and several other champions

whose hard fate placed them in her path, and after exhibiting the greatest valor, she fell herself under the sword of the champion Hjalti. After her fall, great events happened in a short time, first one array, then another, getting the upper hand. Hundreds of men on either side were doomed never to return home, and great was the host which was to enter Valhalla.

When the evening came, the white shields were raised and the truce proclaimed. The combatants went to their tents and dressed their wounds.

Early the following morning the conflict was renewed. After the battle had raged fiercely for a season, Ivar attacked the apex of the array of Starkad. His father's sword Hrotti shone like fire, and he cut down the host of Starkad like saplings. Neither helmet, chain-armor, nor shield could withstand his blows. He went through the host with his foster-brothers, and slew all those who were in his way. The shield-maiden Heid, seeing the appalling death of men in the array of Starkad, rushed towards Ivar. Many men engaged in single combat stopped by common accord to see the conflict. Her fiery steed, white with froth, seemed to enjoy the fray. Heid's hair was loose and dishevelled, and swung to and fro, following the motion of her body; her eyes seemed to send out flashes of fire; lightning seemed to spring from her sword as it struck that of Ivar. Never in his life had Ivar been so hard pressed, but finally the pressure of other combatants separated them.

Ubi the Frisian advanced before the host of Ivar, and all retraced their steps before him, so deadly were his blows. When the archers recognized him, they said, "We will not shoot elsewhere, but let us all aim our arrows at this man for a while, for we will never get the victory until he is dead." The most skilled archers began to shoot at Ubi, and he fell at last, but not before twenty-five arrows had been sent into his body, and not before he had slain six champions, severely wounded eleven others, and killed sixteen Sviar and Gotlanders, that stood in front of the ranks.

After the death of Ubi, the host of Ivar made a fierce attack on the host of Starkad, and nothing could resist them. When Starkad saw this great slaughter of his men, he urged his host not to let one man overcome all, such valiant and proud men as they were. He shouted, "Where is Storkud, who until now has always borne the shield of victory?"

Storkud, who was near, answered: "We will try to gain a victory; though where Ivar is, a man may be fully tried."

He rushed to the front, towards Ivar; a fierce fight ensued, and Storkud fell. Great, indeed, was the slaughter of men.

When Heid the shield-maiden saw so many valiant men fall, she rushed forward, and however valiant and skilful a man was in the handling of his sword, he was almost sure to meet his death while fighting against her.

Ivar entreated his men to take her alive, but she would not be taken, and fell fighting furiously. As she fell, Ivar sang: "Sunk to the ground is Heid the shield-maiden. The Sviar have slain her, and with her many of her champions. She was more at home in the fight than talking with a wooer, or going to the bridal bench with bridesmaids."

When Starkad looked over the wing Heid commanded, and saw how it had diminished, he sang: "Many were we when we drank the mead; now we are fewer, when we should be more. I do not see one among my men who can carry a shield and meet Ivar's host; nevertheless I will carry a shield with what is left of my men, and go and fight the Gotlanders and their followers."

Then he advanced towards the host of Ivar, and at last the decisive conflict took place. Both sides fought with the greatest fury. The field of battle where the swords met appeared like a lurid sheet of fire, and after the most heroic struggle Starkad fell with his standard.

When Ivar saw that the standard of Starkad had fallen, he knew that he was dead; he had the horns blown, the peace shield raised, and shouted an order that the battle stop. When the host of Starkad became aware that he had been slain, the combat ceased, and Ivar offered truce to them all, which was accepted. Several chiefs became his vassals, and promised to pay him tribute

every year, and send men to his standards when
needed, Ivar putting his foot on their necks as a
sign that he had become their ruler.

After the battle a search was made for Starkad,
and his body was found under a heap of slain.
He was buried with his sword Tyrfing, and a mound
was raised over him.

Ivar took the ships belonging to Starkad, had
them dragged ashore, and built on their decks
great pyres. Upon these he placed the bodies of
his champions that had fallen, and he and those
who were present threw into the burning flames
gold and silver and costly weapons to do them
honor.

Hervor was the only daughter of Starkad by
Helga, daughter of Agnar the berserk. When her
father fell she was only ten years old. When
Helga gave birth to Hervor, most people thought
she ought to be exposed, and said that she would
not have the character of a woman if she was like
the kinsmen of her father, who all had been men
of bad repute. She constantly practised riding
on horseback, shooting with bows, the handling
of swords and shields, and all kinds of athletic
games. When she had grown up she became a
shield-maiden, and loved to be under helmet and
chain-armor far better than being occupied in sewing or embroidering. From the age of fifteen she
was wont to say that the kin of Starkad had not all
perished, and she thought to avenge her father's

13

death.   She was tall and strong, and of fair complexion; her long, silky hair was of the color of
red gold, and the people said that it was like the
hair of Sif, the wife of the god Thor.

When Hervor was twenty, she longed to have
Tyrfing, the sword of her father, which had been
laid in his mound with him.   Tyrfing was sharper
than any other sword, and when it was drawn from
its scabbard, rays of light sprang from its blade;
it was a most famous sword, and had been in the
possession of the family of Starkad and kept as an
heirloom for many generations.

One spring Hervor left her home all alone,
dressed as a man, and engaged herself on board of
a Viking ship, whose commander and crew had no
other home than their vessel.   Afterwards they
sailed and plundered in many places, until at last
their leader died, and the men appointed Hervor
to rule over them.

They sailed for the place where her father and
his fallen warriors had been buried, and reached it
towards evening, and anchored their ship in a bay,
and remained on board that day.   After sunset
they saw large fires moving to and fro over the
mounds, for the island was a great burial place.
These fires were will-o'-the-wisps, but the people
believed they were supernatural fires.   The crew
were full of dread, and said that they never would
go ashore in the evening.

The following day, late in the afternoon, Hervor
landed.   At sunset the crew thought they heard hol-

low noises on the island. After a diligent search, Hervor recognized the mound of her father, for it stood high among others, also from the inscription on the memorial stone. As she came near it, she sang: "Awake, Starkad! Hervor, thy daughter, wants to rouse thee. Yield to me the sharp sword Tyrfing, which the Dvergar forged in the days of yore for Vikar, thy kinsman." Then she said in a louder voice: " Einar, Hrani, Hervard, and all warriors that were slain with my father, I awaken you all from beneath the mounds under which you rest —you who are clad in helmet and chain-armor, and with shields, sharp swords, and reddened spears. Much have you increased the mould under which you lie. I call you all to let me have the sharp sword Tyrfing."

Then she opened the mound of her father, and, entering the mortuary chamber, she took Tyrfing, and sailed home. After this her sole object in life was to avenge the death of Starkad. The following year she assembled a great host, and made war against Ivar, but perished in the battle, after performing prodigies of prowess and valor.

Shortly after the events just spoken of, Ivar and all the high-born men of Gotland received from Yngvi, the Hersir of Svithjod, an invitation to attend and participate in the great athletic games, "idrottir," that were to take place the following spring for the championship of the Norselands; for, like the Spartans, the Norsemen thought highly of all games and exercises that give strength and suppleness to the body.

Ivar sent back word by the messengers that he was coming, and that he and the Gotlanders would compete in the different games with those who strove for the championship, also to try to wrest it from those who held it. Then he sent word all over the island, instructing his people to practise the games with great zeal and energy.

CHAPTER XX

THE SESSION OF THE THING

AFTER the departure of the messengers of the Hersir of Svithjod, as was usual at that time of the year, a great Thing, or assembly of the people, took place. As the date drew near, Ivar sent the Thing arrow to all the Thingmen over the island, to call them to the Thing place to punish those who had violated the laws, and to settle other matters and controversies.

Accordingly the Thingmen journeyed to Damp-stadir, either on horseback or in ships, each Hauld or Bondi taking with him a large retinue of followers, according to his wealth and rank. The person of every Thingman was holy. If any one attempted to disturb them on their way to or from the Thing, he was declared an outlaw.

The multitude came without their weapons, for on the Thing plain perfect peace must reign, and any one breaking it by insults or otherwise was accounted without the pale of the law. It was the same as if he had violated the temple peace. He was regarded as a wolf in the sanctuary, an outlaw, or "nithing," in all holy or inhabited places, until he had made reparation for his crime.

The Thing plain where the people met was not far from the temple, and was so holy that it could not be sullied by bloodshed arising from blood-feud or any impurity. The Thing, from the time it was opened until it was dissolved, was under the protection of the gods.

In the centre of the Thing plain was the court, a large circle which was surrounded by hazel poles supporting ropes. These ropes were called "ve-bonds," or sacred bands. Inside the circle sat those who were to judge the case brought before the Thing. No judge when once within these holy precincts was allowed to leave, neither could an outsider enter them.

Before the opening of the Thing, according to ancient custom, Ivar sacrificed a large bull in the temple, in the presence of the people, and filled the sacred bowl that stood on the altar with its blood. Afterwards he took the oath ring which stood upon the altar, and over which men were to take their oaths, and dipped and reddened it with the consecrated blood, and then put it on his arm ; and then he, with the Hersirs and Thing-men, made their way to the Thing plain, and took their places in the court, which stood upon an eminence, from which all who were assembled could see them and all that took place within the sacred precincts.

Ivar then made known the boundaries of the Thing, reciting in a loud voice the following formulary : " With laws shall our land be built, and not be laid waste by lawlessness; but he who will not allow others the benefit of the laws shall not enjoy them himself."

A murmur of assent greeted the last words of the sentence, for the Norsemen were, above all, a law-abiding people. And as obligatory, he recited the declaration of peace by first saying, " I establish peace among all men here."

Then every Thingman that was to judge, or any man who had to perform legal duties, took an oath upon the ring, and said : " I call those present to witness that I take oath on the ring, according to law, to defend or prosecute this case; and give the evidence, verdict, or judgment which I know to be the most true and right and lawful ; so help me Frey, Njord, and Odin."

The first case brought before the Thing was that of a Hauld who had wounded a man in a fit of anger.

"Thou knowest well," said Ivar, "that the higher a man is in station, the greater is the indemnity to be paid by him for breaking the law; he who is of high birth ought to set the example. The judgment of the court is, that thou shalt pay for the wound thou hast inflicted six rings of gold, each ring weighing twelve aurar, which is six times the amount a freeman should pay for the same offence, or half more than a Bondi."

A man was next brought up for stealing while on a trading voyage. This class of thieves were called "gauntlet-thieves." All the crew of the ves-

sel was present. "Thou knowest the law," said Ivar.
" It is, that thy head shall be shaved and tarred,
and eider-down or feathers put upon it. Then the
crew shall make a road for thee and stand on both
sides, and thou shalt run to the woods if thou
canst. Every one shall throw a stick or a stone
after thee, and whoever does not throw shall pay
a fine of nine ortugar."

The thief was tarred and feathered; a road was
made for him between the sailors; he ran as fast
as he could, but he had hardly reached the end of
the road that had been made for him when he fell
exhausted, badly wounded.

A Bondi came before the court, and declared
that he had killed two robbers who tried to defend
themselves. " Well hast thou done, for these men
were unholy, and thou hast no indemnity to pay
for their lives," was the verdict.

Then a man was brought up who had committed
burglary and had been caught with arms upon
him. "Thou knowest the laws," said Ivar again;
"thou art an outlaw and shalt die. Men like thyself the land does not want."

A case was next brought up in which a man
was supposed to have committed murder. One
of the champions of Hjorvard, named Asgrim, had
been slain, and the people who were there were
unable to tell who was the slayer; but it was sus-
pected that a man by the name of Asmund had
done the deed, though he denied the accusation
vehemently. It had been decided at a preceding

Thing, by the kinsmen of Asgrim, that Asmund should take an oath at the following autumn Thing, which was the one now taking place.

Then Ivar took from his arm the oath ring, and, in presence of the Thingmen and of the multitude, Asmund named two witnesses, as was required by law, saying: "I choose Thorvald and Olaf as witness that I take an oath upon the temple ring that I did not redden point and edge of any sword where Asgrim was slain. I know this oath to be most true, so help me Odin, Frey, and Njord."

A man was brought up that had been caught stealing food; he proved that he had stolen to sustain life, and that he had gone to several households to try to get work, but could not get it. Witnesses came forward to testify that he had come to their houses in search of work, but they had none to give him. "Go thy way," said Ivar; "for though the law is that no man shall steal from another, nevertheless it also declares that the man who gets no work to live by, and steals food to save his life, shall not be punished."

One man was brought before the Thing who had been caught stealing for the third time. "Thou art irredeemable," said Ivar. "Thieving is born in thee, and the law of the land is that a man caught three times stealing must be hanged; for thou art a born thief, and must pay the penalty of the law; for the land cannot be burdened with men like thee."

On the fourth day a very important case regarding an inheritance came before the court. There was a bitter feeling between the parties. Angry words followed each other; the litigants in the heat of passion lost their heads, and, to the utter astonishment of every one, had weapons hidden under their cloaks, and suddenly the Thing ground was covered with blood. A great uproar arose; the multitude was horror-stricken; such a thing had never happened before at Dampstadir. The men who had committed this great offence were outlawed, and had to flee for their lives.

Ivar declared that the plain was desecrated by the blood of hate, and consequently no holier than any other ground, and that no Thing could ever take place there again.

Then Ivar with the Thingmen chose another Thing field, after which they made preparations to sail for Upsalir.

CHAPTER XXI

IVAR'S VISIT TO YNGVI

SIGRLIN was extremely desirous that Ivar should appear at the games and before the daughters of the Hersir of Svithjod as befitted his rank and wealth. For several months she had been preparing his outfit. Ivar himself wanted to have his best apparel and weapons, for men who went to the games or to the Thing wore their finest garments and arms. When everything was ready, and before they were packed, his mother called him and asked him to look at his outfit.

First she showed him the cloaks, or rather mantles; these were made of woven stuffs that had come from the Caspian, and were very costly. They were worn over the shoulders, and only by men of high birth; they were similar in shape to the *paludamentum*, or military cloak of the Romans, or the *chlamys* of the Greeks; they were a mark of dignity and honor, and were fastened with most costly brooches. They were of variegated hues—green, red, blue, scarlet, and purple—and bordered with a wide braid of different colors, or with a kind of lace; these mantles were the handsomest and most costly part of Ivar's outfit. The

Norsemen took great pride in them. There were also rain and dust cloaks.

The silk and linen underwear, such as vests, undershirts, drawers; silk, linen, and woollen shirts, were like ours, but without collars attached to them. Those of wool were of varied patterns and colors. Kirtles were also plentiful; they were longer than the shirts, were of silk, linen, and wool. These were put over the shirts, and worn next to the chain-armor, and extended somewhat below it. There were also many pairs of trousers; these were of wool, almost tight-fitting, socks and legs in one piece.

Ivar thanked his mother for all the care she had taken in selecting his outfit, which could not be more elaborate and costly. He himself chose the weapons he was to take with him, for there was nothing of which the Vikings were more proud than their arms. His were unrivalled for beauty and quality. The chain-armor suits, or "brynjas," were marvels of workmanship, and one of them was of gold; the blades of his swords and saxes were all beautifully damascened, and their hilts were gold ornamented, and their scabbards also ornamented with gold; his shields were gold-rimmed, and adorned with superb designs, representing warlike deeds of great Vikings.

There was a rich assortment of leather belts, with buckles of gold, inlaid with precious stones. Some of these buckles were enamelled in red, green, blue, and black. The Norsemen excelled in the art of enamelling. A large collection of brooches for fastening his mantles were in a special box.

His toilet-box contained combs, ear-picks, and tweezers of gold.

But the gems in jewellery were the fastenings of his chain-armor. These were of bronze, covered with a sheet of gold of exquisite *repoussé* work.

One of the fastenings had a rosette in the centre, surrounded by nine heads, but the other circle was of a richness of design in which the artist had displayed his greatest skill and taste. In that were four rosettes at equal distance from each other ; between each of these was a figure of a man in a sitting posture, which perhaps represented Ægir, the god of the sea. Each figure was surrounded by fishes, ducks of different sizes, etc.

His riding accoutrements could not be excelled for beauty : the stirrups were of silver, inlaid with gold ; the spurs were of solid gold, ornamented with exquisite filigree work ; the bridle was a gilt-bronze chain.

All those who were to go with him were also to dress with great magnificence, and their riding gear and weapons were to vie with those of the richest men of the land.

The fleet of dragon-ships which took Ivar and his retinue to Svithjod were the finest ships of Gotland, and no handsomer ones could be seen in the Viking lands. Their red-burnished gold dragons

glowed as fire when the sun shone upon them, and
some of them were so much ornamented that
their entire hulls seemed to be of gold. They
carried handsome striped sails of different colors,
red and blue stripes predominating. Their pen-
nants and standards were gold embroidered. The
shields that were to hang outside, along the gunwales, had gold rims, and were painted in yellow
and black, or red and white, so that their effect, as
they lay side by side, overlapping each other, was
very striking.

Fifteen provision ships followed the fleet. Two
of these carried some superb horses which Ivar
intended as a present for the Hersir of Svithjod,
for Gotland was celebrated for its breed of horses.
Among the horses were thoroughbred stallions of
dark chestnut color. Ivar was to present him, also,
with a new dragon-ship sheeted with thin gold
above the water-line.

Hjalmar, Sigurd, and Sigmund had joined Ivar,
each with a handsome skeid.

After an uneventful voyage, the fleet sighted
the shores of Svithjod, and soon afterwards arrived opposite the fjord leading to Lake Malar.
The fastest vessels let down their sails, cast anchor, and waited for those lagging behind; and
when they had come in sight of each other, the
shields were hung outside of the gunwales of
every vessel. The peace shields were hoisted,
and the standards of the different Vikings were
seen floating gracefully on the breeze. The fleet

remained at anchor for the night, and next morning the horns were sounded for the anchors to be
raised and to move forward. The wind was fair
and fresh, and as the ships sailed they passed by
many small hamlets nestling in nooks along the
picturesque shore. Slaves in their white garments
were seen tilling the soil, or cutting down trees
that were to be used in the construction of houses
or vessels. The harvest had taken place, and rye,
barley, and oats were still stacked in the field.
Everything was peaceful, but behind these hills
and these forests lived the Sviar, or the Sueones
of the Romans and their kindred, the bravest and
most daring people the Roman Empire had ever
come in contact with.

The fjord leading towards Lake Malar had, in
those days, about the same appearance as to-day.
Their granite walls protected them against the
daughters of Ægir and Ran. Island after island
lined the coast and the entrance of the fjord, and
the shores were clad in many places with woods
and forests of gigantic oak and pine, and some
which witnessed the scenes I describe are still to
be seen here and there. When evening came, the
horns sounded for the vessels to cast anchor for
the night.

The following morning, at dawn of day, the ships
were again under way. The voyage drew towards
its end, Lake Malar was entered, the old town of
Sigtuna came in sight, and soon afterwards they
cast anchor for the last time.

Then Ivar, two of his uncles, his three foster-
brothers, and the men of high birth who had followed him, left their ships and landed. All were
splendidly attired. Ivar wore over his shoulders
a superb red cloak, and his followers likewise.
These cloaks were so long that their swords could
not be seen under them. They mounted their
horses, which had been sent ashore. They rode
slowly along, with their hawks resting on their
shoulders or on their wrists. Ivar's hawk was
called Habrok, and was very famous on account
of its skill in catching large birds and hares.

Every man in that retinue looked every inch a
warrior; their mustaches, which only high-born
men could wear, gave them a martial appearance;
their hair hung gracefully on their necks from
under their shining, bright helmets. Ivar wore a
golden helmet.

The watchmen in the towers at Upsalir had
seen Ivar and his following coming, and told
Yngvi of their approach, saying to him: " There
glitter in the sunshine, helmets, splendid shields
and chain-armor, axes and spears. The men look
very valiant. Those must be some of thy guests,
and from their bearing they are high born."

The people watched them as they rode towards
Upsalir. When they arrived in front of the gate
they stopped, and after it was opened they entered the large square, or town, and went to the
great banqueting hall, dismounted near the door,
and then went in.

Yngvi was seated on his high seat, and received Ivar and his kinsmen and warriors with great courtesy, and bade him be seated, as a mark of honor, in the second high seat. Yngvi was of medium height; he wore a long, flowing, white beard, for he was of that age when Hersirs wore beards, instead of a moustache; he had deep blue eyes and a benevolent countenance, and was clad in a long, flowing robe of great beauty, embroidered all over with gold. He looked at Ivar intently for a while. What were his thoughts nobody could tell; but probably he was trying to read the character of the son of Hjorvard, his kinsman. He, perhaps, also thought that one of his daughters would make a good match by marrying the son of Hjorvard.

Ivar was tall and strong; his physique, under the constant training of athletic games, was superb. His features were regular, his cheeks rather prominent; his nose was aquiline, his eyes of a most beautiful deep blue, and, when looking at you, seemed to search your innermost thoughts; and his long hair was fair and silky.

In the evening there was great feasting and drinking, but the daughters of the Hersir of Svithjod did not make their appearance.

Wonderful, indeed, was Upsalir, and it was not strange that its fame extended far and wide, for it was the most beautiful burg in all the northern lands. The buildings and houses that faced the

immense quadrangle which they surrounded made
an extraordinary sight; there were houses with
wooden walls that had stood the storms of centuries, some of which, it was believed, had been
built by Frey himself. What immense-sized oaks
and fir trees had been used in the construction of
these buildings! The timbers had become so
hardened on account of the resin having been ab-
sorbed by the fibres of the wood, that they seemed
indestructible. Gold and silver had not been
spared in the inside ornamentation of many of
these structures; the best architects and artists of
those days had been employed in their construction, ornamentation, and carvings. Many of these
houses looked very weird and fantastic, and were
of the same style of architecture as those of
Dampstadir, but of an earlier date.

Among those structures stood one finer than
all the others; this was the great banqueting hall,
famed all over the Norselands on account of its
splendor, size, and peculiar outside ornamentation
of gargoyles. The two doors leading into the interior were marvellous specimens of carving. The
door-jambs represented the different ceremonies
attending the funeral of Baldr, according to Norse
belief, and a heavy gold knocker adorned each
door.

The hall itself was superb; the walls were
adorned with carvings, and represented a sacrifice
made to Odin, and many other religious subjects.
Shields hung all along the walls, and these were all

adorned with gold, and with beautiful designs, many telling of the great deeds of the heroes of the race. They had been collected by each successive ruler of Svithjod, or had been given to them as presents by the most renowned smiths of the day. Tapestries hung where there was no carving, and these had been chiefly embroidered by the daughters and wives of the Hersirs who had ruled over Upsalir. Here was a tapestry representing ships gliding over the water with their gold-ornamented dragons; another represented a body of men dressed in war costume, ready to land. Many were hunting scenes with dogs or hawks.

The collection of Grecian glass gathered by different rulers, such as bowls, cups, beakers, and drinking horns, was exquisite. There were goblets with Greek inscriptions upon them; a beautiful bowl of glass, of sapphire color, was partly encircled with an delicate open silver work, showing the color of the glass behind. All these objects illustrated the great taste and refinement of those who had collected them, and told of the high civilization of those times in the North. There were numbers of Roman and Greek bronze vessels of most graceful forms, showing the Roman and Greek art at its best in that particular branch of industry. Some of these vessels were fluted on the sides, and the fastenings of the handles represented winged women's heads, lions, or other graceful figures. Upon one of these vases was a Latin inscription in letters of silver. Roman and

Greek statuettes of bronze, of men and women, were scattered here and there.

But the objects which Yngvi prized more than any others were a collection of Roman coins anterior to Augustus, of the time of the republic; these had been coined by patrician families, and showed that the Sviar made voyages to the Mediterranean, and incursions along its shores, long before our era. As Yngvi showed them to Ivar, he said: " Many of our kinsmen have been buried on the Mediterranean, for in the time of the Etruscan they traded there, and their graves are seen to this day in that country, and can be easily recognized, for they are exactly like those found in the Norselands."

Among the valuable objects from the North were two large and superb drinking horns, made of bands of gold, with figures in *repoussé* work, having strange mythical representations, among which were three-headed men, shields, swords, horned men, men on horseback, stars, pigs, snakes, fishes, deer, and other animals. Each of these horns weighed between seven and eight pounds. There were other vessels of silver, with beautiful *repoussé* work in gold near the rim, representing deer, birds, and animals, which were of Greek or Roman origin.

In this hall the most sumptuous entertainments were given, but only on great occasions, or when mighty chiefs came on a visit, or when a wedding took place. Then the scalds recited in the evening, by the light of heavy wax candles, the deeds of the forefathers and the great warriors of the race, or the old and wise taught wisdom to those who were around them. The high seats were of gold. Above the high seat of Yngvi hung his sword, with the peace-bands round it ; under it were his helmet and shield.

Not far from Upsalir were the "idrottir" grounds, or athletic fields, a place famed all over the North. The name idrottir was applied to all bodily and mental exercises. Men practised there all kinds of games and gymnastic exercises.

The most important championship games took place in the spring, before men left upon Viking expeditions, and in the autumn when they had returned home. Old and young were equally eager for these contests. When a ship was at anchor near the shore, the crew always landed to play games ; no opportunity was ever lost when the occasion allowed them to practise. To gain the championship of the herad was considered a great honor, but a still greater one was to gain that of several herads, when many men were pitted against each other. But the contest that was to take place for the championship of all the Norselands was on a far greater scale, and was to be a memorable occasion in the lives of those who were to become contestants.

CHAPTER XXII

YNGVI'S POETS AND CHAMPIONS

YNGVI had gathered round him the greatest champions of the Northern lands. When a warrior had achieved great fame and had obtained the championship in any game of strength or dexterity, or was a great berserk, and gained the victory over some celebrated warrior, he made his way to Upsalir, for the Hersir of Svithjod was convivial, liberal, and lavish of his gold to his men. No one had ever repented of serving him, or of following him in battle. Some of the storehouses where his wealth was kept were literally filled with gold and silver, fine swords and beautiful weapons, costly garments and cloaks, and other things, which were to be given away to those who served him faithfully or who came to visit him; for it was the custom never to let the guest depart empty-handed. The best goldsmiths of the land were constantly working for him.

Yngvi, as was customary with great Hersirs, kept always twelve champions. Every one of these was a famous berserk; and the Hersir of

Svithjod prided himself on the fact that his champions were the strongest, most agile and skilful warriors in the land, though once in a while a new man would come and show that no one can be best in everything.

It was the custom of the berserks, when they were in Upsalir and came to the hall, first to go and salute Yngvi; then to walk up to every stranger, and ask him if he thought himself their equal; and if any one dared to say that he was, then their anger and eagerness to fight increased.

They began to frown and shout, loudly saying to the man: "Darest thou to fight us? Then thou wilt need more than big words or boasting. We will try how much there is in thee."

But if Yngvi interposed, saying: "These men are my guests, and have come to see me," then there was no fighting. Most of them, in time of peace, went about the country and challenged men to fight duels if they would not do their will, or went on expeditions in far-off countries to gather wealth.

It was their custom, when they were only with their own men, and found the berserk fury coming over them, to go away and wrestle with trees or rocks, as I have already said, otherwise they would have slain their friends in their frenzy, for when they were in that state they lost their reason; but in every day's life they were not so bad to have intercourse with if they were not offended, though they were most overbearing if their pride or re-

nown were at stake. All of Yngvi's berserks had
drunk of the blood of wolves and eaten of their
hearts in order to become fearless, and they had
succeeded very well in that respect, for they were
feared and dreaded everywhere ; but now and then
they found a man to be their equal, and they had
to admit him to fellowship with them.

They had made a vow never to flee from fire ;
and it was told of them that one day when they
were visiting in the country with Yngvi, the cheer
was so good and the drinks were so strong that they
fell fast asleep, and then fire was set to the hall by
some enemy.

One of the champions woke first, and seeing
the hall nearly full of smoke, called out : "Now it
will suffocate our hawks," and then again lay down
to sleep.

Then another saw the hall burning, and said :
"Wax will now drop from our saxes," and then
lay down again.

But when Yngvi awoke, he rose and roused the
warriors, and told them to arm themselves. They
then rushed at the walls with such force that the
joints of the timbers broke, and then the berserk
rage came at once upon them ; but those who had
set fire to the house had fled, and there was no
enemy to fight, so they wrestled with trees and
rocks while their berserk fury lasted.

Yngvi thought a great deal of his berserks, and
allowed them a great deal of latitude, for he knew
that in life one must overlook many things in

order to be happy, and he knew their disposition. They, in return, loved him dearly, and everyone was ready to lose his life for him at his bidding; but rulers who had good champions were very shy of risking their lives unnecessarily. One of his favorite champions was Svipdag, and the way he had come to him was this: His father, the Bondi Svip, lived far away from other men; he was wealthy, and had been one of the greatest of champions, and was not at all what he looked like, as he knew many things and was very wise. He had three sons, Svipdag, Geigad, and Hvitserk, who was the oldest; they were all well-skilled, strong, and fine-looking men.

When Svipdag was eighteen winters old, he said one day to his father: "Our life here in the mountains, in far-off valleys, and unsettled places, where men never visit nor receive visits, is dull; it would be better to go to Yngvi and follow him and his champions, if he will receive us."

Svip, who wanted to persuade him from doing so, answered: "I do not think this advisable, for his men are jealous and strong."

Svipdag answered: "A man must risk something if he wishes to get fame; he cannot know, before he tries, when luck will come to him."

His father finally gave him a large axe, and said to his son: "Be not greedy, do not boast, for that gives a bad reputation; but defend thyself if attacked, for a great man should boast little, and behave well in difficulties."

He also gave him good war accoutrements and a good horse.

Then Svipdag rode, and at night came to Up-salir; he saw that games were taking place outside the hall; Yngvi sat on a large gold chair, and his berserks were near him. When Svipdag came, the gate of the burg was shut, for it was then custom-ary to ask leave to ride in; Svipdag did not take that trouble, and forced open the gate, and rode into the town.

Then Yngvi said: "This man comes here reck-lessly, as this has never been done before. It may be that he has great strength and has no fear."

The berserks at once got very angry, and thought that he asserted himself too much. Svipdag rode before Yngvi, and saluted him well, in a skilful man-ner. Yngvi asked who he was, and he answered: "I am the son of the Bondi Svip."

Then Yngvi soon recognized him, and every one thought he was a great and high-born cham-pion. The games were continued; Svipdag sat and looked on. The berserks eyed him angrily, and said to Yngvi that they wanted to try him; and Yngvi answered: "I think that he has no little strength, but I should like you to try whether he is such a man as he considers him-self."

When every one came into the hall, after the games were over, the berserks walked toward Svipdag, and asked him if he was a champion, as he made so much of himself. He answered that

he was as great a champion as any of them. At
these words their anger and their eagerness to
fight increased, but Yngvi told them to be quiet
that evening; they began to frown, and howled
loudly, and said to Svipdag: "Darest thou to
fight us? Then wilt thou need more than thy
boasting. We will try how much there is in
thee."

Svipdag answered; "I will consent to fight one
at a time, and will see if more can be done."

In the morning a great duel began, and there
was no lack of heavy blows. The new-comer knew
how to use his sword with great strength and skill,
and the berserks gave way. Svipdag killed one,
and then another wanted to avenge him. Yngvi
stopped the fight, and made peace between them,
and then he made them swear foster-brotherhood,
after which he said to Svipdag: "Great loss hast
thou caused me by killing one of my berserks,
but I see that thou canst more than fill his
place, and henceforth thou will be one of my body-
guard."

But of all his body-guard and men Yngvi valued
his scalds the most ; they were placed on the second
high seat when no strangers were entertained, so
that he could see them. One of them was Odun,
the Satirist, so named because he only recited and
composed satirical songs; he was the oldest bard,
and had been the scald of Yngvi's father. But his
greatest scald was Haldor, who was not quick of
speech when he spoke in prose, but poetry was

very easy to him, and he always answered in verse, and songs flowed from him as fast as he could think. All the scalds of Yngvi were also famous warriors, and while he went into warfare they were always in his shield-burg, looking on and singing the praises of the most valiant one.

CHAPTER XXIII

YNGVI'S THREE BEAUTIFUL DAUGHTERS

THE three daughters of Yngvi were renowned all over the Northern lands for their accomplishments and their beauty; the eldest was named Astrid, the second Randalin, and the youngest Gunnhild. Randalin, "Ran's dale," had been named after Ran, the goddess of the sea; Gunnhild after the two Valkyrias, Gunn and Hild. It was the custom in those days to make one name of two. Astrid was twenty-two, Randalin twenty, and Gunnhild nineteen years of age.

Astrid was so fair that wise men of the country said that she was the most beautiful maiden in all the Northern lands. Her hair was so long and thick that she could cover her whole body with it; it was as fine as silk, and of the color of amber with a tinge of gold. She was somewhat tall, being above the average height, and had a graceful and slender figure; on her shoulders rested an extremely handsome head; her features were perfect, her nose was Grecian in shape, like those of her ancestors, and her eyes were soft and dreamy, deep blue, contrasting charmingly with her clear and fresh complexion; the bloom of her cheeks had that exquisite, soft pink tinge which diffused itself into her white skin, as delicate as apple blossoms floating on milk, or the hues of the most lovely carnation; her teeth were so even that they seemed a row of pearls set between two lovely cherry lips; her hands were slender, not too small, and her feet were in perfect proportion to her size, with a high instep; both foot and hand showed the characteristic elegance of generations of wealth and cultivation. Her walk was dignified for a girl of her age, and to add to all her charms, she had a sweet and soft voice, without which no woman is perfect.

Randalin was of medium height, somewhat stouter than Astrid, with a well-knit body, due to constant exercise, for she was fond of riding and walking. She had the features of her father, and was very much like him in many ways. Her eyes were also blue, but her cheeks were ruddier than those of her eldest sister. She was very accomplished and learned, and had been taught to speak Greek by one of her bondwomen who had been captured in Greece. She loved the society of the wise and of scalds, and admired, above all, valor in men. Good looks to her were nothing without courage, accomplishments, and good manners.

Gunnhild, the youngest daughter, was of the same height as her eldest sister. She had thick chestnut hair with darker streaks here and there. She had blue eyes, which people said were exactly like those of her mother. Her nose was

straight, her mouth small, and when she talked or
smiled, showed two rows of beautiful small teeth ;
her complexion browned easily in the sun during
the summer months, and her pink cheeks looked
the more beautiful through the darkened skin.
She was by far the most coquettish of all the sisters, and extremely lively and witty, and loved to
see men, young and old, captive at her feet. She had
the faculty of making the last man that she spoke
to believe that he was the favorite ; but though
much courted, she did not know what love was,
and could not have loved, even if she had tried.

These three sisters had very aristocratic manners. They seemed to have been born to rule,
and appeared in every way descended from high
lineage, and were every inch daughters of Hersirs.
They were so beautiful that the people believed
that the Nornir had, at their birth, fated them to
be the fairest among the fair daughters of earth,
and had also gifted them with all the loveliness,
charms, and accomplishments which make women
attractive to men, and lead the bravest, highest,
and the most intellectual, captive at their feet,
and their willing slaves. Their presence at the
games always incited the players to greater feats ;
the scalds became more inspired, and every guest
tried his best to be foremost in their good graces.

Many a great warrior, sons of powerful Hersirs,
and foremost in all kinds of athletic games, had
undertaken daring and dangerous expeditions in
the Roman Empire and elsewhere, and had chal-

lenged the greatest champions of the land to combat, and performed acts of great valor and prowess,
in order that their deeds might be sung by the
scalds before the daughters of the Hersir of Svithjod, for they were considered the greatest prizes in
the Viking lands, and no one but those of Odin's
kin could ever aspire to become their husbands.
No chief's son had yet been so bold as to ask one
of them in marriage, for they all feared that they
had not accomplished deeds of valor great enough
to permit them to hope to win their hearts, for
there was nothing in the world which the Vikings
admired more than charming women; towards
all they were the soul of chivalry.

These three sisters lived in their skemma, or
bower. There they sewed, embroidered, and did
other handiwork, attended by their free servants
or bondwomen; and there they received their
friends.

Each of them owned several bondwomen, to
whom they were much attached, and who were
regarded as part of the family. These had been
captured, with their parents, when young; two of
them came from Britain, two from the northern
shores of Gaul, and two had come from the Mediterranean. One of the latter was the daughter
of a citizen of Rome, and the other was a Greek.

Astrid had superintended the household of her
father since her mother's death, two years before.
She attended to the brewing of ale, and vied with
other women of high lineage who should brew

the best ale ; and she prided herself upon weaving the finest of linen and spinning the best spun wool for clothes.

For some reason, the sisters had not made their appearance in the hall since the arrival of Ivar, and there was great curiosity to see them among those who had never been to Upsalir ; and every day many eyes were turned towards their bower, trying to get glimpses of their fair forms. Men dressed in their best, groomed their moustaches, and parted their long hanging hair carefully, and were most particular in their toilets when they went out, so that they should not be seen at dis-advantage if perchance they were to meet the three sisters.

The skemma in which the three daughters of the Hersir of Svithjod lived was an ex-tremely handsome house, with others attached to it. The lower floor was accessible through a beautiful, pointed porch ornamented with fine carving ; the door led to the large every-day room, which contained several looms and spinning-wheels. It was used for meals also, and along the walls were shelves where beautiful dishes, drinking horns, cups, and table ware were dis-played to advantage. There were, besides, other large rooms on that floor, one of which was the sewing and embroidering room. The upper story was accessible through stairs leading to the veran-das above, from which one had access to the bed-rooms.

15

Astrid had a bedroom to herself, while Randalin and Gunnhild slept in another room. Their
beds were built along the walls, and between them
was a large closet of the same depth as the width
of the beds; heavy home-made woollen curtains of
bright color were hung to hide the beds, and were
very ornamental. Two steps led into each bed.
Tables, carved chairs, cupboards, movable closets
with elaborate carvings, made up the furniture of
these bedrooms.

Several smaller rooms on this floor were entirely
devoted to the wardrobe of the three sisters, and
contained several large wooden, painted chests to
store many different articles in.

One room contained their dresses. Here hung
their "slœdurs," or festive gowns, with their long
trains; these were worn only at great feasts.
Many of them were of brocade or costly woollens,
and gold and silver embroidered. These festive
dresses were made very wide, and the sleeves
reached to the wrists. When worn, the waist was
generally adorned by a beautiful belt of gold,
from which a bag, often gold-embroidered, was
suspended for rings or other precious ornaments.

Opposite these hung their kirtles, or every-day
dresses, which were much shorter than the festive
ones, and were generally of linen or wool, and of
varied patterns.

The mantles were of many kinds. The finest
ones were called "skikkja" and "mottul." These,
like the cloaks of the men, could only be worn by

women of high birth. They were without sleeves,
usually fastened at the neck by a beautiful and
costly brooch, or valuable hooks. They were of
different colors—red, brown, purple, blue—and ornamented with wide braid or with lace on their
edges. There were other cloaks, used for winter,
lined with different varieties of fur. In a smaller
room was their linen and silk underwear.

Exquisite small boxes, with hinges of gold,
were for their jewels; some of these boxes were
of box-wood, and beautifully carved, and contained
long hair-pins, to fasten the hair when arranged in
a large knot on the back of the head. Some of
these pins were of gold, others of silver, ornamented with gold tops of various designs; there
were also diadems of gold, some with the ends
ending in snake-heads, on which the names of the
owners were written in runic letters; numerous
necklaces of gold, some of gold rods, ornamented
with crescents. Gold Roman coins, with loops attached, were fastened to gold chains to be worn
round the neck. There were also other pendants
of gold of exquisite filigree work. The bracelets
were many, and of various patterns, some so graceful that even to-day no jeweler could excel them.
Many of these were spiral in shape. Two of these
bracelets on account of their beauty were called
" sviagris " and " hnitud," and no goldsmith had
been able to rival them. They had been heirlooms
in the family for generations. The collection of
gold and mosaic beads was something extraordi-

nary. The mosaics were lovely and of most skilled workmanship. Besides these were crystal balls of wonderful clearness, with Greek inscriptions upon them, and amber beads. Gold buttons for sleeves, and hooks of varied patterns, were together in a large bowl.

The brooches were most remarkable; some of them were very old, and had been in the family for generations. Among these were cruciform fibulæ of bronze, ending with heads of horses, or other animals; circular ones, and others in the shape of the "Svastica," a peculiar cross, a sign seen among the relics of Troy, and to-day on the foot of the image of Buddha, in India. Many others were circular, of bronze, covered over with a sheet of *repoussé* work of gold, upon which were lovely designs. There were other brooches entirely of gold, or silver gilt, and of various patterns.

But the finest of all the jewels were the gold "bracteates." These were worn hanging on the breast. They were round in shape, and varied very much in size, from one inch in diameter to seven and eight inches, and were of the purest gold, very thin, and remarkable for the originality and peculiarity of their designs.

CHAPTER XXIV

THE daughters of the Hersir of Svithjod had many of their young kinswomen visiting them at this time. They had arrived during the summer months, having been invited to be present at the games. Among those were Thora, daughter of one of the great Hersirs who ruled over one of the largest herads in Gardariki; Alfhild, daughter of one of the Hersirs of Holmgard, which realm, together with Gardariki, comprised a great part of what is now known as European Russia.

Hildigunn was the daughter of a powerful Hersir of the island of Funen, almost the equal of the Hersir of Zeeland in power. Randgrid, Geirlaug, Ingegerd, and Sigrid, were also daughters of great Hersirs.

One of the prettiest and most intelligent of their kinswomen was Thorny. She had attained her eighteenth year the preceding spring. Her large hazel eyes were full of poetry and fire, and when she looked at one it seemed as if she read the inmost thoughts of one's mind. Her broad forehead showed intellect, and her head was adorned with a mass of light brown hair. When she smiled she showed a bewitching set of pearly teeth. She was full of life, and was not ashamed to say that she preferred men's society to that of women.

The third evening, when the men of highest lineage had assembled in the great banqueting hall and were seated in their respective seats, Astrid, her two younger sisters, and all their feminine guests entered the hall. A murmur of admiration greeted them, and no wonder; for it had never happened within the recollection of the oldest men that so many high-born and beautiful maidens, daughters of chiefs who ruled over powerful realms, and who were of Odin's kin, had been in Upsalir at the same time. It was certainly the greatest gathering of men and women within the recollection of anyone. The flower of womanhood was there, and all that was chivalrous and brave in the land had come also.

Each maiden had in her hand a drinking horn of gold, filled either with mead, ale, or wine, and she offered it to the guests. Afterwards, lots were drawn by the warriors to decide where they were to sit, and fortunate were the men who had drawn the lots which permitted them to be by the side of maidens. Ivar had as a seat companion Randalin; Hjalmar, Astrid; Sigurd, Svanhild; Sigmund, Solveig. They talked much to each other during the evening, and were delighted at their good fortune; and all hoped to have the same chance again, so pleased were they with each other.

It happened thereafter that almost always the four foster-brothers had as companions the same maidens, which attracted everyone's notice; and, as they enjoyed so much each other's society, many began to think that more than one wedding would take place within a year among them.

The day before the games took place Astrid had a dream, in which her Disir appeared to her. Every family in these Norselands had, like the Etruscans and Romans, their guardian spirits. Their belief and worship of them corresponded somewhat to that of the Lares and Penates of the Romans. The Disir were supposed to watch over every individual member of the family. These were thought to be the representatives of the departed, and when there was danger ahead often made their appearance in dreams to warn them in time. They always appeared in the shape of women.

Astrid had dreamt that, as she was standing outside of her house, and while looking over the sea, she saw a woman walking over the waves and directing her steps towards her house. She was so very tall that she seemed as high as the highest mountains. Astrid went to meet her, and invited her to come to her home.

After the guest had seated herself, she said: " Thou, Astrid, and thy two sisters, must be most careful at the games not to fall in love with the sons of a great berserk who are coming to Upsalir."

Then she saw twelve eagles tearing the flesh of men. Then the tall woman told her to receive Ivar and his foster-brothers well; after saying this she rose, and as she was ready to depart she said: "I will continue to protect thee and thy family. Now we will separate for some time. Fare thee well."

Thereupon Astrid awoke. She was very much concerned in regard to this dream, and went to Thorhalla, a woman who was reputed very wise in the interpretation of dreams. When she came to her door, she said: "I should like thee to explain a dream which I have dreamt."

Thorhalla said: "I will not hear thy dream. Go away as quickly as thou canst to the house of Bryngerd; she will explain it to thee."

Astrid wondered why Thorhalla would not explain her dream, but she did as she was bidden; and, after walking quite a while, she came to the house of Bryngerd, and told her dream to her.

Bryngerd listened very attentively, and said to her: " This forebodes great events. The woman thou hast seen is thy Disir, and has come to forewarn thee of danger. The twelve eagles mean the twelve sons of the berserk Hervard, and many valiant men will fall on thy account."

On her return home, Astrid told of her dream to her father and to her sisters, and made preparations for a sacrifice to her Disir, or guardian genius. The sisters had a special hall near their skemma, with a stone altar in the room, for sacrificing to their Disirs. Two beautiful black oxen and a very handsome favorite horse were to be sacrificed.

Ivar and his foster-brothers, unaware of the preparations for a sacrifice that were being made by the three sisters, wended their way towards their bower, just as they were beginning to sacrifice, and were ready to redden the altar with blood. As they approached the house, the bondmaid who was watching saw them, and went into the hall to warn her mistresses that some one was coming.

On hearing this, Astrid, full of alarm, came out of the door, and as she saw Ivar and his foster-brothers she exclaimed: "Do not come here, for this place is holy! We are making a sacrifice to our Disirs. Do you not fear the anger of Odin, that you dare to come to us?"

Ivar replied: "We are not afraid to incur the anger of Odin, fair maidens of Svithjod. We would brave it for your sake, but we will not come within the holy precincts when you are making a sacrifice."

After saying this, the foster-brothers went off in another direction.

Astrid returned to the room, and with her sisters reddened the altar with the blood of the sacrificed animals, and asked their Disirs to continue to watch over them.

CHAPTER XXV

THE day when the " idrottir," or athletic games, began had come. All the warriors and champions who intended to take part in these contests had arrived either by land or by water. For several days before, wherever the eye turned, men were seen training and preparing themselves for the games, and tents were scattered in every direction. The fairest women and maidens of all the Viking realms were in Upsalir; they also had come to witness the games. Many of them were of great beauty, and daughters of Haulds and Bondi who owned vast tracts of land, and rivalled in power some of the Hersirs. There was also a vast multitude of commoner people who always collected on such occasions. These brought their tents and provisions with them, and put up at any place they could find. At dawn of day, when the games began, a great crowd had already collected on the idrottir fields.

Among the daughters of Hersirs and high-born men who were present were Signy, Ragnhild, Helga, Hjordis, Sigrid, Ingebjorg, Thora, Sigrun, Gudrun, Herborg, Bryngerd, Randgrid, Kara,

Thorhalla, Bergthora, Grimhild, Brynhild, Gudrod,
Asta, Hildirid, Thorgerd, Thordis, Ingigerd, Thurid, Hungerd, Hallgerd, Hildigunn, Asgerd, Ulf-
hild, Gyda, Thyri, Olrun, Svanhild, Hrefna.

Women were always one of the most interest-
ing features at the games. They came to applaud
and cheer the contestants, and to urge the men to
their utmost. No wonder that there was a saying,
that at the games many lost their hearts, and that
numerous engagements and weddings were sure
to take place during the year that followed.

At sight of them, Ivar and every other man
was filled with ambition. "I must become a
champion," was the thought of every one, "so
that these fair creatures may admire me." It
was no wonder that so many handsome girls
and women had sent such a thrill of admiration
through the vast multitude, for before them stood
the representative of all that was beautiful, graceful, and accomplished in the Norselands.

A parterre of exquisite flowers could not have
presented a more lovely view. They were clad in
their most becoming day or walking dress, which
came to just above the ankles. Their foreheads
were adorned with diadems of gold, and their
necks and arms with necklaces and bracelets of
gold. Their waists were surrounded with belts
of gold of variegated patterns and exquisite workmanship, showing the taste and skill of the goldsmith. Every one wore her mantle; these hung
gracefully over their shoulders, and were of differ-

ent colors, red, purple, blue, brown, and white predominating. All were more or less embroidered
with silver and gold, and made fast by artistic
brooches of gold.

"What a beautiful sight!" Sigmund exclaimed.
"Look, foster-brothers, at their thick and glossy
hair!" All the tints of blonde type were here
represented, from the lightest flaxen, amber, and
burnished gold, to the dark auburn and chestnut.

Sigurd, pointing out to Ivar a maiden who had
superb hair, said: "See how luxuriously her hair
of gold glows against the azure of the sky. Look
at her eyes; they are as the deep blue of the sea
we meet when we are far away from the land."

"Look at this one," said Ivar, pointing to him
one of the loveliest maidens in this bevy of beauty.
"See her hair hanging on her back, and swaying
in the breeze; it is the color of a field of wheat
moving in the wind, and gilded by the rays of the
sun."

"Look at this other one," said again Hjalmar;
"her hair is as black as that of the raven. Her
eyes seem to send forth flashes of fire. Some of
the kin from which she is descended must have
come from the land of the Huns; I think she must
be from Gardariki." She was unique among all,
with her raven hair, and much admired on that
account, for the fair hues generally predominated
over the dark.

Sigurd said: "Foster-brothers, have you ever
seen such eyes as those that are here together?

They are like a bunch of arrows in a quiver, ready to be shot at us poor mortals, and to make us feel the pangs of love. Some of them are dreamy, some are twinkling with mischief, some are piercing, some are so loving, a few are so fiery, that one feels that it is better not to excite the ire of the maiden who possesses them. Look at their color —from the deep blue to the amethyst and greenish tourmaline. Look at the hazel ones; there are but a few of them, but oh, how lovely and poetical! They seem at times to send forth flashes of genius, then to return again gently to their dreamy mood. Well may the eyes be called the mirror of our thoughts, for they tell of our love, sorrow, or anger.

Among the great Vikings who had come to compete for the championship were Haki, Starkad, Ingvald, Sigurd, Bodvar, Hervard, Ingimund, Heidrek, Thorolf, Hallvard, Asmund, Agnar, Ragnar, Hodbrod, Gunnar, Volsung, Thorvald, Siggier, Thoris, Einar, Bjorn, Ulf, Sigmund, Ogmund, Vemund, Thormod, Gautrek, Thorbrand, Indridi, Gauti, Vikar, Fridthjolf, Hrolf, Hjalmter, Halfdan, Eirek the Red, Alrek, Ottar, Visbur, Refil, Adils, Ingald, Havar, Randver, Hogni, Arnvid, Grammar, Kolbak, Jorund, Arnkel, Skeggi, Hromund, Hord, Gisli, Thorkel, Egil, Ketil, Ingolf, Leif, Erling, Glum, Ogvald, Viga.

These men, and many others present, were the embodiment of all that was chivalrous and brave in the Norselands. Many of them had passed a great part of their lives at sea or in foreign lands, conquering and fighting, carrying their victorious standards before them everywhere. Their ruddy faces told that they were the sons of the sea, who had fought many a time, with great skill, the daughters of Ægir and Ran. What tales many could tell of the terrific gales they had encountered with their ships while on their expeditions, voyaging on either the North Sea, the Atlantic Ocean, or the Mediterranean, and almost every one could say that some of their kinsmen had gone to the hall of Ran on their way to or from home! Fear was unknown to them all.

What superb specimens of manhood they were! The finest the world could show! Spartan-like in appearance, for all the weak at their birth had not been allowed to live. What splendid proportions their bodies had! What strong chests and powerful frames! What muscles! For from their childhood these men had been trained, and practised athletic games, and all had lived much in the open air. Many were tall, but there were also many of medium height. A few were short. These were often the hardiest and most agile, and could stand hardships much better than their taller friends. Most of them were fair, but some few had dark hair and beards.

Yngvi, with his three beautiful daughters, a bevy of young maidens, and wives of Hersirs and Haulds, and other guests, when they arrived on the field took their places on an elevated spot, from which they could survey the games.

Astrid was dressed in a red, ornamented kirtle, and over it a scarlet cloak, ornamented with lace. Her long, fair hair reached down far below her waist. Randalin wore a blue woven mantle, and under it a scarlet dress, with a gold belt. Her hair reached down to her waist on both sides, and she tucked its tresses under her belt. Gunnhild wore a kirtle, a dress fitting the waist very lightly, and short, and over her dress a close-fitting blue jacket.

Among the distinguished women were Drifa, the wife of the Hersir of the island of Zeeland. She came, followed by three of her bondmaids. She had a red dress, narrow below, long and tight at the waist, with long sleeves, and wore a band of gold cloth round her forehead; her hair was long and fine. Over her shoulders hung a white, gold-embroidered cloak. Hallgerd, a beautiful woman, widow of the former Hersir of the island of Fyen, who was very much sought for on account of her wealth, was dressed most tastefully, and her belt of gold showed her graceful form to advantage.

Yngvi, the Hersirs, and many prominent men and scalds, stood by themselves, near them, and were to be the umpires. As soon as Ivar and his foster-brothers had arrived on the fields, they went to salute the daughters of the Hersir of Svithjod and all the fair maidens who were their guests. A shower of smiles and bows from them told how the compliment was appreciated, for many blushed.

Ivar and his foster-brothers saluted Yngvi and the other Hersirs. Yngvi asked Ivar if he was a man of many athletic games.

Ivar replied: " My foster-father thought I knew many things well ; but I have not shown my skill to others, and I think thou wilt find it slight when compared to that of some men."

Ivar replied in this way, for he remembered the advice which his father had given him, that a man with a thinking mind should not boast, but rather be heedful in his mood, and beware, because the tongue is the head's bane.

Then all prepared themselves for the contests that were to begin—wrestling, jumping, leaping, running, different games of ball, swimming, and warlike exercises with spears, swords, bows and arrows.

CHAPTER XXVI

THE contests began with wrestling, which was one of the most popular of the games. The simplest form of this sport was for the wrestlers to take hold of each other's arms or waists, as best they could, and by the strength of their arms endeavor to throw each other off their feet.

The Sviars and the Gotlanders were pitted against each other; the former had kept the championship for several years, and Ivar and other Gotlanders intended to wrest it from them if they could. The competitors divided themselves by lot into two parties, each of which was drawn up in a row, headed by its leader. These were to pair off their men to wrestle in the arena, between the two rows, one after the other. Ivar's side was the weaker, having two men less, so two men were taken off from the Sviars' side.

Before beginning, every man threw off his outer garment in order to be more free and agile, and kept only a slight covering. The beholder could see at a glance what early gymnastic and athletic training did for the body; broad chests, strong and muscular limbs were the chief characteristics of every man.

16

The crowd watched with intense eagerness the preliminaries of the contest. Twenty-two men on each side were to take part. The contest was quite even; here a man on the Sviar side fell, then one on the Gotlander side. At times the wrestling was very severe between combatants, and the spectators watched with great interest the expansion or contraction of the muscles of the rivals.

The fourth man before the last on the Sviar side had been victorious, and had thrown the last three men but one of the Gotlanders, and Ivar was the only wrestler left. So he and his antagonist wrestled for a long time, until at last the Sviar fell. Then Ivar had to wrestle with the three others, and threw them one after the other, when a great cheer, like the sound of distant thunder, greeted his victory, and his foster-brothers came to congratulate him with great joy.

After this, Ivar and his foster-brothers went to the day meal, and on the way to the hall Sigmund saw among the bevy of young women one that looked at him intently. She was fair of face, and beautiful to look at; she wore a red dress, ornamented all over with lace. Her hair was flaxen and glossy, and fell over her shoulders. Sigmund asked who she was, and about her family, and was told that she was the sister of Thorir, a Hersir who ruled a large herad, and that her name was Thora "Hladhönd," which means lace hand. To Sigmund she was the most beautiful woman on the grounds. Then he went to speak to her and

found that they had met before at a mid-winter
sacrifice.   After their meal they rested a while,
and then went back to the games, and looked
on.

The second day the contest was to be a more
difficult form of wrestling, which consisted in grap-
pling and attacking according to certain rules, by
systematic turnings and grip movements with arms
and legs, each seeking to bring the other to the
ground.   Ivar did not wish to be recognized, as
he had been the successful champion the day
before, and the weather being chilly he had put
on a cloak with a hood which partly hid his face.

Among those who took part in the game was a
man of very powerful frame, of the name of Thorbjörn.   He would walk and look round the crowd,
and any one he wanted to take part in the game
he seized by the hand and pulled forward into the
field; and one after another these fell before him,
to the great amusement of the crowd.   When
almost all had wrestled, except the strongest, the
people began to ask themselves who should contend against Thorbjörn.   Thorbjörn himself was
looking round, puffed up with pride, thinking no
one could be stronger than he, and challenged the
champions who had fought against each other the
preceding day.   Noticing among them a man of
large size, whose face he could not clearly see on
account of a hood he wore, he came towards him
and took hold of his hand.   At first he pulled hard,

and then with all his strength, but the man sat still and could not be moved. Then Thorbjörn said in an angry voice: "No one ever sat so firm before me as thou dost. Who art thou?" Then pulling his hood down, so that his face could be seen, he exclaimed: "Ivar Hjorvardson!" and added, "If thou wilt take part in this contest with me, thou art a welcome guest."

"I have ceased to wrestle," answered Ivar, whose feats of the day before Thorbjörn had not witnessed, "but there was a time when I enjoyed wrestling greatly."

Soon after, the contest between the two began. Thorbjörn rushed at Ivar, who stood firm, without flinching, and then stretched his arms around the back of Thorbjörn, caught hold of his breeches, lifted him off his feet over his head, and threw him behind him, so that Thorbjörn's shoulders struck the ground with a heavy thud. This was a magnificent exhibition of strength, and it was hailed by the crowd with great acclamations.

Then one of Thorbjörn's brothers, called Angul, challenged Ivar, who said: "Let me rest a little while, and then I will be ready for thee."

This new challenger was also of great strength, and each had the better of the other by turns. They fell twice together on their knees. They grasped each other so tightly that both became blue from the pressure, but finally Angul fell.

Ivar had shown that he was so strong that the people were eager to see two champions attack

him at the same time. This was against the rules,
but was allowed if any contestant was willing to
encounter such odds. Ivar said he thought he
could do so in the afternoon, after a brief rest.

In the afternoon two champions who were
thought the strongest wrestlers attacked him at
the same time ; they wrestled valiantly, but could
not throw Ivar, and after awhile both men fell.
All the people were greatly delighted at this
spectacle. When the wrestlers stopped they
thanked them for their exhibition, and it was
the opinion of all that Ivar's two opponents together were not as strong as he, so Ivar was
proclaimed the champion in wrestling.

That evening the scalds sang before an admiring crowd the deeds of great warriors, and every
one present was dressed in his best attire.

The games of ball were by far the most popular of all ; they were to last two days, for there
were so many competitors. There were three
kinds of ball games, called Knattleik, Soppleik,
and Skofuleik, respectively. This last game was
a winter one, and was played on the ice, week
after week, by the people of a single herad, and
was a source of great amusement. All these
games were considered more or less dangerous,
as the balls were of wood or of scraped horn
enclosed in leather, and were sent back with
tremendous force by the bat.

Hord, a great ball-player from the island of

Zeeland, had sent a challenge to the men of Gotland to compete for the championship. Men of
equal strength were chosen on both sides, so that
the chances might be even.

The game was played in this way: A man
threw the ball into the air, and then struck it
with a bat, sending it a long distance; another
caught it with his hands, and sent it back, but
this the opposite side sought to prevent by shov-
ing him aside, or by throwing him down, or striking the ball away from him. If the ball went
beyond the bounds, or fell on the ground, the
man who had knocked it had to go and fetch it.

Hjalmar was a great ball-player, and wherever
he had competed for the championship in ball
games he had been victorious. It was generally
conceded that he was the best player in Engel.
Hord was considered the best ball-player in Zeeland; he was very popular and a very strong man.
The contest began very eagerly; both sides had
ten men each, and were very jealous of each
other, and the game became very rough. The
Gotlanders won the victory, but four men of Zeeland and three men of Gotland had been badly
hurt in the contest.

Other games of ball were taking place in different parts of the field at the same time.

The fourth day the crowd seemed greater than
ever, and many other men wanted to play.
Among these were two unknown men, who came

to Yngvi, and, after saluting him, said their names were Hrafn and Krak, and they hailed from the island of Bornholm; they boasted that no one could play better than they did. After hearing their boasting, many invited them to play; they said that they were rather rough-handed players, but that they could not help it, for they were strong men. The champions of Yngvi said that they did not mind that, and would take care of themselves, whatever might happen. The two brothers went to the games, and generally had the ball; they played very savagely, as they had said, and pushed men and knocked them down roughly, so that when the evening came many were bruised or maimed.

The following morning Sigurd prevailed upon Sigmund to play with him against them. Hrafn and Krak were already in the fields, challenging. Hrafn took the ball and Krak the bat, and they played as they were wont.

When they had played for a while, Sigurd got hold of the ball from Hrafn, and then snatched the bat from Krak, and sent it to Sigmund. They kept the ball for a long time, and Hrafn and Krak could not get hold of it; so Sigurd and Sigmund were victorious, and they kept the championship to the end of the games, at which Yngvi, Astrid, her sisters, and a bevy of maidens were constantly present.

The running games were of two kinds: men

running against fast horses, or against each other.
In this game there were many competitors. The
fleetest horses in Upsalir, or rather in Svithjod,
had been picked out for the contest. Men who
competed were dressed in tights only. Hjalmar,
who was one of the fleetest men known, was to
run against the fleetest horse. When the signal
to start came, he started with the horse, and
though the animal kept abreast of him nearly all
the time, he finally reached the starting point
somewhat ahead. One of the spectators was so
surprised at Hjalmar's feat that he said to him :
" Didst thou not hold the strap of the saddle-
girth, and let the horse pull thee along?"

" Not in the least," replied Ivar, hotly indig-
nant at the distrust expressed of his foster-
brother.

Yngvi had a very fast horse, which was next
entered against Hjalmar. The two started together, and Hjalmar ran ahead of the horse the
whole way. When the race was finished, Hjalmar
said : " Did I this time take hold of the saddle-
girth ? "

" I think thou didst start first," replied the
umpire.

The horse was allowed to breathe a while, then
his rider pricked him with his spurs, and he sprang
off anew. This time Hjalmar stood still until the
umpire shouted : " Run now." Then Hjalmar
himself started, and soon outran the horse, and
kept far in front of it all the way to the starting

point of the course, which he reached long in
advance. The vast multitude loudly applauded
Hjalmar ; and as he passed in front of the daughters of Yngvi and the bevy of young women,
they too cheered him, and he bowed gallantly to
them. Astrid had been watching him since the
games had begun, and admired him much, and as
he passed by her she shouted, " Well done, Hjalmar Gudbrandson of Engel." She had hardly
said these words, when her face became crimson,
and she wished she had been able to restrain herself.

Then all the men that had run faster than the
horses came and competed for the championship.
Hjalmar ran so fast that his feet did not seem to
touch the ground. He distanced all his competitors, and was proclaimed the champion runner, to
the great joy of Astrid, who already loved him,
though she was, maiden-like, only half conscious
of the fact.

The two following days were to be devoted to
warlike exercises, and the next morning Yngvi
asked Ivar: " Art thou skilful in warlike exercise ? "

Ivar replied in his usual modest way : " My
foster-father and my foster-mother thought so,
but I have not shown my skill to others, and I
think thou wilt find it slight compared with that
of many men. I have now won several championships since the games have begun, but I do not

think I shall be the foremost in warlike games, for it would be strange if my luck was to continue. Nevertheless I will strive for the championship, and do my best."

Then Ulf, a great Viking, who was said to be the best shot with the bow and arrow in all Norway, came up to Ivar and said to him: " Let us try our skill. Thou art younger than I, but I hear thou art very skilful with the bow."

Upon this, Ulf took a spear, and put its point into the ground; then he placed an arrow on the string, and shot into the air; the arrow turned itself in its course, came down with its point in the end of the spear-shaft, and stood there upright. Ivar next took an arrow and shot. It went very high, then the arrow-point came down into the shaft of the arrow of Ulf, that had stuck on the shaft of the spear. Then Ulf took a spear, and threw it so powerfully and so far, and nevertheless so straight, that all wondered. But Ivar threw still farther than all, so that his spear socket lay on the point of Ulf's spear. Ulf took the spear again, and shot another time, and the spear went beyond that of Ivar's.

" I will not throw any more, for I see it is useless," said Ivar.

" Throw," said Ulf, " and farther if thou canst."

Ivar threw, and this time far ahead. After this, Ulf placed an arrow on the bow-string, and took a knife and stuck it into an oak. He then shot into the back of the knife-handle, so that the

arrow stuck fast. Ivar next took up his arrows,
while Ulf stood near him and said : "With gold
are thy arrows wound round, and a very ambitious
man art thou."

"I did not cause these arrows to be made;
they were given to me, and I have not taken any
ornaments off them," returned Ivar, shooting, and
hitting the knife-handle, and splitting it, the arrow-
point sticking in the upper point of the blade.

"Now we will shoot farther," said Ulf. Then
he laid an arrow on the string, and drew the bow so
as to almost bend its tips together. The arrow flew
very far, and stopped in a very slender bough at
which he had aimed. Every one thought this a
most excellent shot; but Ivar shot still a little
farther, and, besides, his arrow pierced a nut that
had been put up as a target. All present wondered at this.

"Now the nut shall be taken and placed on the
head of Björn," said Ulf, "and there thou shalt try
if thou canst hit it, if thou art willing to do so.
Thou shalt not shoot from a shorter distance than
before. Björn is my slave, and for his boldness
and willingness I will give him his freedom after the
trial, if his life is spared."

Björn was delighted and willing to risk his life
for his freedom, for where is the man that does
not love to be free?

"Wilt thou stand still and not shrink, if I shoot
at the nut?" asked Ivar.

"Certainly," said Björn, who had witnessed the

skill of Ivar, and therefore had great confidence in
his aim.

"Then Ulf shall stand at thy side," replied Ivar,
" and see if I hit the nut."

Ulf assented, and Ivar made ready and took aim.
The arrow flew swiftly, and skipped over the
crown of Björn's head and under the nut, and
Björn was not wounded.   The nut rolled backward
from his head, but the arrow went much farther.

When Yngvi asked if the shot had hit the
nut, Ulf replied: "Better than hit; for he shot
under the nut, and it rolled down, and he harmed
not Björn."

This extraordinary feat of Ivar was greatly
applauded, and by none more than by Randalin.
Björn the slave was made free.

After this, Ivar took his sword, and handled it
equally well with the right and the left hand, and
moved it so swiftly that it seemed as if there were
three swords in the air at a time.   Then he threw
his sword high up, caught it with his left hand, having the shield in his right hand, and dealt a terrific
blow upon a shield which a man held for the purpose, before the people could see what he was
about to do.   The enthusiasm of Randalin was
unbounded when she saw the great skill of Ivar.

Then came the leaping games.   Many leaped
as well backward as forward, more than their
height, in full war apparel, and the championship
was undecided when Ivar came forward in full

war dress, with helmet, chain-armor, sword, and
shield, and leaped far above his height, which was
nearly six feet, and then leaped backward quite
as high as he had done forward. This feat was
cheered tumultuously, and all agreed that to Ivar
should be awarded the championship.

On the last day of the games, the twelve sons of
the powerful and famous berserk Hervard appeared
on the scene of the contest for the championship in
swimming. Thorgrim was the eldest; the second,
Gisli; the third, Bui; the fourth, Seming; the
fifth, Hadding; the sixth, Thorolf; the seventh,
Brani; the eighth, Angantyr; the ninth, Ketil;
the tenth, Grim; the eleventh, Barri; the twelfth,
Asbjörn. All these brothers were equal in
strength and skill, with the exception of Thorgrim, who was much the strongest; they were
all great berserks, and had inherited all the warlike
qualities of their father and kin, and most of them
had also the same temper. They had all gone
into battle before they were fifteen years old, and
since had ravaged far and wide, and had met no
equal in strength and courage. They had won
great renown, for never did they engage in battle
without gaining the victory. These twelve brothers
always went together in one ship, with no other
champion on board, but often they had a great following of ships and men. Their father, who had
been a very great warrior, had given them many excellent swords, which he had taken in war. Thor-

grim had the sword Mistletoe, Gisli the sword
Thegn, Bui the sword Rangvid, and all the other
brothers had swords equally good and celebrated
among Vikings; besides these, they had other
excellent duelling swords. They went on warlike
expeditions during the summer, but during the
winter they remained at home with their father.

It happened that the preceding Yule all these
brothers were at home, and on the evening that
the men were to make vows over the horn of
Bragi, they came into the hall of their father, and
after many vows had been made, they made theirs.
Bui made the vow that he would marry Astrid, the
eldest daughter of Yngvi, the Hersir of Svithjod,
and never allow any one to possess her in case
her father or herself should refuse him. His
eleven brothers vowed that they would stand by
him.

They had come to take part in the games, and
to win championships, after which they intended
to ask for the hand of Astrid, at the feast which
was always given at the conclusion of the games.

The brothers had noticed with no little jealousy
that Astrid and Hjalmar seemed to love each
other, but no one knew of their errand, for they
had kept it secret. They had resolved to try to
drown Hjalmar in the swimming contests.

Yngvi and all high-born women and men of the
land were present when the swimming began.
Among the most remarkable swimmers was a man
of the name of Olvir, who went to Ivar and said

to him: "What thinkest thou of our having a swimming match?"

"I think well of it," replied Ivar, "for I am told that thou and I are about equal as swimmers."

Ivar and Olvir swam off, and played a long time with each other, alternately dragging each other down, and finally they were so long under water that the spectators did not expect them ever to come up again. But at last Olvir rose and swam ashore. He went up and rested himself, but did not dress. No one knew or dared to ask what had become of Ivar. But after a still longer time, he too appeared above the surface. He had caught a very large seal, and sat on its back. He clung to it with both hands by its bristles, and thus steered it, and when he came near the shore let it go.

"Why didst not thou kill the seal with the knife thou didst carry in thy belt?" asked many people.

"Because," answered Ivar, "if I had done so, Olvir, or those who witnessed our contest, would have said that I had found it dead."

Though Olvir had been the first to come ashore, while Ivar had taken time to capture the seal, it was decided by the umpires that the best swimmer of the two was Ivar, to the great satisfaction of all the maidens and women that were present, and of all his male friends as well; but none was as pleased as Randalin.

Then came the contest in swimming clad in full war dress. Not many dared to try this contest. Hjalmar took his helmet, chain-armor, and sword, wrapped them in his cloak, making a bundle of them, which he tied on his back. Then he broke off his spear handle and threw it far off into the water, and swam towards the broken handle. He caught it, then swam farther, to an island far away. No one swam as far as he, so he won the championship that morning, to the great delight of Astrid.

After the day's meal and the drinking hour were over, Thorgrim, the eldest son of Hervard, called his brothers, and they went down to the shore ; and Thorgrim said to Gisli : " I trust to thee to drown Hjalmar while competing with him to-day."

Gisli answered that it would be difficult to do so, and then Thorgrim asked Bui to undertake it. Bui replied that he was doubtful of success, but consented to try. Then Bui went to challenge Hjalmar, and Hjalmar accepted, saying to himself: " Now I need not spare myself, as I should like better to contend with him than with any other of these berserks."

Bui asked if they should try a long swimming match.

"We may do so," replied Hjalmar, "as thou mayest have the better of it in the other modes of swimming."

When they had been swimming for a long time,

Bui seemed anxious to go back, but Hjalmar kept on. Bui swam somewhat more slowly, and asked, shortly after: "Art thou to swim longer?"

"I think thou wilt be able to swim alone towards the shore," replied Hjalmar. "I will swim farther."

"Very well," said Bui, "I will risk going back;" and he turned, but had not gone far before he became exhausted. Hjalmar swam to him, and asked how it went with him, but Bui's pride prevented him from acknowledging his weakness, and he told him he might go his way.

Hjalmar replied: "I think thou deservest that we both go together, for I do not want thee to be drowned. Lay thy hands on my back, and thus support thyself;" and in this way they came to land.

Bui walked up the bank, but had become quite exhausted. Hjalmar sat down upon a boulder at the mark of high water. Thorgrim asked his brother how he felt. Bui answered, "I should not be able to tell if Hjalmar had not been a good and generous man."

"Now Ketil," said Thorgrim, unmoved by hearing of this chivalrous conduct, "thou shalt try to drown Hjalmar."

"I will not try," answered his brother, "for it seems to me that Bui, who has tried the swimming, has won little glory, and that all the fame of the contest has gone to Hjalmar."

Then Thorgrim himself challenged Hjalmar, and threw off his clothes. Hjalmar rose from his stone, and went into the water with Thorgrim,

17

and as soon as they met, Thorgrim thrust him
down into the deep. No one on shore could see
what they were doing, for they were both far under
water, though the sea boiled above them. After a
while it became quiet, and Thorgrim swam ashore.

Ivar and his two other foster-brothers began to
feel very anxious, as Hjalmar was not seen any
more. They thought Thorgrim had drowned him,
and they swore to avenge him. Astrid fainted
on her seat, and there was great sorrow among
the women, maidens, and men that had seen the
contest, and many friends mourned the death of
Hjalmar, who they thought had surely gone to
the hall of Ran without being prepared to appear
there as befitted his rank.

There was little merriment over the beer in the
hall that evening. Yngvi was overcome with
anger, for if Thorgrim had drowned Hjalmar by
hurting him, it was murder; but Thorgrim declared that if Hjalmar was drowned, it was from
exhaustion, and he was ready to take his oath on
the temple ring that he was innocent of any foul
deed. Lights were kindled, and the second high
seat reserved for Hjalmar was empty. Suddenly
the door of the hall opened. Hjalmar entered,
greeted by great shouts of joy, and, advancing
towards the seat of Thorgrim, he placed on his
knee the knife Thorgrim had worn in his belt
when swimming; then everybody knew that Thorgrim had carried a knife, which Hjalmar had taken
from him, and yet had spared his life.

Hjalmar had swum under water for a while, and landed the other side of a small island, where nobody could see him from the shore. After a time, hearing the good news of Hjalmar's safety, Astrid entered the hall, followed by her sisters and girl friends, with a golden horn in her hand. She paused before Hjalmar and said : "Hail to thee, noble Hjalmar ! thrice hail to thee on account of the danger thou hast escaped!" and then seated herself by his side, and with a frowning look eyed the twelve sons of Hervard. These were more angry than ever against Hjalmar, and bore him no good will, but nothing could be seen of this in their countenances.

The hall became full of clatter and cheer ; the beer was drunk freely. All felt happy that Hjalmar had not lost his life ; the only unhappy ones were the twelve brothers, who, nevertheless, tried to appear merry.

CHAPTER XXVII

THE FOSTER-BROTHERS FALL IN LOVE

THE meeting of so many people at the games played havoc with the hearts of many a maiden and many a warrior who had come to Upsalir. Tales of love had been whispered in the ears of many trusting and confiding Viking daughters, and many had sworn to love each other until death. Vikings who lived far away, or in distant lands, had promised to come with their ships and visit the fair ones who had inspired them with admiration and love. Of course, they were coming to see their fathers and mothers, or their kinsmen, with whom they had become friends. These brave warriors and doughty champions deluded themselves, as men often do on such occasions, with the idea that the people would not understand that their object in coming was to see the daughters, instead of their fathers, mothers, or kinsmen. It is true that some men had become fast friends, and had sworn foster-brotherhood to each other during the games.

The time was near at hand when the lovers were to part; sleepless nights told of the anguish many felt at the thought of going away; and no won-

der, for how many had felt love budding for the
first time. What delightful days had just been
passed! What new friends many had made!
How many old friendships had been renewed!
How many beloved faces had been seen again,
after years of separation! How many slumbering
loves had awakened!

But the games were also to leave many heart-
burnings. There had been broken friendships
between men or women who had been fast friends
before; for, if there is one thing in the world
that the friendship of two men cannot support,
even if they are brothers, it is for both to love
the same woman; and it is the same with two
women, even if they are sisters, who love the
the same man. Envy and hatred are sure to follow, for love cannot be shared. Many had also
taken an oath beforehand that they would marry
such or such a girl, or challenge their successful
rival to mortal combat; and many a duel was to
take place on that account, for it had happened
that the maidens they admired had not always
reciprocated their feelings, and, indeed, loved
some one else better.

One evening the foster-brothers did not go to
the hall, and were together in their house, and
for quite a while had not uttered a single word,
when suddenly the silence was broken by Sigurd,
who said to Ivar: " Foster-brother, thou seemest
to be in a meditative mood. What dost thou
think on?"

"I was thinking," replied Ivar, "of love." And he continued: "Love was born in the beginning of all things, and came with the world. Atoms kissed atoms, and were made one. The pollen of a flower wanders in the air, over sea and land, to kiss another flower, and say ' I love thee.' The sea kisses the shore; the moon and the stars kiss the night; the breezes, the water and the land; the sun, the earth; the dawn, the day; the twilight, the night; the heat, the cold; the dew, the flowers, the meadows, and the woods; the rain kisses all life. Men and women were born out of love, and both wander in the world until they meet their mates, for love is part of their own being. Life without love might as well never have existed."

"Yes," exclaimed Hjalmar, "to us men, woman is the incarnation of love, of all that is sweet and beautiful in life. To us she is the most sublime conception of the creative power of the gods." He was thinking of Astrid when he uttered these sentiments. "We forget Odin for the woman we love; for her we would give our last drop of blood. We would die before her eyes that she might see our manliness and bravery, and learn that we are worthy of her love."

Then, with great animation, he exclaimed: "O Love, embrace me with thy giant's strength, and stay with me until my life ebbs away! Bring thy vivifying breath close to my lips, until thou becomest part of my own being, for I care not to live without thee. When Mother Earth, who has fed me and loved me so tenderly, folds me within her embrace, and hides from me forever the light of the sun and of this beautiful world which I have loved so much, O Love, envelop me with thy immortality!"

"Thou must surely be in love," exclaimed the three foster-brothers, "to utter the sentiments thou hast just expressed."

"The fact is," said Sigurd, "that love is lurking in the heart of you all, my foster-brothers."

"That is true," they shouted with one voice, and began to exchange confidences.

Ivar spoke first, and declared that he loved Randalin, Yngvi's second daughter, to distraction. "When she speaks," he added, "her voice sounds to me as the softest tones of the harp; from her lips come the scented perfume of the roses of the Caspian, or of the flowers of our own land."

Then, in a fit of enthusiasm, he said, with great earnestness: "Foster-brothers, I tell you that honey is sour compared with the sweetness of Randalin." A merry laugh of approbation greeted Ivar's last sentence.

Then Hjalmar said: "Foster-brothers, I love Astrid, the eldest daughter of the Hersir of Svithjod, and the goddess Sjofn has turned her mind and mine to mutual love, and I have taken an oath that no one shall marry her unless I fall by his hand."

"We will stand by thee, Hjalmar!" shouted again all the foster-brothers.

Sigmund declared that he loved Solveig the Fair, so called on account of her beauty. Solveig was very retiring and bashful, but her dignified manner and charms had not escaped Sigmund. She was the daughter of Björn Hersir, who ruled over a large herad, and resided at Gaular, close by the temple. The foster-brothers had met her there at an autumn sacrifice at which they were present, and at that time Sigmund fell in love with her; and now that they had met again at Upsalir, he was more desperately in love than ever.

"I knew," said Ivar, addressing himself to Hjalmar, "that thou wast in love with Astrid, and that she loved thee, for in a hundred ways that passed unnoticed to others, I saw that she showed her preference for thee over all her other suitors. The ancient saying proves true," he added: "'The eyes cannot hide it if a woman loves a man, or if a man loves a woman.'"

Hjalmar replied: "Ivar, I can say the same thing of thee. We, thy three foster-brothers, saw how much thou and Randalin were in love with each other. As for thee, Sigmund," said he, laughing, "this saying proves true in regard to thee: Many a man acts strangely when in love, but blame not man for that, blame love instead."

"Dear Sigurd," said all the foster-brothers at once, "thou hast said nothing to us yet about the maiden thou lovest; and thou art our elder, and we know that no one has a greater admiration and regard for women than thou hast, nor loves their society more than thou dost."

" I have wandered, as you know, more than any of you," returned Sigurd, " in our and many other lands, and have not yet seen the maiden of my destiny. I have never met her whom I wanted to marry. Once or twice in my life, if nothing had happened to prevent me from meeting again the maiden I had begun to love, I should have probably been married to-day; but the Nornir have not shaped my life thus far for me to be passionately in love. We must wait for time and for their decrees."

After hearing his words, the foster-brothers said: " Sigurd, marry; for thou art the only one left of thy kin. And it is not wise for a man to die and leave no scion to inherit his virtues and his fame."

After this talk, each foster-brother went his own way, and Ivar, without taking notice of it, walked unconsciously towards the bower of Randalin, and saw her coming towards him on her way to the house of her father. A thrill of joy ran through him as he perceived her. She turned pale and red alternately at seeing him; she was ready to sink to the ground. An indescribable feeling told her that Ivar was about to propose to her. The bondwoman that followed her fell back, and Ivar and she walked on together.

After a little pause, Ivar said to her : " Thou

knowest, Randalin, that the goddess Var listens to the oaths of men, and to the private engagements which men and women make between themselves in regard to love, and punishes those who break them. I want her to hear me to-day, and to listen to what thou hast to say to me." Then, looking at her intently, he continued : " Rememberest thou, fairest of maidens, the day when we met for the first time ?"

"Yes," replied the daughter of Yngvi. "I remember it as if it were to-day."

" Canst thou recollect," continued Ivar, " how we looked at each other as soon as we met, and how our eyes seemed to melt into each other's ? At that time an indescribable feeling seized me ; thou didst seem to entrance me. I felt as I never felt before in my life. I loved thee, and I thought that thou also didst love me ; and when thou didst continue thy way, my eyes were riveted upon thy fair form, and I remember that before thou didst disappear thou didst turn thy head once more towards me, as if some magic impulse compelled thee to do so, and told thee that I was still spellbound at thy sight. We gave to each other a farewell look, as if to say, ' Yes, we will meet again.' "

" I remember all that well," said Randalin, for her honest heart could not deny it.

" Since then," said Ivar, " I have thought of thee by day, and often dreamt of thee by night ; and now I feel that before I return to Dampstadir

I must tell thee of my love, and ask thee if thou wilt give me thy heart and marry me. If thou sayest no, life then will have no more charm for me; the clatter of weapons on the field of battle will no more sound pleasantly in my ears; ambition for renowned deeds will never stir me more; I feel that without thee I could not live."

Randalin's feelings, as she heard the burning words from Ivar's lips, were such that she could not speak. Taking his hands, and looking with her beautiful blue eyes into his face, she said: "Ivar, thy wife I will be, and no other man shall ever possess me."

In the evening the foster-brothers met, as was their custom, to talk matters over before they went to the banqueting-hall to drink with the high-born men and champions of the land. All agreed that they should ask the parents of the young girls for their consent to the different marriages, for the laws regarding marriage were very strict, and there was nothing in the world in which Vikings were more particular, or more revengeful, if the honor of one of their kinswomen was attacked.

CHAPTER XXVIII

BETROTHAL OF IVAR AND RANDALIN

THE next morning Ivar went to see two of his uncles, Randvir, a brother of his mother, and Visbur, a brother of his father, who had come to Upsalir with him, and said to them: "Kinsmen, I desire you to ask for me in marriage Randalin, the second daughter of Yngvi, the Hersir of Svithjod."

"Well done, Ivar," said his two uncles with one voice. "Thou art wise in thy choice, for Randalin is beautiful, and most accomplished in all that pertains to woman, and will be a wife worthy of thee; she is one of the greatest matches in the Northern lands, and we hope sincerely that both her father and herself will consent to your union."

"I have told Randalin how much I loved her, and she has said that no one shall ever marry her but me," replied Ivar.

The same afternoon the two uncles of Ivar went to Yngvi, and said to him: "Kinsman, we have to talk to thee on a very important matter," and then explained their errand. Visbur was the spokesman, and said: "We are allied to thee by blood and kinship, and we wish furthermore to cement more closely our friendship, so we have

come to ask the hand of thy second daughter,
Randalin, for Ivar. Thy daughter is high-born,
and of all the pedigrees of the Upsalir families,
hers is the highest, for she is descended in direct
line from the gods themselves. We wish, if it is
thy pleasure, that Ivar should be thy son-in-law."

After a pause, in order to allow Yngvi to reflect
upon his proposals, Visbur continued : " Ivar is
valiant, has been in many battles, has travelled far
and wide, and is, we think, very wise for his age.
More than all this, Ivar loves thy daughter Randalin, and we think it will be a happy union for
both our families, and will cement the friendship
that exists between Gotland and Svithjod."

Yngvi received their request favorably, and replied : " I know that there will be no disparity in
the match, for both Ivar and Randalin are of
Odin's kin ; Ivar is a renowned warrior, and rules
over one of the powerful realms of the North.
There is no obstacle to their marriage, for though
they are related by blood, it is only in the fifth
degree, and this is the degree in which marriage
is allowed between kinsmen and kinswomen. This
is one of our wisest laws, which has been adhered
to by us Norsemen from the most ancient times ;
by this we prevent the degeneration of our race."

" But," continued Yngvi, " Randalin is wise, and
I will not betroth her to any one without her consent. Besides, she is of age, according to law, since
she is over fifteen ; and as she owns entailed lands
in her own right, she can betroth herself to whom

she likes, though it would be very unwise for her to do so without my consent. But before I speak to her on the subject, we must find that we are of one mind in regard to the conditions of the marriage concerning property. You are aware that Randalin has, even to-day, a great deal of property in her own right, and that she owns a third of her mother's inheritance, which includes many large landed estates, and that in the course of time a great deal of wealth is to come to her. Marriage is a civil contract, owing to the relation which man and wife hold towards each other in regard to property. Let us see what will be 'the dowry,' or 'home following,' and the 'counter dowry'; if we agree on these points, I see not what should prevent the marriage if Randalin is willing. Her brothers are waging war in the Mediterranean, and they will be delighted to hear of their sister's marriage with their comrade and remote kinsman, Ivar Hjorvardson."

Then he added : " According to the laws of our land, a woman has to be provided with a dowry, otherwise her children are not 'inheritance born,' and no marriage is valid without dowry ; and that dowry, and the counter dowry which we give her, belong to her for life, and afterwards to her children, or to whomsoever she wills them, and her husband must not touch them. If she dies childless, her estates go back to her kinsmen, but the dowry is then returned to her husband ; and she is entitled to a third of the property, both personal and real, earned by her husband during their married life."

"Thou speakest fairly," said the uncles. "Ivar will give as dowry to Randalin the estates of Bjolstad, of Lis, of Hof, and five hundred marks of gold."

"This dowry is acceptable to me," answered the Hersir of Svithjod.

"What counter dowry wilt thou give to Randalin?" inquired the uncles of Ivar.

"I will give her," replied Yngvi, "the large estate of Rodelsvellir and five hundred marks of gold."

"This is generous on thy part," said Visbur and Randvir. "We will not discuss the trousseau which Ivar ought to give Randalin, for we know him to be most generous, and proud of his rank and dignity, and that he wishes Randalin to have such an outfit as becometh the daughter of the Hersir of Svithjod."

Randalin was sent for, and Yngvi said to her: "I have a marriage to propose to thee, my daughter, which I think will suit thee well. I did not wish to betroth thee without thy consent. What thinkest thou of marrying Ivar Hjorvardson, the Hersir of Gotland? No better union couldst thou form in all the Northern lands."

Randalin replied: "Father, no one could better please me, and the goddess Var has listened to the vows made between us, for Ivar and I love each other."

Then Ivar was summoned to the conference, and Yngvi addressed him thus: "I would not give my daughter to thee, Ivar, if I did not like thee; and I would rather have thee than any of the other men in our Northern lands marry Randalin, for I consider thee the foremost in mind, courage, and daring." Ivar thanked Yngvi for his kind words and for his consent to his marriage with Randalin.

After all the conditions were agreed to, each side called six men of high rank, and the agreement of the marriage was recited before them, as the law required, and they stood as witnesses of the contract.

It was agreed that the betrothal should not be for more than twelve months, unless unforeseen circumstances occurred.

Yngvi then said to Randalin: "I betroth thee according to law, as thy father and guardian. It is a complete betrothal."

Then Ivar advanced toward Yngvi, who declared Ivar betrothed to Randalin, his daughter, and then they named witnesses to their betrothal.

Randalin next came forward and said: "Thou, Ivar, in presence of these witnesses, hast betrothed thyself to me lawfully; give me the counter dowry, and clasp my hand as the fulfilment and performance of the whole agreement, which a little while ago was recited before us without fraud or trick. This will be a complete and lawful match."

"According to law," said Ivar, "we name

witnesses, Randalin, that thou hast betrothed thyself to me, Ivar Hjorvardson, lawfully.   I give thee
the counter dowry, with handshaking to seal the
agreement, as the fulfilment and performance of
the whole contract, which was but just now recited
between us."

Then, laughingly, one of the uncles of Ivar said
to him: "Thou knowest, Ivar, that the breaking
of a betrothal by either party is punished, and
whichever party breaks it forfeits the dowry promised."

"No fear of this," exclaimed Ivar and Randalin
at the same time, as they stood side by side.

Then said Yngvi, addressing Ivar, "Randalin
has no faults or blemishes on her person.   If thou
findest faults or blemishes in her which I have not
told thee of, it is because I do not know them.
Her mother, as thou knowest, is dead, and she is
the one that could tell.   Randalin herself says
she has no blemish.   If she has, thou canst refuse
to marry her ; and if thou canst prove that I knew
it, thou mayest claim the dowry according to law."

They all separated, very happy, and when Yngvi
was alone with his daughter, after the kinsmen of
Ivar had departed, he said to her: "Daughter,
thou thinkest that Ivar is perfection.   A short
time after thou art married to him, thou wilt find
that he has faults, and thou wilt perhaps regret
that thou didst not marry Thorstein, who, like
Ivar, loved thee, and who aspired silently to thy
hand ; but I assure thee that if thou hadst married

Thorstein, thou wouldst also find fault in him, for there is no man, no matter how good and brave he is, that is without a fault. So be satisfied, though thou mayst find some fault in Ivar, and though the ideal thou hadst of thy lover before thou hadst known him well and lived with him is broken. Many dreams of youth vanish in life. The Nornir are wise, and none of us knows his fate beforehand."

The following morning Ivar, accompanied by several of the highest-born men of Gotland, and followed by the kinsmen of Hjalmar, went to Yngvi and explained their errand, which was to ask Astrid in marriage for Hjalmar.

The Hersir of Svithjod listened to them, and said: "It was my intention to betroth my daughter to another man, for I did not know that Hjalmar and Astrid loved each other. I think much of Hjalmar, for he is valiant, and is one of my land defenders, and I think the marriage a good one, as his family is also descended from Odin."

The conditions of the marriage and the length of the betrothal were then agreed upon before witnesses. Sigmund was also betrothed in the same way, and for the same length of time, to Solveig, leaving Sigurd the only one of the four foster-brothers with free heart and hand.

CHAPTER XXIX

Two days after the termination of the games, a great feast was given by Yngvi to all his kinsmen, and all the high-born men and women who had come to Upsalir to witness the contests. The three large festive halls were filled with guests, and many lots were drawn among warriors for seats, there were so many men of equal rank and dignity. At this feast the announcement of the betrothal of Ivar and Randalin, and of Hjalmar and Astrid, was made by Yngvi, their father; and that of Solveig to Sigmund, by Bjorn, her father.

All the Hersirs and many of the high-born men and women were invited to the wedding of Ivar and Randalin, which was to take place first.

When Bui heard that Astrid had been betrothed to Hjalmar, he remembered the vow he had made the preceding Yule. Accordingly, when the feast was at its height, and while Astrid was seated by the side of her father, Bui entered the hall and advanced to Yngvi's side, told the vow he had made the preceding Yule in regard to Astrid,

and explained that his errand to Upsalir was to
ask her in marriage. In a loud voice, and looking defiantly towards Hjalmar, he said that he
requested an answer on the instant. A profound silence had succeeded the chatter of voices,
and all waited to hear the reply of the Hersir
of Svithjod; but, before he could answer, Hjalmar stepped forward, and said: "My mind has
always been bent upon marrying Astrid. Remember, my lord, how I have defended your
realm and increased your possessions in far-off
lands. You have betrothed your daughter Astrid
to me, and I know not why this man should come
to ask her hand, when he knows that she is betrothed to me. I also have made a vow upon the
altar ring that I will marry Astrid, and allow no
one else to possess her. Besides," he added, hotly,
" I think the land will be better off if it gets rid
of these twelve brothers."

The Hersir of Svithjod, after hearing these two
men, turned towards Astrid, and said to her:
" What sayest thou ? "

Astrid replied: " I am betrothed to Hjalmar,
and I love him. I love Hjalmar, and I will never
marry any one else but him, for he is good and
brave. I have heard but evil reports of Bui and
all his brothers. Besides, our Fylkja has appeared
to me in a dream, and told me to beware of the
twelve sons of Hervard."

When Bui had heard her words, he challenged
Hjalmar to a duel, and said, in presence of all the

guests, that he would be called a "nithing" by
every man, if he married Astrid without accepting
the challenge. As it was considered cowardly not
to accept a challenge, Hjalmar said scornfully, that
he was quite ready to accept his defiance; and the
time of the duel was appointed, and the island of
Samsey was fixed on as the spot where it was to
take place.

This challenge had hardly been given, when a
great Hersir and mighty champion named Ketil
rose up before Yngvi, and said: "I have just
arrived at Upsalir, and the games are ended; contrary winds have followed me all the way, so I
have not been able to take part in the contests.
I am much disappointed, for I wanted to win several championships, and have trials of strength
and agility with Ivar, before the eyes of Randalin,
thy daughter. I have made a vow that I will
marry Randalin, and that no one else shall marry
her before stepping over my dead body. Whoever
is wooing her must fight a duel with me. I challenge Ivar to a duel, to take place at Arhaug
on the first day of Yule," and he shouted so loud
that everybody in the hall heard him: "Thou,
Ivar, shalt be every man's nithing, if thou comest
not to the duel!" Ivar at once accepted the challenge as Hjalmar had done.

At Arhaug, Ketil and his men sacrificed. He
practised witchcraft much, and the people believed that no weapons could pierce his chain-
armor or hurt him. He only made sacrifices to

the sun and to his guardian spirits, for he did not believe in Odin nor in the other gods.

After the feast was over, Ivar and his foster-brothers left Svithjod, together with all who had come to the games, all having received valuable gifts.

The sons of Hervard had gone, immediately after the challenge of Bui to Hjalmar, not in the best of moods, on account of the failure of their mission in regard to Astrid. They went home and told their father of the result of their errand and of the challenge of Bui to Hjalmar.

Hervard answered: " Never have I been so anxious about you before now. Nowhere do I know of men equally brave and so skilled in the handling of weapons as Ivar and his foster-brothers Hjalmar, Sigurd, and Sigmund."

They talked no more of the matter that evening, but the anxious brow of Hervard told of his anxiety in regard to the duel, and how much he feared for the lives of his sons.

After the departure of Hjalmar, Astrid became very sad. Her sumptuous home seemed to have no charm for her, and she could think of nothing but the duel which was to take place between Hjalmar and Bui. One evening as her father was all alone, he saw her come into the hall with a face so pale that he called her to his side. She responded with a smile, trying to hide her feelings, for she did not wish him to notice how sad she was.

"Come sit by me, daughter," said he, in a tender and sympathetic voice.

After seating herself by her father's side, Astrid laid her head on his breast and remained silent, hiding her face in the folds of her cloak. Yngvi took her hands in his; they were hot and feverish, and, as he petted her, he asked her, not knowing what was the trouble, if the marriage that had been arranged between her and Hjalmar was not to her liking, and if she regretted her betrothal. Sobs were the only answer he got; but when she had relieved her overburdened breast in copious tears, and had recovered sufficiently, she replied: "Father, I am pleased, and I would marry no one but Hjalmar; but, I do not know why, I think I shall never see him again alive."

"Why so?" said Yngvi.

"I had a dream before the games," replied Astrid, "in which our Fylkja appeared and forewarned me of Hjalmar's danger, and told me that the twelve eagles I saw in a preceding dream were the twelve sons of Hervard, and that these would cause me great sorrow; and afterwards she called me towards her, and said: 'Follow me.' I think this forebode the death of Hjalmar and, perhaps, mine. The decrees of the Nornir must be fulfilled, and none of us know what they are."

Yngvi did his best to cheer his daughter, and tried to persuade her that her dream was not deserving of so sinister an interpretation, but it was difficult to comfort her. Randalin, too, was anxious about the result of the duel between Ivar and Ketil.

Nevertheless there was no way of preventing these duels, and the time for that between Ivar and Ketil soon arrived. Ivar made ready two ships, and asked many doughty champions to follow him. He had sent word to Svithjod, to men of high renown to meet him at Arhaug to witness the duel, so they might tell on their return to Upsalir of his victory, or that he died with honor and valor. He sailed for Arhaug, the appointed place, and arrived there three days before the time with his foster-brothers. On his arrival, Bodmod, the son of Ketil, invited him to his hall, and there he and his men were entertained with great splendor. In the course of conversation, Ivar mentioned the name of Odin. At the mention of Odin, Bodmod became angry and sang: " Odin I have never worshipped, though I have lived long. I know that the head of Ivar will fall sooner than mine or that of my father."

But Ivar sang in answer: " I love Odin and all the gods, and sacrifice to them, and I know that Odin loves me."

On the day appointed for the duel, Ivar and his foster-brothers took a boat, and rowed to a small island where the conflict was to take place. Ketil was there already, waiting for Ivar.'

A great crowd had assembled on the shore of the mainland to witness the contest, or ordeal, between these two famous champions, for the people believed that the judgments of the gods were decided in this way.

"What kind of duel dost thou wish us to have," asked Ketil of Ivar, "the Holmganga or the Einvigi? Thou art the challenged man, and thou hast the right to choose which of the two thou wilt have."

Ivar answered: "I choose the Holmganga, for there is more honor and fame in this than in the other; and when I left Gotland for Upsalir, to participate in the games, it was to win more fame than I had before. There are two alternatives before me: the one, to get bravely the victory in fighting against thee; the other, to fall with valor; and that is better than to live with shame and dishonor."

"But," said Ketil, "why dost thou choose the Holmganga instead of the Einvigi? Thou art young and inexperienced, and in the Holmganga there are difficult rules, but none in the Einvigi."

Ivar answered: "I shall not fight better in the Einvigi, and I will risk the Holmganga, and in all be on equal footing with thee. Though much younger than thyself, and of less experience, I am not afraid of the Holmganga rules. I have handled the sword many a time, though I have never done so in a duel. My foster-father taught me well its use, and the rules of duelling also."

Then the laws of the Holmganga were recited by Sigurd, this being obligatory before a duel took place.

"This is," said he, "the Holmganga law: The

cloak must be ten feet from one end to the other, with loops in the corners, and in these pegs must be put down. The one who makes the preparations must go towards the pegs, hold his ear-lobes, and, bending over, stand with his feet apart, seeing the sky between them. Three squares, each one foot wide, must be marked around the cloak. Outside the squares must be placed four poles, called hazel poles. The place is called a hazelled field when it is prepared thus. Each man must have three shields, and when these are made useless he must stand upon the cloak, and thereafter defend himself with his weapons. He who has been challenged is to strike first. If one is wounded so that the blood falls upon the cloak, he is not obliged to fight any longer. If either steps with one of his feet outside the boundary, it is held that he has retreated ; and if he steps outside with both feet, he is held to have fled, and is accounted vanquished.

" Have you, Ketil and Ivar, taken heed of the Holmganga law which I have just recited to you ? " asked Sigurd in conclusion.

" Thou hast recited well and correctly the laws of the Holmganga, Sigurd," replied Ivar.

As customary in the Holmganga, one man held the shield before each of the combatants. The one who received most wounds was to pay an indemnity for being released from the fight, for it was the law of the Holmganga that if he who challenged another man, in order to get something, gained

the victory, he should have the prize for which
he had challenged; if he was defeated, he should
release himself with as much property as had been
agreed upon; if he fell, he should forfeit all his
property, and he who killed him was to take all
the inheritance.

It was the custom of duellists not to draw their
swords on the place of the Holmganga, but let
the sword hang on the arm, so that it should be
ready at once, when wanted.   At the outset Ketil
said to Ivar: " It seems to me that the sword
that thou carriest is longer than the laws of the
Holmganga allow."

" Thou canst measure my sword," replied Ivar,
" and thou wilt find that it is of the proper length,
and according to the regulation."

Then Ivar said to Hjalmar: " Foster-brother,
thou must hold the shield before me."

Hjalmar replied : " I have done that for no one
before, my beloved foster-brother.   Rather ask
me to go into Holmganga against Ketil, for I am
afraid thou riskest too much.   I do not want to
part from thee, and hope the Nornir have fated us
to die the same day."

Ivar thanked his foster-brother, but said that
what he asked could not be granted.

Hjalmar answered: " In case of thy death,
none of us would go back unless thou art avenged,
for we foster-brothers have sworn to avenge each
other's death "

Then he advanced towards Ivar, and took the

three shields that he was to hold before him, and
handed two of them to Sigurd and Sigmund;
then he said to Ivar : " Foster-brother, let us hope
that victory will be thine ; but thou hast to fight
against one of the greatest champions of our land,
a man very skilled in the handling of the sword
and of the sax."

" Now it is better to stand by one's word, and
not to be the first to ask for peace," Ketil
said.

"Thou art right," replied Ivar. Then he sang:
" Lovely maid of Svithjod, to-day I fight for thee;
I will come to thee victorious, Randalin ; to-day
Ketil will die."

Ketil began to shout fiercely, and the berserk
frenzy came upon him. He bit the rim of his
shield, and looked like a wild beast; foam came
from his mouth, but after a while he became himself again.

Ivar and Ketil, after shaking hands, went inside
the boundaries of the duelling place, and placed
themselves on the squares that were marked on
the cloak.

First Ivar sang: " Thou, Ketil, wilt to-day lodge
with Odin."

And Ketil sang back : "I do not put my trust
in Odin, but before night thou, Ivar, wilt be among
the dead."

Hjalmar held the shield of Ivar, and Bodmod
that of Ketil, his father. Ivar had the sword
Hrotti, and when it struck Ketil's shield, it was as

if lightning came from it. Ketil, seeing the sparks, said: "I should not have fought against thee if I had known that thou hadst Hrotti with thee. It is most likely, as my father said, that we brothers are to be short-lived, except the one of us who is named after him."

Heedless of this complaint, Ivar struck at Ketil's shield, and dealt blow after blow so quickly, that Ketil could not strike him, having to shelter himself behind his shield-bearer; then Ivar drew back to get room to wield his sword and aim a blow at Ketil, but Ketil was too quick for him, and Ivar's shield was cut asunder. New shields were provided, and these were equally cut to pieces. Each side had now spoiled two shields, both combatants had only one shield left, and the fight was to be decisive.

Then followed the fiercest of combats. Ketil sang: "There is courage in Ketil. My sword Hviting is sharp; it will belie the word of Odin. I tell thee, Ivar, it is unsafe to trust him; use thy arms and hands well before we part, for soon thou art to fall."

Ivar replied : "Soon, Ketil, wilt thou fall to the ground."

Here Ketil drew back with a swift motion, to wield his sword more easily, and deal a death blow at Ivar. But Ivar sprang towards him just at this instant, and struck him a blow which almost cleft his shoulder in two, and he staggered outside the mark, and fell mortally wounded.

Thereupon Ketil died, having fought and fallen valiantly. According to ancient custom, a large bull was led forward, and sacrificed by Ivar as the victor.

Ivar then went back to Dampstadir, and the Sviar to Upsalir to tell Randalin of the great victory of Ivar, who on account of this deed obtained still greater renown than before.

CHAPTER XXX

DEATH OF HJALMAR AND ASTRID

A SHORT time after his return from Arhaug, and his memorable duel with Ketil, Ivar made preparations to leave Dampstadir with his three foster-brothers for Samsey, in order to be there at the time appointed for the duel between Hjalmar and Bui. Before sailing, Hjalmar made a solemn sacrifice to Odin for victory. They sailed with two small ships of the kind called "ask" to the island, and after an uneventful voyage arrived there, and cast anchor in a bay called Munarvog.

The sons of Hervard likewise made their preparations. The night before they sailed, Thorgrim had a dream which he told his father.

"It seemed to me," said he, "that we brothers were in Samsey, and found many birds there, and killed them all. Then we went to the other side of the island, and two eagles flew against us. I had a hard fight against one of them, and at last both of us sat down, and were badly wounded. The other eagle fought against my brothers, and overcame them all."

When Hervard heard this, he became more concerned than ever in regard to the lives of his sons, for in this dream he saw a warning of their death. He said to them: " This dream needs no unravelling, for it is plain enough. I am sure it concerns you, and I fear that the men who fell mean yourselves."

The sons replied that they did not fear that, for they had always obtained the victory before.

"All men go the day they have been fated to die," rejoined Hervard, and they spoke no more on the subject that day.

The next morning the twelve brothers went to their ship, and their father followed them to the shore, and gave good armor and weapons to them all. " I think," said he, " you have need of the best weapons now, for you are to fight against most valiant champions," after which he bade them farewell, and they departed. They reached Samsey, and landed at a bay called Unavog, on the other side of the island from where Hjalmar and his men were.

After the sons of Hervard had landed, the berserk fury came over them all, and they wrestled with trees, large rocks, and boulders, as they were wont when this madness seized them. After a time they became quiet again and rested, for they had become weak, as was always the case after the berserk fury.

The next morning they walked all over the island to see if they could discover traces of Hjalmar and his foster-brothers' arrival. After crossing to the other coast, they saw two ships, and

knew that they must belong to Hjalmar.   Then
they drew their swords, bit the edges of their
shields, and the berserk fury came over them all
again.   They boarded the ships in an onset of
irresistible rage, six of them attacking each ship in
the centre.   So brave were the men on them that
no one fled from his place, or spoke a word of fear,
or changed color.   Six of the brothers went forward
to the bow, and the other six towards the stern,
and slew every man they encountered.   After
this they went ashore, howling and shouting.

Hjalmar and the foster-brothers had gone
ashore also, and walked over the island to see if
Bui and his brothers had come.   When they
reached a hillock from which they could see their
own ships, they saw men coming out of them
with bloody weapons and swords, and recognized
the sons of Hervard.

When Hjalmar perceived them, he said to his
foster-brothers: "Our men are slain; and they
were so brave and so skilful in the handling of
weapons, that it seems to me most likely that
we shall all lodge with Odin in Valhalla to-night."

This was the only word of fear that Hjalmar had
ever spoken in his life, and his foster-brothers wondered why he had done so.   Had he a presenti-
ment that his Disir would prove faithless to him?

When Ivar heard this, he said to Hjalmar:
"Courage often is better than a sharp sword, and
many a dull sword has won the victory.   We will
be victorious over the sons of Hervard, though

19

they have slain all the brave men who were on board of our ships."

"Never have we fled from our foes," said Sigurd. "Let us rather fall under their weapons, and die with honor, for this is better than to live with shame; and we will fight the berserks one after another."

Then Hjalmar sang: "We will not lodge with Odin to-night. I must wed Astrid before I die, and ere evening comes all these men who come to fight against us will be dead, and we four foster-brothers shall live."

The sons of the berserk Hervard and the four foster-brothers met. The duel was to be the Einvigi; they could advance or retreat as they pleased, and no shield was held before the combatants. Bui was armed with the sword called "Rangvid," and Hjalmar, "Dragvandil," the sword which his father had given him when he became of age. As they met in the arena, Bui said: "If either of us escapes, he shall not take the other's weapons. I desire to have Rangvid in my mound, if I die; Hjalmar shall have his shirt and his weapons. He who lives shall raise a mound over the other."

Then the combat began in earnest, and was fought with the greatest violence. Both struck hard and often.

When Ivar and Sigurd and Sigmund had looked on for a while, they went to a place some distance

away, and made ready for the fight with the other
eleven sons of Hervard. Ivar said to the berserks : " We will fight according to the custom of
warriors, and not that of thralls. One of you,
and no more, shall fight me at a time, if your
courage fails not."

They consented, and then Seming came forward,
and Ivar went against him. Hrotti, the sword
which Ivar had chosen, and which belonged to
his father, was so good that it cut steel as if
it were cloth. It was not long before Seming
sank dead to the ground. Olvir then came forward to meet Ivar, and after a short fight he too
fell dead. At this the rage of the berserks was
overpowering, for they had always been victorious before. Then Gisli came forward. He was,
next to Thorgrim, the strongest and most skilful
of the eleven brothers. He attacked Ivar so
fiercely, that the latter at first could do no more
than defend himself. They fought for a long
time, during which the victory seemed doubtful.
All their armor was cut off, but the charmed shirt
which Randalin had made for Ivar protected his
body, so he was not hurt. Finally Gisli fell, after
receiving many wounds. Then Thorgrim fought
against Ivar. The fight was very severe, and
lasted long. Finally Thorgrim lost so much blood,
that he fell down suddenly, and at once died.
One brother rose after the other, but Ivar slew
them all. He was completely exhausted, but he
had refused the help of Sigurd and Sigmund,

for he thought he could gain the victory over Hervard's sons more easily than they could, and he did not wish to risk their lives.

After this the foster-brothers repaired to the spot where they had left Bui and Hjalmar fighting, and they saw that Bui had fallen, and lay motionless on the ground, and that Hjalmar sat with his back resting against a rock, and was as pale as a corpse.

Ivar approached him and sang: " What ails thee, Hjalmar? Thou hast changed color. I see that deep wounds weaken thee. Thy helmet is cut, and thy chain-armor is pierced near thy heart. Thy life, alas! is soon to finish, and ere long thou art going to Valhalla."

In reply, and in a faint voice, Hjalmar sang: "I have sixteen wounds and rent chain-armor. It is dark before my eyes; I cannot see to walk. The sword of Bui has touched my heart, the sharp point hardened in poison. I owned five burgs, but I never enjoyed them, as thou knowest well that I cared not for occupation on land. Soon I shall lie deprived of life, its thread sundered by the sword in Samsey. I would I could have married Astrid before going to Odin, but the Nornir decreed at my birth that this should not take place. I left the young Astrid on that fated day, destined never to see her again. How well it is for man not to know his fate beforehand. For sorrow would have followed me, and instead I thought only of victory."

Then he called Ivar to his side and said : " Draw from my hand, my foster-brother, the red-gold ring, and take it to Astrid. I know that it will be to her a lasting sorrow that I do not come back to Upsalir."

Then, after another pause, he continued : " The women on land will not hear that I sheltered myself from blows. The wise maidens in Upsalir will not laugh because I succumbed in the fight, as well as my adversary, whom I slew first."

Then raising himself, he continued : " Seest thou, Ivar, from a high tree a raven flying from the east ? An eagle follows ; that is the last eagle to which I give prey, and it will taste my blood. It is my wish that thou carry my helmet and chain-armor into Yngvi's hall. The heart of the daughter of the Hersir of Svithjod will be moved deeply when she sees my chain-armor cut upon the breast. I behold the daughters of Yngvi in Upsalir. How beautiful they look ! Hjalmar will not look again upon them, neither will he cheer with ale and speeches the warriors who sit in Yngvi's hall."

Then came another pause, for Hjalmar was suffering intensely from his wounds, but he had made a vow never to shriek from pain. Finally he said to his foster-brothers : " Two of you must go and hew a stone coffin for me, while another shall sit by my side, and write upon wooden tablets that song which I will compose about my deeds in life."

· Then he began to dictate the song, and Sigmund carved it, and the nearer the poem drew to its end, the more the life of Hjalmar ebbed away. Then came a deep silence, his voice had ceased. He was dead !

Then Ivar said solemnly : " It will be told far.and wide that few nobler and more famous men have ever lived than Hjalmar Gudbrandson of Engel."

After the words of Ivar, the foster-brothers looked at each other without saying a word, but all felt the great and irreparable loss they had sustained. They placed the berserks in a heap, near the sea, and piled boughs upon them. They put with them their weapons and clothing, divesting them of nothing. They covered the pile with turf, and cast earth over it, thus raising a great mound. They then went out to their ships, took ashore every one who had fallen, and there threw up another mound over them.

After the burial of the berserks, the three foster-brothers carried the body of Hjalmar on one of their ships, and sailed to Svithjod. They landed not far from Upsalir. Ivar carried Hjalmar on his back, followed by Sigurd and Sigmund, and then laid down their beloved dead foster-brother at the door of the great hall, chanting, as they walked there, the praises and great deeds of valor of Hjalmar.

After entering the hall, they marched towards the high seat where Yngvi was seated, and then put down on the floor and in front of him Hjal-

mar's pierced armor, his sword, helmet, and sundered shield.   These tokens told, without words,
of the death of Hjalmar the Brave.

Ivar and his two foster-brothers then went to
the bower of Astrid.   She was seated on a chair,
and was embroidering a cloak for Hjalmar, and
thinking of him.   Then Ivar sang again the great
and valorous deeds Hjalmar had accomplished
during his life, and said: "I have to tell thee,
Astrid, a sad tale;" and he gave her the ring
which she had given to Hjalmar before they
parted, and told of the greetings sent her by him
before he expired.

Astrid took the ring, looked at it, and knew
that Hjalmar was dead.   She uttered not a word;
her face changed color and turned very pale.   She
sank back lifeless into her chair.   She did not stir
for so long that her attendants became alarmed.
Bending over her, they saw that she was dead.

" Nothing better has occurred for a long time,"
said Ivar.   " Let us, foster-brothers, welcome the
event, though it causes great sorrow to the Hersir
of Svithjod."

Then he took Astrid in his arms, and carried
her to the door of the hall, and laid her in the
arms of the dead Hjalmar, and then went to tell
Yngvi of the death of his daughter.

When Yngvi came out, he saw, with profound
grief, the sad scene before him, and he mourned
greatly the deaths of his daughter Astrid and of
Hjalmar.

A large mortuary chamber was built for Hjalmar and Astrid ; a bed of down was laid on the floor, and upon it was put a pillow for them to rest their heads upon. They were not to be burned, for there were many since the death of Frey who did not wish to have a burning journey to the world they were going to. Hjalmar was dressed in his finest war clothes, clad in his pierced armor, his shield placed on his breast, and his sword by his side. Astrid was laid by him in the white bridal dress intended for her wedding, decked with costly jewels. Then a high mound was built over them.

Hjalmar the Brave, and Astrid the Fair, lay silently, side by side, in the embrace of death. Their grave stands to-day by the granite shores of the Baltic, looking silently out upon the ships that sail to and fro on that sea they loved so much ; the wind and the murmur of the waves sing a continuous requiem over them. Every year when June returns, its soft and fragrant breezes, passing over fields, meadows, and pine forests, blow over them. Butterflies and bees, rejoicing in the sunshine that brings new life, flit over the flowers growing upon their graves, and birds sing their love-songs by their side, just as in the days of old Hjalmar and Astrid sang theirs.

We are born, we grow, we love, we die. Love is the best of gifts that has been given to us ; then friendship, the foster-brother of love. Astrid has gone to live with the virgin goddess Gefjon, upon whom all those who die maidens wait. Hjalmar

went to Valhalla, and from there he sees his
beloved every day.

Ivar, Sigurd, and Sigmund mourned greatly the
death of Hjalmar, and there have never been
within the memory of man four men more attached to one another. For a long while they felt
their irreparable loss, but time assuaged their sorrows as the years passed away; but the remembrance of the noble qualities of Hjalmar came to
cheer them, and at every sacrifice and feast, when
they drank to the memory of departed kinsmen,
the name of Hjalmar the Brave was always
remembered by them. The people to this day
love to tell the story of Hjalmar and Astrid.

CHAPTER XXXI

THE WEDDING OF IVAR AND RANDALIN

About a year after the sad events just recorded, the day of the union of Ivar and Randalin approached. Great preparations were made in Upsalir for their wedding. The most costly tapestries that had been embroidered by the successive wives and daughters of the Hersirs of Svithjod had been taken out from the store-rooms where they had been sacredly kept, for these were only used for adorning the walls of the halls at weddings. Many of them represented romantic episodes in the courtship of the maidens who had embroidered them. Likewise the bridal bench ornamented with gold and silver and with rich carvings was brought out. How many beautiful daughters of the Hersirs of Svithjod had been seated upon those benches since Upsalir had been founded! What an array of illustrious maidens could be named! What a history could be told to us of the race descended from them! What a diversity of character and temper these women possessed! But, in despite of that splendor of life, many a young heart had been disappointed, for their union had not proved as congenial and as happy as they expected. Many of the girlish vis-

ions and dreams which belong to youth had not
been fulfilled as they had hoped. The Nornir had
woven a thick mist before their eyes to hide the
future. Many had found that station, fame, wealth,
and power did not give happiness, and had often
envied the merry laughter that came from the
house of the humble, and even from the cabin of
the slave.

For two weeks preceding the wedding, the
guests began to arrive in great numbers. The
Hersirs of Gardariki, Holmgard, Fyen, Zeeland,
and from the herads of Norway, were received
with great honor; large houses, well furnished,
were given to each high-born guest, and the
servants took care that they should lack nothing.
Ivar arrived with a large number of men of high
birth four days before the wedding.

The day of the wedding came at last. After the
guests had all assembled in the great hall, Randalin, under snowy bridal linen, entered by the
woman's door, followed by her bridesmaids. Her
beautiful features were seen but dimly through
the gauzy drapery, fastened with great skill, with
a jewel of exquisite beauty, upon her head. On her
neck could be seen through the transparent linen
a necklace of gold beads, upon which the artist
had lavished his greatest skill; from her belt of
gold hung a bunch of keys, showing that she was
to rule the household of Ivar. With a slow and
majestic step she advanced towards the bridal
bench, then seated herself in the midst of her ten

bridesmaids. These were Alfhild, daughter of one of the Hersirs of Holmgard; Thora, daughter of one of the Hersirs of Gardariki; Hildegerd, daughter of the Hersir of the island of Funen; Svanhild, niece of the Hersir of the island of Zeeland; Randgrid, daughter of the Hersir who ruled on the southern side of the present Christiania fjord; Geirlaug, whose father ruled over a large island in Friesland; Hildigunn, the daughter of Grammar of Britain; Ingegerd, Sigrid, and Thorhalla, cousins of the bride, and daughters of very powerful Haulds, who had the blood of Odin in their veins.

Each bridesmaid seated herself according to the order of precedence. Alfhild was on the right of the bride, and Thora on the left, and then came Hildigunn and Svanhild, and the others followed. Great care had been taken to seat them according to their rank, for women were most particular in that respect, and were very jealous of their privileges, and when not properly seated often considered it a personal affront.

The bridegroom entered next, followed by his groomsmen. These were Sigurd and Sigmund, his two foster-brothers; Thorbrand, the brother of Alfhild; Thord, the brother of Thora; Geir, the brother of Hildigunn; Skeggi, the brother of Svanhild; Ingolf, the cousin of Geirbaug; Ali the Bold, and Hunding, Hroar, and Bard, who were powerful Vikings.

Ivar seated himself on the high seat opposite that of Yngvi. On his left sat Sigurd, and on his right, Sigmund ; then came Thorbrand and Thord, and the rest seated themselves according to their rank. By one accord, they had given the precedence to Sigurd and Sigmund; not that they were the highest, but because they knew the love that existed between Ivar and his two foster-brothers, who had shared so many dangers together. On the side of Yngvi were the highest Hersirs of the land, and great number of lots were drawn on that day by men of equal rank for seats of honor.

The scene was one of great splendor. The women were magnificently dressed, and vied with each other in the richness of their gowns and in the beauty of their jewels. After entering the hall, they took off their festal mantles, embroidered with gold, and displayed their lovely toilets.

They all wore the "slœdur," or festal dress, with long trains sweeping the ground. These were made of the costliest material that could be procured on the Caspian or from Greece, and embroidered with gold and silver. The bodices of the dresses in many instances did not reach so high as to cover their shoulders ; and that part was covered by a guimpe of pale blue or snowy white silk, and showed dimly, to great advantage, their milk-white skin. Some wore a wide, loose, unattached collar, almost hiding the neck, richly embroidered with gold. The married women wore graceful head-dresses. The shoe-cloths were also richly embroidered, reaching nearly as high as the knee.

They wore their hair in different styles; some had it twisted in a large topknot, which was made fast with long hair-pins of gold and silver, with heads of exquisite workmanship; others had their hair pushed back, and tied in a short, loose knot, made fast with a ribbon of gold ; a diadem of gold adorned the forehead of almost every woman. They wore necklaces of gold beads or mosaic, or of gold Roman coins, separated from each other by elongated beads of gold. On their arms were graceful gold bracelets, most of them spiral in shape, and upon their fingers were many rings. Belts of gold contrasted with their dresses, and showed to advantage the waists they encircled. From these hung leather or velvet bags embroidered with gold.

The groomsmen of Ivar were dressed in their most costly garments, and all wore their cloaks of dignity and rank. All the male guests were likewise in costly attire.

Then Yngvi, as high priest of the temple, consecrated the bride, and wedded Randalin to Ivar, by making over them the sign of the hammer of Thor, and invoked the goddess Var, who had listened to their vows. After this Randalin was holy, as a wife, in the sight of every man.

This ceremony ended, the bridegroom advanced

towards Randalin, and presented her the "lin-fee," or trousseau, in which were included beautiful bracelets, necklaces, and diadems of gold. There were several mantles of different colors, and various head-dresses, gloves, shoes, underwear of silk and linen, and night-dresses with long sleeves, of the finest linen the land could produce. Some were of silk, the material for which had been brought by Ivar from the shores of the Caspian.

Then the gifts called the bridal bench gifts followed. These were called bench gifts because each guest presented a gift to the bride while she was seated on the bridal bench. Guest after guest lay before Randalin the beautiful presents that he or she had brought for her.

A great-aunt, from the island of Fyen, gave her with her bench gift a gold coin of Tiberius, who was Roman emperor 14–37 A.D., which had come into the possession of her ancestors during the life of that emperor.

Another aunt sent her, among her presents, a gold coin of Claudius, 41–54 A.D., that had been in the possession of her kinsmen since that time.

Among the many gifts of Sigrlin, Ivar's mother, was a gold coin of Titus, 79–81 A.D., which had been got by the ancestors of Hjorvard in the Mediterranean at the time Titus took Jerusalem.

A cousin gave her a gold coin of Decius, 249–251 A.D.; another, a gold coin of Aurelian, 270–275 A.D.

An uncle of Randalin, from southern Svithjod,

gave her a gold coin of Probus, 276–282 A.D., which his son had given to him.

There were many exquisite jewels, necklaces made of rods of gold; diadems of gold, with Randalin's name in runic letters upon them; spiral bracelets of gold; belts of gold and of silver; beautiful hairpins of gold and silver, with ornamented tops highly finished; necklaces of mosaic beads of great beauty, and gold beads; and bracteates with gold chains of beautiful workmanship.

Gurid, an aunt of Randalin, sent her, by her son, a woman's headgear, carefully put in a bag of velvet all embroidered with gold.

Sigurd gave her a large quantity of Grecian fabrics, and many jewels of gold. Sigmund likewise gave the rarest glassware that could be procured in Greece, or on the island of Cyprus. Gudbrand, the father of Hjalmar, had brought her many dishes of gold and silver. Sigrid, his wife, sent her beautiful tapestries which she had embroidered herself.

Thora gave a beautiful piece of tapestry which Astrid had embroidered before her death, representing Ivar playing at the ball games that had taken place the year before, while she was in Upsalir. In the background were Yngvi and the women who were looking on.

Gunnhild, her youngest sister, gave her a gold embroidered bag.

Yngvi gave his daughter as a bench gift a dower of gold and silver, and many costly objects, and

also two landed estates, one in the present Cour-
land, and the other in Venden in the present Pome-
rania. The presents which Randalin received that
day represented a large fortune in gold and silver.

Immediately after all the bench gifts had been
presented, great preparations were made for the
wedding feast which took place soon afterwards.
The Hersir of Svithjod had spared no expense.
New vats for beer and ale had been made, and
an extraordinary quantity of ale and beer had
been brewed, and wine was not lacking. The
tables were set with great magnificence.

The three halls had a gala appearance. The
tables in front of the seat were covered with beautiful embroidered table-cloths, and were adorned
with the most costly Grecian and Cypriote glasses.
The dishes containing the viands were of gold and
silver. The drinking horns, or vases, were of many
kinds, some of solid gold, others of silver ornamented with gold, and Grecian cups of cut glass
were very abundant. At night, light was furnished
by big wax candles.

The great Hersirs that were present agreed to
sit in turn on the high seats, to the great relief of
Yngvi, who feared a contest for precedence. The
viands spread on the tables were beef, roast veal,
pig, venison, birds, and fish. All these were served
in gold plates, and all the plates set before the
guests were of silver.

Special servants, called "fillers," saw that the
20

horns were always full, and carried them round.
The throng was so great that slaves had to be
called in, who wore clean, new, white " vadmal,"
or woolen, and all had their hair newly close-
cropped.

Among the female slaves some were of great
beauty, and had been brought from Britain, Gaul,
Greece and Rome. They also filled the horns, and
carried them round.

There was great drinking and much merriment,
and also invocation of the gods. The wedding
lasted six weeks, which corresponds to a period of
a month with us. Scalds recited poetry every
day before admiring audiences; and, as at the
games, this feast was to be the cause of other weddings in the near future, for during it many men
and women had fallen in love with one another.

No man ever heard of a greater feast. When it
ended, all the guests departed with costly gifts.

The time when Randalin was to leave Upsalir,
to part from all that had been dear to her in her
girlhood, had arrived. A new epoch of her life
had dawned upon her without her being aware of
it. Her girlhood's careless joys had departed forever. All had been so bright in her youth, that
she fancied it would continue to the end of her
life. She possessed Ivar, and happiness was as-
sured to her forever.

Skuld had carefully concealed from her gaze the
future. Little did she dream of the stormy bil-

lows of life ahead, of the sorrows that befall every mortal man and woman. Ivar was all to her, and for him she was willing to sacrifice even her life. Love was her own. O Skuld, how kind thou art to hide from man the decrees of the Nornir, who have shaped our lives from our birth! We came into the world through no will of our own, and we know not in the beginning of the day what fate will bring forth before night.

Randalin's eyes, full of hope, were looking into the future. Hope and the Future, those twin sisters, were brighter in her eyes than the rays of the sun. Ivar belonged to her, and Love owned them both.

The dragon-ship that carried Ivar and Randalin to Dampstadir, carried the sweetest, the loveliest of wives, and the manliest and wisest of husbands.

LONDON:
PRINTED FROM AMERICAN PLATES BY WILLIAM CLOWES AND SONS, LIMITED,
DUKE STREET, STAMFORD STREET.

www.ingramcontent.com/pod-product-compliance
Lightning Source LLC
Chambersburg PA
CBHW020935030726
47496CB00005B/1208